After a hate crime leaves one of them near dead, Veterinarian, Josh Nolan and Cop, Connor Vincent are starting a new life in Black Creek, a remote town on the edge of the Adirondack State Park, Vermont.

Josh is taking over his grandfather's practice and Connor settles into working in the sheriff's office covering the area.

When Connor pieces together a whole list of unsolved crimes going back fifty years he puts his life, and that of his partners, in danger.

A dangerous lone wolf is intent on destroying the beginnings of a pack and when Connor is attacked and near death there is only one thing that can save him. A wolf shifter's bite.

One Bratty Omega

Donny left his childhood pack behind him when his father couldn't accept the fact that his son was just an Omega. Destined to be the lowest on the pecking order of the pack, Donny acts out in ways that are sometimes not too healthy for his wellbeing.

Proctor is coming to Black Creek to visit an old friend. The last thing he expects is to find himself hanging out with some young, blond brat. What's more, Proctor doesn't expect himself to be attracted to the little troublemaker.

But things aren't what they seem to be in Black Creek, and as Proctor digs deeper, he discovers secrets that are explosive.

Will he be able to accept the truth? And more importantly, will he be able to accept Donny?

The Alpha's Only

Tiberius, Alpha of the Black Creek pack, is tired of being alone. When Keir, a new Beta joins the pack, Tiber is startled to learn he's found his mate. Keir isn't interested in becoming one of a couple of Alpha mates. He plans to be the one and only. First, however, they need to defeat their enemies and weed out the ones who are trying to destroy them from within.

eXtasy Books

This work is copyright. Apart from any use as permitted under the Copyright Act 1968, no part may be reproduced, copied, scanned, stored in a retrieval system, recorded or transmitted in any form, or by any means, without the prior written permission by the publisher.

>Building the Pack Books 1, 2 and 3
>RJ Scott, Stephani Hecht, Amber Kell
>ISBN: 978-1-77111-693-0

Copyright © RJ Scott, Stephani Hecht, Amber Kell 2013

First Edition published 2013
www.extasybooks.com

eXtasy Books Incorporated
P.O. Box 2146
Garibaldi Highlands, B.C. V0N1T0
Canada

Cover Art by Angela Waters
Cover Design by Angela Waters

EXTASYBOOKS.COM

The New Wolf
Building the Pack One

By

RJ Scott

*To Stephani and Amber . . . they'll know why
And always for my family.*

Chapter One

"Talk to me, babe" Josh Nolan asked. "You look so sad."

He hugged Connor from behind and was relieved when the big man, after initially stiffening in protest, finally relaxed back against him. They'd been here four days and the tension in Connor had gone past the irritability stage and on to the deadly silence phase. Josh hated it when his partner of five years went quiet—it often meant something was really wrong, and tall, dark and silent Connor was the last man to suggest talking his issues out.

"I was just thinking," Connor's voice rumbled.

Josh's heart sank. He had been waiting for Connor to say something ever since they'd set foot in the town a few days earlier. Shorter than Connor by two inches, Josh couldn't see past him to the fixed point his partner was staring at. Their red roofed white wooden house with the wraparound veranda backed onto the edge of the forest and there couldn't be much to see. The house was at the furthest point west in this small town of Black Creek. Josh knew the view was one of trees and more trees, a dark wall in this late evening light.

"You think we did the wrong thing moving here?"

Connor shrugged.

Josh rested his forehead between Connor's shoulder blades and inhaled the familiar scent of his lover. Guilt consumed Josh. He was the one with the ready-made business to come to. Taking over his grandfather's veterinary practice was perfect for him. He didn't want to specialize in family pets, he wanted to expand and cover the myriad of animals taken to the surgery as his grandfather had done up until he died ten years before. The clinic had been in the hands of his grandfather's partner since then. One call to say he was retiring and Josh knew moving here was the next step in his life. But whereas he had been ready to go on, he wasn't entirely sure Connor agreed with the rapid change in their life

"No, I don't think we did the wrong thing," Connor said. His voice was firm and brooked absolutely no argument. "I needed out of the city." He turned in Josh's grip and leaned back against the window sill before tugging Josh closer and pressing his head into Josh's chest. Josh cradled his lover's head and wondered what to say next.

This last year had been hard. Too hard for either man to have come through it all unscathed. Consciously he sought out the scar at the back of Connor's neck where the knife had sliced through muscle. Josh had almost lost the only man he'd ever loved and the scar was the sole visible reminder. Didn't mean their hearts weren't scarred with fear and anger though, and that was what worried Josh. Albany PD had pushed Connor through counseling, but the unprovoked attack left Connor a different man—quiet and reserved in a way that sometimes Josh couldn't break through.

"Then what is it?" Josh asked softly. "You've been so quiet since we got here."

Connor moaned gently and pressed a kiss to Josh's naked skin. They'd not long taken a shower together in the temperamental old cubicle off the main bath. They'd laughed and fooled around pre the main event back in the bedroom and Josh *had* felt at peace. A quick check around the house and he'd come back in the room to find Connor all twisted up in his own thoughts.

"Promise you won't laugh?" Connor mumbled. Josh gently pried Connor's forehead away from the skin contact and looked down into green eyes filled with emotion.

"Never," Josh promised.

"It's too quiet," Connor began. "I keep waiting for the shit to hit the fan and for the sirens, and I'm just on edge."

Josh considered Connor's quiet words. For Josh, nothing had changed except the type of animals he had treated. From dogs, cats and hamsters, he had moved on to equine care, wild animal treatments and even had his hand in the ass of his first cow. The learning had been steep and he'd been challenged every day, even though Edward went with him everywhere to ease the transition. Connor had moved from Albany with its crime stats and the sprawling city with all its secrets to this back-of-nowhere town, where he and the other deputies in the sheriff's department shared vehicles and patrolled larger areas.

"I wouldn't laugh at that, Con," Josh said finally. "I can't imagine how hard it is to give up the city and come here. I'm sorry you had to leave and move here just because of me. You had a career..."

Connor shook his head which stopped Josh talking. "I'd go anywhere to be with you and I was ready for a change in my career," Connor said. He spoke firmly and deliberately again. Like he was expecting Josh to argue with him and wanted to leave no room for discussion. "I love you."

"But... I want us to both be happy," Josh said unnecessarily. The decision that they had made to leave Albany had been an easy one for Josh. When Connor had been attacked it made both men take a step back and re-evaluate everything. Connor hadn't even been hurt when he was on duty,—he and Josh were at the cinema, and had left with the crowd. Lost in talking about the film, they'd not realized they were being followed. The reports labeled it a mugging, but Josh and Connor knew better. The young guy, high on something, had been shouting language of hate. Far more probable was that the fact Connor and Josh were holding hands had been the cause of the attack.

Josh couldn't even think about that night without feeling sick. Holding Connor in his arms as he bled onto the sidewalk in front of a McDonalds, he had felt every part of his life fracture. There was prejudice everywhere, and Josh wasn't stupid. Moving to Black Creek didn't mean that they wouldn't still find bigotry. Still, his grandfather and Edward had been in a committed relationship until Josh's grandfather's death two years ago. Zachary Nolan had loved living here, said no one thought twice of having a gay couple in the town. Josh assumed—more like hoped—Black Creek would be accepting of Josh and Connor as a couple.

They could be *out* here, in a way that wasn't possible in the city with Connor's job.

"I don't mean to worry you. I promise you I am happy," Connor said gently. "I just looked at my phone and Proctor left a message. It pulled me back into everything he is going through."

"Is he okay?" Josh asked quickly. Proctor was a good man, Connor's ex-partner on the force, and working with a new guy now.

"He's doing well. The newbie spilt coffee over his back seat—he was just telling me this story, is all."

"But you still miss it? The city?"

"I don't miss a thing," Connor stated. "I just haven't lost that city instinct yet. I can't fully relax." He huffed a laugh then added, "It's too damn quiet."

Relief flooded Josh—Connor wasn't regretting things, he was just adjusting to the new life. He slid to his knees in front of Connor and shuffled in between Connor's legs. He looked up and used every ounce of his puppy dog eyes to make the unsuspecting Connor laugh. Then he lifted one eyebrow as Connor began to smile.

"Would it help if you fucked me into the mattress?" Josh asked innocently. Connor groaned again, obviously this time not in disappointment at himself, but at Josh's words. They switched when they felt like it, but it was Connor who ran the show most of the time. The dynamics of their relationship were perfect. Connor mostly thought he was in charge and Josh let him think that. It worked for them.

Connor palmed his cock under the towel then slipped the pale blue fluffy material to one side and revealed a sight Josh could never tire of. Cut and hardening rapidly Connor's, cock was a thing of beauty. It was heavy and thick, and Josh loved tasting and touching it and the feel of it stretching him.

He didn't hesitate or tease. In seconds he had Connor's cock in his mouth and he used every trick in the book to take the half hard length to full hardness and leaking in no time at all. Tasting the single pearls of pre-come had him near losing it himself at the sounds of encouragement and praise from Connor. When Connor rested the palms of his hands on Josh's head, Josh knew this was the sign of how close Connor was. He either pulled off or sucked him down farther and tasted his come.

With deliberation he released the sucking hold and instead clambered to stand, ignoring the whine of disappointment from Connor whilst dragging his lover to the bed. They fell laughing onto the cool crisp white sheet and pushed the quilt down off the bed with their feet. These July nights were too hot to be covered in the heavy material.

Josh shuffled so he could reach the lube and in seconds he was stretching himself with Connor watching. They did this together—Connor reached out and pressed a finger alongside Josh's. When Connor slid home and they began to move, Josh knew how close he was, within seconds. Orgasm tugged him inside, threatening to have him spilling quickly.

Connor seemed to notice and he didn't hold back. "Finish it," he groaned.

Josh did as he was told and circled his cock with his hand. A few strokes and he was coming just as Connor pressed home with a yell of release.

They fell onto the bed in each other's arms with laughter and words of love.

Connor held Josh tight then whispered. "Wherever we are, as long as we are together, that is all that matters."

Chapter Two

Connor climbed out of the car and stretched tall. He'd been up with Osborne checking out the ridge. Some campers had reported seeing blood, but it turned out the blood was no more than what remained of a deer and there wasn't a lot the sheriff's department could do about that one.

"You want coffee?" Adam Osborne asked as he slammed the car door. Connor winced at the loud noise. Proctor had babied his car back in the city, and Connor had learned to shut car doors carefully.

"Cream. Lots of cream, and four sugars," Connor replied.

Osborne jogged to the small diner at the far end of what could be called the main street of Black Creek. It was nothing more than a diner serving meals to travelers who used this road as a rat run off the main road, and doubled as the place to get coffee. That was probably the only thing he missed—Starbucks. His daily fix of cream and sugar with a hint of caffeine was what got him started when he began shift.

He turned a full three-sixty and checked out the street. There was a store, with apartments over, and a gas station at the opposite end. He could see the red of the roof on their place through the trees and warmth flooded him. Josh would be there, doing what he did best. Other than that there were two boarded shops, a beauty parlor and a cash converters place. Money wasn't as freely gained in this place as it was back in New York. People struggled in the recession. Still, everyone he'd met so far were happy and settled. He wanted that for him and Josh.

When he'd awoken in the hospital, the first thing he'd seen was Josh at his bedside, his lover's eyes red rimmed and his face gaunt with exhaustion. That single image haunted Connor even to this day. So close to death it wasn't real, he'd made a lot of decisions in that moment. He wasn't ready to leave this life, or Josh.

If only he could settle into his new work as easily as Josh was doing in his. Josh was so damn content—up to his elbows, literally, in animals, he was happy.

A noise from beside the beauty parlor had him zeroing in on the source. Someone shouting—blurred indistinct words and another voice pleading. Connor's instincts went into overdrive and in seconds he had his weapon drawn and he was edging to the corner to get a better look. He assessed the situation. A tall broad dark haired guy had a smaller, much smaller, guy pressed up against the wall. The smaller of the two was blond and slim and seemed to be whimpering.

"... if anyone finds out—"

"They won't, Tiber, I promise—"

"Don't fuck with things, Donny. Don't go hunting without me. You hear me?"

"Someone has to find it, not like you're doing anything—"

The large guy, Tiber, gripped hard to Donny's arms and lifted him off his feet before shaking him. Donny whimpered again and tilted his neck before lowering his eyes. He stopped talking and Tiber was clearly furious.

Connor contemplated what to do. This Tiber was a similar size to him, broad, strong and Connor couldn't see weapons. This could be a local issue and, not for the first time, he wished he knew more about how the town worked. Maybe this

The New Wolf

Tiber was a drunk and needed to be pulled away and sent home? Maybe Connor should use his weapon.

He stepped into the alley and kept his weapon at his side. Tiber reacted immediately. He dropped Donny who stumbled to remain upright, then let out a groan.

"Is there a problem here?" Connor asked quickly.

"No problem, officer." Tiber stepped towards Connor but Connor didn't stand down. He may not be pointing a gun at the guy, but he was determined to stand his ground and show his control of the situation in other ways. "Is there, Donny." The last wasn't a question, more of an implacable statement.

Donny shook his head and came to stand next to Tiber.

"Just a misunderstanding," Tiber added.

"Didn't look like that to me," Connor said evenly. "Seems to me you were shaking Donny here down."

Tiber sighed and his tense figure relaxed a little. "The brat did something he shouldn't have. It's dealt with, and it won't happen again, will it, Donny?"

Donny didn't hesitate. "It's finished," he said quickly.

Osborne turned up next to Connor and chuckled. "Morning, Tiber, Donny, what's up?"

Connor relaxed a little. Osborne was only twenty-three, but he knew this town and its people like the back of his hand. If Osborne wasn't concerned, then Connor didn't have to have weapons drawn. Yet, something in the way Donny stood next to Tiber screamed possession. Connor wasn't so sure about this. Was this a domestic situation?

"I fucked up," Donny said immediately. He glanced up at Tiber and Connor inhaled sharply. There was such a look of love on Donny's face, adoration, and when Tiber focused on Donny's look, he smiled, then shook his head.

"The usual," he said. "It's done."

"You may want to keep this off the streets," Osborne warned the two men. Connor saw Tiber bristle a little at the admonishment, then visibly rein in what looked like irritation. Donny just grinned broadly and, with a wave, jogged away from the situation. With a curt nod, Tiber turned on his heel and left in the same direction. Connor waited until the two men were out of ear shot, then turned to Osborne. He had questions.

"What was that about?"

"Cousins. Family stuff." Osborne summed up the situation with an added shrug for emphasis. He glanced down at the weapon in Connor's hands. "You don't need to draw your weapon quite as quickly," he admonished. "It's not all drugs and gangs in Black Creek you know."

Embarrassed, Connor pushed his gun back in the holster. "Old habits die hard," he said in defense. Osborne didn't say anything else, instead he walked over to the small sheriff's office and Connor followed.

Something about the situation he'd just seen wasn't right. The young kid, couldn't be more than twenty, had looked terrified. No, not terrified. What had he looked like? Regretful? Resentful? Submissive? The whole way he looked and acted around Tiber was reminiscent of some of the same sex partnerships he'd seen over the years. Not everyone had an equal relationship like he and Josh did. Maybe those two weren't cousins, but partners?

"Something in your head?" Osborne asked as they reached the door.

Connor pushed it open and gestured for Osborne to go in first. "No, not at all. Are there any more *family situations* I need to know about?"

Osborne shook his head, then sat at his desk. "No," he said firmly. "None."

Connor trusted his instincts. Osborne was lying, that much was sure.

Interesting.

Connor pushed aside the last of the mandatory paperwork on the call out and saved the data to the PC. The internet was so damn slow and he tapped his fingers idly on the desk while he waited for the submission progress bar to raise from three, to ten, to fifteen percent. At this rate he'd still be here at dinner time.

"Heard you met Tiber and Donny."

Connor leaned back in the chair. Ellis Cross, sheriff and Connor's boss, rested his ass on the corner of Connor's desk.

"Yeah. Family problems," Connor said carefully. He wasn't yet ready to question what his partner had told him. He needed to find out more about the two men he'd seen. See if they were actually cousins.

"The family is notorious around here," Ellis pointed out. He crossed his arms over his chest and appeared determined to talk.

"Notorious for shaking each other and pushing them against the wall?"

Ellis sighed, then chuckled. "Don't tell me, Tiber had Donny off the floor?" Connor nodded. "Tiber doesn't know his own strength sometimes. I'll have a word with him."

"Is that the way it works here?" Connor asked. Suddenly the sheriff stating he was taking on something that had been Connor's case was pushing him to ask about protocol. Hell, it wasn't even a case, but something about the whole thing was wrong and it had Connor's hackles up.

"What do you mean?"

Connor could read people, and there was definitely tension in Ellis' shoulders even as he tried for easy

"Just that I come across this big guy holding a smaller guy off the ground and threatening him and so far I have had Osborne dismiss it with explaining they are cousins, and you dismissing it with an *I'll deal with it*. Just wondered how it worked around here is all." Connor sat back in his chair and waited. He wanted to see how the sheriff dealt with him questioning procedure on what was only his second day on the job.

Sheriff Cross quirked a smile and the smile reached his gray eyes. "Yes," he said simply. "That is kinda the way things work."

Connor looked at the guy steadily. "Good to know," he said.

The sheriff pushed himself up and away from the desk. "Back this afternoon," he said, then left the office. The noise of the door shutting behind him echoed in the otherwise silent rooms. Connor shifted uncomfortably in his chair. Silence again. Where was the arguing and shouting, the perps demanding to be released, the sound of keyboards being thumped in frustration and the phones constantly ringing.

"You'll get used to it," Osborne offered helpfully. He was finishing the last of his coffee and typing slowly at the same time. "Small counties an' all," he added.

Connor considered the statement. Would he get used to it? Not only the new procedures unique to this county, but the quiet? He hoped Josh was having a better day. Picking up the file on his desk, he made his way to filing. This he could do in his sleep. Each call they answered needed an audit trail—he was used to that.

He'd even had time to fill in this paper backup to the main database in his neatest handwriting. Proctor would be proud of him—his old partner forever bemoaned Connor's lack of penmanship. He placed the file in the right drawer,

The New Wolf

then randomly pulled some open. He wanted to get a feel for the kind of issues he may need to get involved in. He would imagine it was mostly domestic issues, maybe disagreements over land, nothing as evil as the kinds of things he'd dealt with in the city.

The system of filing was fairly clear, but it was only after really looking that he found the section for unsolved call outs. Maybe a fresh set of eyes on cold cases may be just what he needed to ease him into a slower life. Surprised at the amount of folders in the drawer, he realized it was because they spread back over sixty years. The oldest files were brown with age and the details inside the first one he picked up were sketchy and only two pieces of paper thick.

"What you doing?"

"Jeez, Emma," Connor snapped. He hadn't heard the secretary come in behind him and spun on his toes to face him, the folder held close to his chest. "Warn a guy. I thought you worked nights. Shouldn't you be home now?"

She waved a bag at him, "Forgot my jacket. Didn't mean to startle you. Osborne said you disappeared into the file room and you never came back." She shrugged, "He thought the bad guys had got you."

"I was familiarizing myself with the system," Connor defended.

"Cool," Emma said. She peered at what Connor was holding. "The Black Creek Creeper files. Spooky."

"Spooky how?" And who the hell called a case The Black Creek Creeper?

"You haven't heard the story of the house in the woods?" Emma crossed to the drawer and pulled out a whole slew of paper. "Black Creek's very own urban legend. Murders, disappearing men, bodies of hitchhikers found in pieces. Lasted five years from late sixties to seventy-two and they never had an idea of who it was." Emma looked around conspiratorially and waggled her eyebrows, "Or what it was, come to that."

Connor gripped the papers tight and pushed the drawer shut. This was probably less urban legend and more unsolved cold case. Maybe a serial killer? Random events sixty years old. Something for him to get his teeth into and to learn more about this town. "I'll take a look. I like a good urban legend."

"It's your dime, just don't let Sheriff Cross catch you, he's all about living in the modern day and ignoring the ancient cases that are, in his words, not worth our time."

Connor glanced pointedly around the file room then out to the quiet offices. He hadn't been here long enough to get any sort of paperwork mountain to contend with. Emma caught the look and smiled wryly.

"Guess you have time," he said with a laugh.

He had a couple of hours, barring phone calls, and he laid out the paperwork on his desk. First, he put everything in date order, where before it was in alphabetical order which made no sense. Then he pulled over a notepad and lost himself in doing what he did best. Investigation.

Chapter Three

Josh wiped his hands and tossed the towel to Edward who caught it deftly. They exchanged goofy grins. They'd just saved a cat brought in all bitten up and bleeding. The little tabby had been put into isolation under sedation and was very likely to live. It was always good to have a win.

"It's good to have you here," Edward said. He'd said it a few times before and each time Josh felt the insistent prick of guilt. He'd visited Black Creek for his grandfather's funeral, but since then he hadn't been back. He and Edward had kept in touch by letter, then by email, but he'd never visited. Edward and Josh's grandfather had been in a strong committed relationship for fifteen years, but it was an odd thing when Josh's gran was still alive to justify Josh's relationship with the older man.

"I'm sorry I didn't come back before," Josh replied with the same thing he was saying each time. It used to be that he would visit his grandfather every few months for a night or two, catching up on him and talking shop.

"I understood the difficult position you were in," Edward offered gently. He wasn't accusatory in his words, instead he was understanding. His dark brown eyes filled with compassion.

"My gran never quite got over the whole thing with gramps taking up with another man after they divorced."

Edward chuckled. "We shocked a lot of people," he said. "Not least, your family and mine."

Josh went into the small office next to the operating room and grabbed two bottles of beer from the fridge. The cat had been an emergency that had extended their normal day by two hours and the evening had darkened the sky. They were done for today. He indicated with the bottle and when Edward nodded in agreement, the two men moved to the back exit and the small decked area beyond. Under the half moon, they sipped the beer and sat in silence for a good five minutes.

"Do you miss him?" Josh finally asked. He immediately wished he could retract the question. Of course Edward missed his partner. Zachary was, or had been, a big part of Edward's life. "I'm sorry, I didn't mean to . . . you don't have to answer that."

Edward dismissed the defense with a snort. "Hell, Josh, there isn't a day goes by that I don't miss that ornery old git. We met in college, the first time, did you know that?"

"I didn't know that. Gramps never said much and Gran wasn't much for talking on the whole subject."

Edward settled back in his chair and finished his beer. "We fell in love when we were twenty," he began thoughtfully. "But it took us near on thirty years before we got together again. I had just turned fifty and this man knocked on my door, said he had this place he'd found in Vermont where we could have a joint practice. I recognized him straight away and every single feeling of love I had felt before flooded back to me. We were back together in an instant like those years hadn't passed."

"That's a strong love," Josh offered.

"It's what you have with your young man," Edward said. "I see it when you are together. The way he looks at you, and that he moved here to be with you. When I sent the letter I never thought you would take my offer."

Josh hesitated at the change in direction of the conversation. He hadn't told Edward about the attack in the city or the reasons why he and Connor decided to make such a huge change in their lives. He considered telling Edward the whole thing, but Edward interrupted his thoughts before he could.

"I'm pleased you did though." He stood and placed the empty bottle on to the small table between them. "I'll see you in the morning." He yawned and stretched and Josh thought to himself that this sixty-five year old man didn't look much over forty-five. The Vermont air and laid back lifestyle must agree with him.

Josh waved a hand and watched as Edward walked through the clinic and out the front, only relaxing when he heard the sound of Edward's car starting. Edward and Gramps had a cabin about three miles outside of the town and Edward still lived there. Deciding now was a good time to make his way home, which was all of two hundred yards away. He went through the usual checks, locking the back door, then checking in on the injured cat who slept on peacefully.

While locking the front door he could see the lights of the house from here and knew Connor would be waiting. The thought made him smile. This was a nice life, a better life. The screech of brakes and a loud crash snapped him out of his happy space. He sprinted the few feet to the road and looked the way of the noise. A car was piled into a tree and to one side of it a dog lay on its side with two legs at crooked angles.

Instinct had Josh checking the driver, but the car was empty. He dialed Connor's number even though he was probably already on his way, he must have heard the accident. He then crouched by the dog and peered closer. It was dark, but the moon showed him a large dog, with gray fur, almost wolf like. He patted the fur and his hands came away sticky with blood. When the dog suddenly opened amber eyes, snarled and stared directly at Josh, he scrambled back out of the way of the teeth. He wasn't stupid. This was one big dog. He'd have to wait until Connor was here so he could leave it and get his bag.

They eyed each other warily, the dog growling low in his throat, then every so often twitching and whining and Josh staying just out of reach. He'd never seen a dog like this before and his nature told him it wasn't a normal dog. Maybe a wild dog? The snout was longer, the build larger, but if it was a wild dog it was kind of small. He peered closer and reached out a hand to touch the wounds but immediately withdrew it when the animal snapped again. He watched as the poor thing tried to crawl away from the scene just using his front legs, his back one trailing with blood.

"You have to stop. I can help," Josh began to croon. He looked up at the car again. Where was the driver? He hoped to hell that the driver had just gone for help or something and hadn't walked off into the forest injured. He heard steps behind him. Running. Relieved, he half turned.

"Thank fuck, Con, there's a dog, injured."

The hit came out of nowhere, forcing him to the ground, dazed. A kick and he was on his front, eating dirt, another punch and his vision blurred.

Connor left the house at a run. He'd been in the shower and only just picked up Josh's call. Something had happened. He could hear in the call Josh talking low and soft to an injured animal, caught the explanation about a car accident.

He slid to a halt when he came on the scene and a quick assessment had him falling to his knees next to a body on the ground. Feeling for a pulse, he cursed the dark night and only when he moved to the other side in the illumination of the single working car headlight did his heart near stop. Josh.

"Fuck. Josh? Can you hear me?" A wound on his temple seeped blood, but he didn't seem injured anywhere else. Had Josh been hit by the car? He thought it had been an animal? Josh groaned and blinked his eyes open.

"Con? The hell?"

"What happened, Josh?"

Connor helped his lover to sit and gingerly tested for any other injuries.

"Check the driver," Josh slurred. "Couldn't find 'em, jus'the wolf." His words were forced.

Connor could see more blood darkening Josh's skin around his mouth. He was torn. The cop in him needed to check the scene, the lover in him wanted to not move an inch from where he was.

"Go," Josh said. He crawled to the car and used it to stand.

Connor was up and checking the driver's seat. Nothing. He used the flashlight on his cell to check around the car, but apart from the blood on the ground, there was no sign of a driver or an injured animal. He put a call in to Emma who manned the phones at night and she passed the report on to the sheriff and deputies. They would be with Connor in five.

Connor crossed to Josh who leaned wearily against the car. "What happened, J?" he asked immediately. He had to get a fresh idea of what the hell kind of scene he had just run down to.

Josh coughed and wiped blood from his forehead as it slid into his eyes. "Heard the crash," he started shakily. "Ran out, no driver, an animal on the ground," Josh summarized. "I heard you . . . thought it was you . . . then someone hit me, kicked me on the ground . . . you showed up."

"Okay," Connor attempted to reassure Josh. "Looks to me like the car swerved to avoid something and it couldn't get out of the way quick enough."

"I need to go and find the injured animal," Josh said determinedly. He walked two steps into the forest before Connor stopped him.

"We can't in the dark," he said firmly. Josh looked at him with damp eyes. Josh hated to think anyone was in pain, human or animal. And Josh's expression cut Connor to the core. "Tell me what you remember. You said it was a wolf?"

Josh blinked away the moisture and looked confused. He wrapped his arms around his chest and shook his head.

"It couldn't be a wolf. Wolves were wiped out of Vermont in the 19th century," he said. His words were clear but his voice had an uncertain edge to it as if he wasn't entirely sure what he had seen. "There's only been one proven case of a single wolf in Vermont," he added. Then he shook his head and winced in pain.

Connor held him close and pressed a kiss to the top of his head. The noise of two approaching vehicles had Connor pulling away from Josh and assuming the stance of someone in control of the situation. The sheriff was in the first car, Deputy Osborne in the second.

"What happened?" Sheriff Cross asked.

"Single auto accident, avoiding an animal and hitting a tree. Driver absent and seems the animal, whatever it was, has crawled into the forest."

"We need to find the wo—dog," Josh insisted. "It's injuries were severe, it will need help."

"The car belongs to one of the Brent kids. Osborne, go pay them a visit," he ordered the other deputy. "We need light."

Osborne climbed back in his car and pulled away and Cross maneuvered his vehicle so that the bright lights lit into the forest. Josh pulled away from Connor and this time he let Josh go. Stumbling a little, Josh moved into the dark and Connor followed him. He found Josh crouching on the ground and when Josh looked up at him, Connor saw the injuries to Josh's face were quite extensive. Whoever had knocked him out hadn't made it pretty.

"The blood just stops here," Josh said pointedly.

"This is definitely the direction your dog went?" Connor looked about him to see if it was possible Josh could be confused.

"Definitely. I watched it drag itself away. And there's blood here, but look, it just stops."

Connor looked at what Josh was pointing at. He nodded. It did appear that the blood, instead of trailing away, simply stopped.

"Was it possible it was a rabbit, and a predator picked it up?" Connor suggested.

Josh huffed a laugh. "Damn dog was huge, for a while I thought it was a wolf. Gray. Beautiful amber eyes. But I guess it was a little small for your average wolf."

"We don't have wolves here," Sheriff Cross said from behind them. Josh scrambled to stand and Connor helped him.

"It was probably a dog," Josh agreed. "A cross breed maybe."

With this consensus, they moved back to the car.

"Who are the Brent kids?" Connor asked carefully. He was aware he was asking a question that probably had an obvious answer for a local. From the way the sheriff described them, Connor imagined they were the town mischief-makers.

"Local family, kids are in and out of trouble, nothing major like leaving an accident though. I'll finish up here with Osborne," Cross appeared thoughtful, then nodded at Connor. "Take him home."

Chapter Four

Connor watched Josh sleep. He'd been told to take the morning off to keep an eye on Josh and for the first time he allowed himself to consider just how awful it had been for Josh when Connor had been attacked.

When he'd realized it was Josh unconscious and bleeding on the ground, his heart had stopped in numbing terror. Was this what Josh had felt? He felt the scar on his head and sighed as his fingers found the ridge of skin. They'd said in the hospital that the scar would be covered when he grew his hair back, and they weren't lying. He deliberately left the hair a little longer in the nape of his neck so that it wasn't immediately obvious, but he knew it was there.

Sighing, he sat back in the chair, staring at Josh, whose breathing was deep and even. He reached for all his notes from yesterday and shuffled them on the bed covers. Something niggled at the back of his head but he couldn't make a connection between the cases. He split out the ones where there were animals involved, two maulings and three disappearances. The first in 1962, the last only ten years ago.

"What you doin'?" Josh asked sleepily. He shuffled to sit upright in the bed.

Connor had to withhold comment on the color of Josh's face. A purple bruise covered him from temple to cheekbone and he would surely be a wide variety of greens and yellows by tomorrow.

"Research," he answered as he filled a glass with water. He passed two pain pills to Josh, then handed him the water. Satisfied that Josh had swallowed the meds, he sat back in his chair. "How you feeling?"

"Like I've been knocked over by a car," Josh deadpanned.

Something twisted in Connor's chest, "Don't joke. When I saw you on the ground . . ." He pushed the paperwork aside and clambered onto the bed. Pulling Josh close, he held him gently and breathed in the scent of his lover. The faint citrusy woodsy smell was all Josh. "I love you, Joshua Nolan."

"I love you, too," Josh said with a wide yawn. "So what are you researching? Did they come back to say they'd found the dog? Or the driver?"

He sounded more alert which was a key reason why Connor felt Josh could handle everything in one go.

"No sign of any animals. Edward went out at daybreak—"

"He shouldn't do that, he's not young anymore," Josh protested.

"He insisted. Osborne went with him. They didn't find anything. And as for the car? It was stolen. All three of the Brent kids were at home playing video games under the watchful eye of both parents and the local priest. Seems they were grounded so that strikes them off the list for now."

"That's probably why the driver ran. That's one thing though, means he wasn't hurt too bad. I just wish we could find the dog he hit."

Connor tightened his hold momentarily to reassure Josh, then immediately eased off. He'd checked his lover out pretty thoroughly but apart from the two head scrapes and the bruise on his thigh about the size of a boot, he'd come away unscathed. At least there were no chest injuries.

"What worries me is who knocked you unconscious. Whoever that is . . . they're on my list. There's nothing there we can use as evidence though. The scene is pretty empty for something so rare in this town."

"What time is it? I need to get over to the office."

"Edward is covering you," Connor said. "We both have the morning off, it's a little after six and I can make breakfast."

"Pancakes, eggs?" Josh asked hopefully.

Connor pressed a gently barely-there kiss to Josh's split lip. "Tell you what, because I love you I'll even do you some bacon."

Josh huffed a laugh, "I can't believe I ended up falling in love with someone who doesn't like bacon."

"We're clearly not compatible." Connor smirked. It was an old joke between them. Familiar and normal.

They clambered out of bed and split up, Josh for a shower and Connor to begin breakfast. He was nearly done when Josh joined him in the kitchen.

"Tell me about your research." Josh stole a piece of crispy bacon.

"Over breakfast. Sit. I made coffee."

"Now I know why I love you."

"You love me because I am the best you ever had in bed," Connor said seriously. Another familiar exchange of words.

"I've had better," Josh said.

"How come we've been together for so long then?" He slid the plate heaped with bacon, eggs and pancakes in front of Josh, then with his own plate, sat down opposite Josh. They ate breakfast pretty much in silence and it was only when Josh concentrated on coffee that Connor felt he was awake enough to talk.

"This research is pretty interesting," he started. "Couple of deaths, some missing people, a few hitchhikers who seemed to vanish after leaving Potsdam and thumbing in this direction. All unsolved cases, or at least cases with nothing but hearsay as evidence. Emma, remember her? She covers the office at night."

"I remember her."

"Well she had me listening to his local bullshit about the Black Creek Creeper." He chuckled when he recalled Emma's serious expression.

"The Black Creek Creeper? Sounds like the title to a B Movie."

"That's what I thought. Rumors had an old guy living up in the forest, usual backstory, home from war, lost his mind, and took to eating human flesh. It's all pretty fantastic in the retelling and every word of it is actually in the official files. Seemed to me every witness saw something different and every single one said the deaths were due to this Creeper."

Josh sat forward over his coffee. "I love urban legends. Was this Creeper a cannibal, or did he eat animals, too? 'Cause if he was only eating people, then he could be a Wendigo? But if it's animals as well... I don't know what he'd be called."

"I know what he's called," Connor said dryly.

"What?"

"Imaginary. The imaginary Creeper."

Josh shook his head. "First you don't eat bacon, and now we find out you have no soul for stories. I think I'm going to have to find a new guy to cook me breakfast." He moved a little in his seat, then kissed Connor.

Josh tasted of bacon and coffee and Connor was so in love with this man it was freaking ridiculous. If it meant something to Josh, then maybe he could research some more local legends. He enjoyed the kiss and chuckled as they separated. He saw a small pearl of blood on Josh's split lip and shook his head.

"You are officially banned from kissing until your lip heals."

Josh touched his lip and looked down at the wet on his finger. Then he frowned. "Why would someone do this? To me? Knock me out? You think it was the driver?"

"I'm guessing so. They thought maybe you'd seen something? I don't know. Our working hypothesis is that someone stole the car for a joyride, one of the Brent boy's friends, knocked into a dog, then hid. Maybe he or she felt guilty or went into shock. Either way that looks like our best direction."

"I hope it was someone local and not someone just going through town."

"Why?"

"'Cause if he or she was hiding in the forest, the Creeper may get them." Josh waggled his eyebrows and stole a pancake from Connor's plate.

"Ass" was all Connor could say.

The weekly meeting was the busiest Connor had ever seen the offices. Seemed like the world and his wife were crammed into the small space, although it was really only staff. He met three other deputies, two men and a woman, as well as Osborne and himself, with Sheriff Cross at the front leaning on the fax machine desk. Connor didn't recall his precinct having a fax machine anymore, but this one regularly churned over marketing faxes for Viagra and lottery wins. Clearly it was being used well. This was his first team meeting and he was intrigued what the town had to talk about.

"Just waiting for coffee," the sheriff said. Then he crossed his arms over his chest and looked directly at Connor. Something about his boss's piercing gaze made Connor squirm and he stared out of the window as he waited for the sheriff to look somewhere else. He focused his thoughts on Josh and how sore his face looked when he'd walked him to the veterinarian clinic.

Josh wasn't complaining though so it wasn't as if Connor could fuss. Anyway, Edward was waiting there with a look of concern and Connor felt like he was leaving his lover in good hands. He glanced back at Sheriff Cross and saw the man was looking at a newly received fax and frowning. Connor wondered if it was Viagra that put a frown on the man's face.

The final person arrived. Emma, with a tray of coffees and cookies, appeared from the small kitchen and there was general chitchat as she passed the drinks around. Then Sheriff Cross cleared his throat and everyone quieted.

"First on the agenda. Bryant, organize getting the damn car out of the tree and have it towed to the garage."

"Will do."

"Jamie Brent is pissed it's totaled, but I'm getting the impression he doesn't want to press us much into finding who took it. It's a heap anyway." Cross shrugged as he said it. Evidently the Brent boys were typical teenage drivers in the back of nowhere. "Connor, how is the veterinarian?"

Connor paused a second to think about what he was going to say. "He's fine, sir. Bit bruised, but he's more concerned about the animal out there that got hit."

Cross let out a thoughtful *hmmmm* noise, then continued. "Osborne, write up the report on this and make sure Joshua Nolan gets a copy for his insurance."

"Will do," Osborne saluted with his mug.

"You've all met Connor now, he's going to be looking to you all for guidance and support while he finds his country feet, so let's keep things moving along there."

A general murmur of noise and everyone turned to face Connor, which in itself wasn't embarrassing except for the suspicious looks in the woman deputy and one of the men. Seems like this was a place that found newbies an object of interest.

"Last thing. It's coming up to that time of the month," Cross sighed and shook his head. "Next Tuesday is Lammas and I'll need Osborne and Vincent to volunteer to cover the whole night."

"I'll do it," Osborne said quickly. Then he turned and looked expectedly at Connor.

"What is Lammas?" Connor asked. He wanted to know what he was letting himself in for even if volunteering probably gave him brownie points.

Osborne grinned enthusiastically. "It's the day in the pagan festival for celebrating harvest. We have ourselves a group of kids from Potsdam who celebrate with beer and God knows what. Couple years ago they ended up in the forest and it got out of hand." He looked excited to be part of what could end up as patrolling nothing.

"Count me in then," Connor said. *Like I even have a choice. Being the newbie did kind of suck.*

Sheriff Cross carried on with normal admin stuff, scheduling, air conditioning, budgets, nothing Connor hadn't heard in his old positions, except here everything was that much more immediate to each deputy.

"Any other business?" Cross asked.

"Just one thing," Connor offered. He knew Emma had said he shouldn't dig into this but he couldn't stop himself. Blame boredom, blame instinct, he wanted something to do. "Why is there no effort made to close down the cold cases in the files."

Cross narrowed his gaze. "We don't have cold cases."

"Disappearances, couple of bodies, spread out over fifty or so years."

"The Creeper cases," Emma interjected with a grimace.

Cross sighed heavily. "You think we have the budget to go messing with things that are long since gone? Each of those files was signed off by previous sheriffs. We live on the edge of a forest where you could go in and not come out for days."

"Is it okay if I have a look at them, fresh eyes and that, on my off days?"

Cross exchanged looks with Bryant and Osborne . The feeling that something was going on here became an itch at the base of his neck. His suspicious nature made him a good cop, and his instincts served him well in the city. Cross and the two deputies seemed unable to say anything definitive about what he saw as open cases.

"I'd rather you spent your time learning systems in the here and now," Cross finally said.

Connor looked at him directly. He could lie with the best of them. "No problem," he said evenly.

"Right, if that is all, meeting is finished." Cross left the outer office and went into the room labeled *Sheriff* and shut the door behind him. Seemed like the moment for discussion was passed.

"We'll need flashlights," Osborne said enthusiastically at his side.

Save me now.

Chapter Five

The first sign of trouble was just after he and Osborne decided to split up and walk the circuit around the clearing individually. The clearing was nothing more than ten or so felled trees, but the way the other trees curved up and around to form a canopy was stunning in the moonlight. Connor didn't call himself a poetic person, but the full moon cast beams of light through the roof of leaves and made the place ethereal. Josh would laugh at him and suggest there were fairies in the glade. He had this way of making some things sound a lot more interesting than they were.

They'd circled the area for two hours. Connor listened to Osborne rambling on about everything and nothing. Life, his family, his college years. He was an interesting guy to listen to. Despite the puppy look about him, he was mature and made a good deputy. Connor felt a little responsible for him, but it was Osborne's idea to split up. There was no sign of teenagers rampaging through the woods, in fact there was nothing up here except for trees, trees, and more trees, and the clearing, of course.

An unearthly howl split the quiet night and the sound of a scream had Connor stopping dead in his tracks and pulling out his weapon. Forget the slower pace of life and assessing a situation before he pulled a gun, he needed to know he could handle this. Running in the direction of the scream, he slid to a horrified stop inches from what was left of Osborne. The young man's eyes were vacant, his neck ripped apart, and his torso shredded.

Jesus, fuck.

Connor circled with his gun stretched out in front of him. Something in the bushes just to one side of him made a sound and Connor fired a shot into the area.

He heard laughing, maniacal laughing, not an animal, but a human. He could deal with humans. They could be ordered to cooperate.

"Sheriff's office, show yourself," he demanded.

More laughing to his left and Connor sent another bullet into the dark. When the laughing continued, he knew he was not going to win this by randomly firing at every source of sound.

He connected to the office. Emma answered and Connor didn't waste time. "Officer down, just off—"

Something leaped at him from the dark, a snarling mass of fur and teeth, and knocked the phone out of his hand. Connor reacted by pushing back against the weight on his chest and let out a yell of shock. He brought the gun up to shoot, but teeth on his hand ripped the gun free and it fell into the darkness. For a second the animal backed away, then looked up at the sky and let out a howl. A wolf. A fucking wolf had jumped him. He scrambled back where he thought the phone may be—his hands reaching in the dark for anything to use as a weapon. This was a big wolf. Fucking big, like the ones he'd seen in movies. It stopped howling then sat on its ass and stared at him. Striated amber eyes met his and he scrambled back farther. Help would come. He just needed to hold the thing off long enough for them to arrive.

His fingers closed around wood and he gripped the fallen branch tight before clambering into a crouch. Maybe he should appear threatening? Stand and wave the wood? Or was it appearing small and harmless with a wolf? He couldn't remember. Outside of a zoo he'd never even seen a real wolf.

Howls in the distance echoed through the trees. *There are more?* This wasn't going to be a fight. This was a pack hunt and he needed to get the hell down to the car. With no further thought, he leapt to his feet and ran with every ounce of energy he had and tumbled headlong into the dark, hoping to hell he was heading the right way. The sounds behind him defied description, snarling, growling, and the noise of something crashing through the undergrowth and it was getting closer with each step.

He wasn't going to make it back to Josh. He was going to die here in this place and he would be the next death on the unsolved crimes list. Panic made him stumble and with inevitability coursing through him, he simply curled into a ball. The wolf was on him and tore at his thigh, then clamped his teeth around Connor's arm, shaking him like a chew toy. When Connor was thrown clear, the wolf lazily padded over, his teeth exposed in a fearsome snarl. Connor waved the stick but the wolf merely used a huge paw to push the stick and the hand to the floor, then used its weight to pin Connor.

Connor wriggled and tried to move, but there was nothing he could do. Teeth glinted in the dark, then the wolf clamped them on Connor's shoulder. The pain was incredible and he could feel his own flesh tearing. Then nothing as the wolf backed away. Connor slid back and away, his vision tinged with red. Blood ran freely from the tear in his shoulder and he was going to die.

A second wolf joined them, leaping into the space between the first and Connor. There was a standoff. Connor wasn't sure what he was watching, but when a third and fourth wolf joined the crowd and stood between him and his attacker, it was clear he was being protected. The large killer wolf snarled and snapped, then in an instant he ran.

Connor closed his eyes. The pain was too much and he was bleeding out. Voices sounded above him. Angry and snappy, they argued.

"Fuck, he needs help."

"We can't take him anywhere."

"We're going to lose him."

"I need to do this."

"You can't. He hasn't made the choice."

"You want me to leave him to die?"

That last voice was familiar. Connor blinked and opened his eyes. Through the blur of blood he thought he saw the guy from the alleyway, Tiber, and the sheriff was there? What the hell was going on. He didn't understand.

"You can't."

"You gonna stop me?"

A wolf stood over him. Beautiful, brindled dark and black with green gold eyes. When the wolf bared his teeth and sunk them into Connor's throat, he knew he was going to die here.

"Come find me, city boy, when you wake up."

Wake up? He was dying. He couldn't breathe.

His last conscious thought was that he wished Josh could hold his hand as he died.

Connor's head was a soft empty space and there was not a single press of pain in his entire body. This must be what comes next. He attempted to move, but nothing worked. He clenched his hand and the fingers twitched, but the pain that shot up his arm at the movement was excruciating.

"Don't move, Con. Stay still. Nurse! He's awake."

Josh? Josh is here? How can he be? I'm dead.

Someone was pushing and pulling and he wanted to tell them all to stop. A prick to his arm and he slid into sleep.

The next time he woke, he felt grounded. Like his body was his and he could focus on who was in the room. Josh.

"Josh?" he whispered. His throat was sore, tight, and the words hurt to push out.

"I'm here," Josh said loudly. So loud that the words hurt.

Connor winced at the noise. "Too loud," he murmured. He felt ice on his lips and he welcomed the cold and wet as it dribbled into his mouth. "Wolf," he said carefully.

"We know," Josh said. Softly this time. "They tried tracking it, but they didn't find anything. The other deputy, Osborne, is dead."

"Saw him."

"Shit." Josh moved until he could press his lips to Connor's head. "Shit, Con, what if it had been you? If I'd lost you . . . I can't handle this."

Grief balled in Connor's chest. Josh sounded so final. "Don't leave," he pleaded. Then coughed when the words cut into his throat again.

"I'm not going anywhere. I want you home. I want you cooking bacon. I want you in our bed." Josh's voice hitched with emotion. "I love you. Just you remember that."

"Always do . . . sorry." He wanted to say sorry. Sorry he and Osborne had split up to patrol that sorry excuse for a clearing, sorry he'd not paid attention when Osborne was talking. Sorry he knew little to nothing about the deputy who died. Sorry that he'd let himself get into a situation where he could die. He should have scouted better. Taken more notice of that instinct inside him that told him not everything was right in the forest.

"Don't be sorry," Josh whispered. "Just be well again. They injected you with more meds, you're going to sleep. I'll be here when you wake up."

"Promise."

"Promise."

The reassurance was enough to allow Connor to relax into the bed and allow whatever made him feel light and floating, to drag him down. He could hear Josh talking, but that couldn't be right, Josh had stepped outside and shut the door. Clear as day he heard the conversation.

"There's still hope?" Josh was asking.

"There's always hope, Mr. Nolan. Always hope."

Chapter Six

Connor transferred himself from the wheelchair to standing as soon as the hospital doors closed behind him. Damn contraption was giving him leg cramps and he'd just lost the pain in his thigh, he didn't want to cause more damage by sitting on his ass. Josh had gone for the car, which he'd had to park at the side of the hospital about as far as was possible to park it.

Connor said he was fine to walk, but the instant flash of concern in Josh's eyes had him changing his mind and giving in to his lover. As it was he'd signed himself out AMA, but hell, he felt better. His wound had healed fast, his head felt clear, and he had the energy to move. All of which meant he did not want to be laid up in a damn hospital bed, which could double as a torture device. A scent hit his nostrils, woodsy and warm it tingled inside him and he frowned.

"How are you feeling?" a voice asked from his side.

He near jumped out of his skin at the sound. He'd been so focused on the unusual scent, which was growing stronger as he stood there, that he hadn't even heard the owner of the voice appear beside him. He turned his head and came eye to eye with Tiber, the guy from the alleyway, and a subdued Donny at his side. The younger man was limping to catch up with Tiber—favoring his left leg. He grinned when he saw Connor—looking up at him from under his lashes. The two men couldn't have been more different. Tiber was tall and broad with three days' worth of stubble, dark hair and brooding brown eyes while Donny was shorter by a head, slim, you could even describe him as twink-like—all blond hair and blue eyes.

"Hey," he said.

"Donny," Connor said in return with a nod of his head. Donny's smile turned into a heart-breaking grin and the smile reached his bright blue eyes. He touched Connor on the arm and Connor inhaled sharply. A warmth trickled from Donny's touch and he found himself swaying closer.

"Donny!" Tiber snapped. Donny immediately stepped back and Connor felt bereft. "How are you feeling, deputy?" Tiber repeated firmly.

"Better," Connor finally answered. He rolled his shoulders experimentally.

"Much better?" Donny interjected with the excited question. Damn, the little guy was near hopping from one foot to the other.

"Really good," Connor offered. Donny's rocking movements were infectious and he wished Donny would touch him again. He'd liked it. "What's wrong with your leg?"

"This?" Donny asked with a wave at his foot. "Got in an accident and the break didn't heal properly. Had to have some uhm . . ." He trailed off and looked up at Tiber.

"Physio," Tiber said firmly.

"Meds," Donny said at exactly the same time. "Physio," he amended quickly. "And meds."

"Wait in the car, Donny," Tiber said sternly. Donny flicked his gaze over to Tiber and pouted. Connor expected him to argue but instead Donny touched his arm briefly, then said his goodbyes and left.

"Why do you talk to him like that?" Connor asked. He still wasn't convinced that the relationship between Donny and

Tiber was healthy. Donny didn't exhibit classic signs of abuse, but he did appear to defer to Tiber absolutely.

Tiber sighed. "I look out for him. He's often in a world of his own and it's like he looks for trouble. He's my cousin. He's got a big heart and he tries to help out everyone. One day he's going to talk to someone who doesn't want to talk back and instead cause trouble for him."

"Your cousin," Connor repeated the bit that interested him most.

Tiber waved a hand, "Twice removed or something like."

They stared at each other and just as it was growing uncomfortable with neither talking, Tiber sighed. He reached into his pocket and pulled out a card, which he held out for Connor to take.

"If you feel..." He paused and frowned. "Unwell," he finally said. "Call me. Or I can check in with you." He looked away from the matched stare at that point. He couldn't look Connor in the eyes and Connor's cop instincts surfaced immediately. What the hell was going on? He needed to do some research.

A horn pulled his attention to the SUV that Josh had parked at the curbside, and when he looked back to ask Tiber questions, the other man had gone. Connor spun on his heel and winced at the ache in his thighs, but there was no sign of Tiber. Damn, that man moved quick.

"You getting in?" Josh called. "You need some help, old man?"

Grumpiness washed over Connor and he couldn't help snapping. "I don't need any fucking help, asshole."

Josh smiled broadly. Fucker. Connor climbed in and pointedly ignored his lover until he'd shut his door.

"Who was that you were talking to?" Josh asked conversationally as they left the hospital and headed back to the house.

Potsdam to Black Creek was only thirty miles, but the roads were winding and it took much longer than it would on a straight road. The intriguing scent of woodland and peat had stayed with him, but instead of the darker notes, he could smell citrus. Strong and sharp it sent waves to his groin and he shifted in his seat.

"You okay, babe?" Josh asked concerned.

Connor huffed a laugh. "Nothing a beer and sleep in a proper bed won't cure."

Lust curled inside him. Maybe a roll on that bed with Josh would be a good addition to the scenario. He missed Josh, the taste of him, and his touch, and the fact that he was cloaked in the citrus fragrance that was usually strongest at the base of his throat. He growled low in his throat at the image of being buried inside his lover, inhaling the smell of him, biting down and tasting him.

Jesus. Fuck. What the hell is going on? Surely I've been off medication for a long enough time to not be doing this crazy weird brain thing anymore.

Josh pressed the palm of his hand flat on Connor's thigh and Connor's treacherous dick twitched under the touch. Josh laughed.

"It's only been a week," he pointed out even as he slid his hand higher and cupped Connor's obvious erection tenting his sweats.

"I swear, Josh, if you don't get us home and inside our bedroom with the door shut soon, then I swear I will get you to pull us over here so I can fuck you on the hood of this damn car."

Josh removed his hand and looked left at Connor with a curious expression on his face. Connor pointedly ignored him and instead stared out the window, feigning interest in the forest as it darkened and thickened when they drew closer to Black Creek. They crossed the river that separated the town in two and were back at the house quickly. Connor willed away the lust. He still ached in his thigh, and his knees hurt, and hell, his elbows ached. How the fuck did you have elbows that ached?

He was out of the cab as soon as the car stopped and at the door waiting. Josh may well have thought he was joking, but the heat inside him to be with Josh wasn't something that was going away.

Josh took the porch steps in one jump and stumbled as Connor grabbed his shirt and pulled him in for a kiss.

God. The taste of him.

Connor deepened the kiss and pressed Josh back against the wooden door, grinding his erection against Josh and near whimpering in the desperation to be inside him. Josh pushed away and temper sparked inside Connor.

What the hell. Where did temper come from? Wait . . . Josh shouldn't be moving . . . I want him still.

"Let's not put on a show for the neighbors," Josh said with a smile. He opened the door and probably imagined that he had slowed down proceedings. Something Connor proved as very wrong when he pushed Josh inside and slammed the door shut behind them.

"What's gotten into you?" Josh said. He wasn't angry or concerned, if anything he looked surprised. Sometimes their lovemaking was tender and drawn out, then other times it was balls deep instant against a wall with come painting stomachs and no words spoken. Josh probably hadn't been expecting the latter on the day Connor was released from hospital.

"Your injury..." The rest of Josh's words were muffled in another heated kiss and Connor pushed Josh back until he was pressed against the wall. Mindlessly he reached for the small ornate box on the hall table. With practiced experience, he flicked it open and grabbed the lube that sat inside. All without breaking the kiss. He had to be inside. Now.

He forcibly turned Josh until his lover was pressed face first against the wall and, in seconds, Josh had his jeans down and Connor was pressing lube and fingers in a messy scramble to stretch Josh ready for him. Josh turned his head and they kissed in the awkward position, tongues and teeth, and Connor could taste the metallic of blood. His heart sang with the lust and passion inside him. Buried inside his lover, forcing Josh's legs apart, shoving him against the wooden walls wasn't pretty or neat or sensual, it was power and dominance and *need right now.*

Josh had one hand flat on the wall, the other holding his cock and fucking into his hand as Connor fucked into him. Connor gripped Josh's hip with one hand and searched for a solid hold of Josh's cock. Finally they were both pressing and pulling and wringing a noisy orgasm from Josh.

"Connor... Connor... Connorrrr..." Josh keened and mewled as he spurted warm and fast over their hands.

Connor closed his eyes in victory and buried his face in the nape of Josh's neck. The scent... the smell... the taste... He pushed and pushed and suddenly he peaked. Orgasm ripped through him, a molten mess of fire and extreme pleasure coiled and spat and he was coming into his lover, marking him from the inside. Finally he stopped and the waves of feeling subsided to a dull roar.

"Connor... that was..." Josh trailed off.

He was breathing heavily, but not as heavily as Connor who felt like he had run a freaking marathon. Carefully he pulled himself free, then removed his t-shirt in one smooth move. They could use it to clean up, although Josh didn't seem to be moving. He had his forehead against the wall and he was bracing his weight. His right hand was slick with come and Connor started there, ignoring his lover's protests. Together they stumbled to the bedroom and cuddled close with breathing finally even and matched and Connor felt Josh fall asleep in his arms.

Connor knew he wouldn't be long after. If only he could relax. Everything was too bright, too loud, he could hear Josh's heartbeat, and he just knew he was heading for a migraine. Josh had brought the meds they'd given Connor into the bedroom and Connor swallowed two dry. He was not going to lie around in pain. He wanted to sleep next to Josh and be thankful he was alive.

The smell of coffee woke him and he reached across the bed to check for Josh. When he reached empty sheets, he assumed Josh was the one making coffee. His feet hitting the floor sent a sensation of pain up his legs and he cursed under his breath. He had issued a check with Josh that his body couldn't cash. Either that or he was getting old. Padding into the kitchen, he blearily rubbed his eyes. Seemed they'd slept through the day and it was after nine in the evening. Josh was wearing sweats that hung from his hipbones and in the soft light of the hall, the dark kitchen was casting weird shadows around his lover. Connor had never seen anything so beautiful as Josh leaning against the counter, waiting for the coffee machine to do its thing.

He yawned widely behind a hand and crossed to Josh, cuddling him from behind. Josh tensed in his arms momentarily in surprise. Evidently he hadn't expected Connor out of bed yet. Then he relaxed back into Connor's hold and finally turned in his arms and pulled Connor closer for a hug.

"How you doing?" he asked gently.

"Ache a bit," Connor answered truthfully. After five years together, Josh could see through Connor like his mom used to be able to do. According to Josh he could tell when Connor was lying, joking, or any other *ing* Connor attempted to pull on him.

"You can probably get some more pain meds." Josh punctuated that with a kiss and, for a second, they stood close and kissed gentle close-mouthed kisses and simply held each other.

"It's weird," Connor started. "My thigh is fine, my chest, fine, but I feel like every muscle in me aches, and my joints, my knees, even my damn elbows. Just ouch. Like I'd pushed too many weights, or run three marathons back to back.

Josh tugged back a little and, even without being able to see into Josh's eyes, Connor knew his other half was probably going to mention the unnecessary sex in the hallway. He wasn't wrong.

"We shouldn't have done that this morning," Josh admonished. "You're not well enough.

"I was fine. You weren't complaining."

Josh huffed a laugh, then turned back to the coffee. Carrying two mugs into the front room, they sat next to each other on the old wide sofa that had come as part of the house.

"I'll be complaining tomorrow," Josh deadpanned. "I'm not saying it wasn't hot, but jeez, look at this." He wriggled a little and pushed down his sweats to expose his left hipbone and five perfect crescent dents that were red and sore.

"Shit, babe," Connor snapped immediately. He placed the coffee down, then touched the marks on Josh's beautiful unblemished skin. "Did I do that?" He leaned down and pressed a kiss to the marks, then sat back up, not really knowing what to say. Should he say sorry? Is that what Josh wanted. Why was it so difficult to read Josh's expression? Normally he could read Josh as easily as he himself could be read.

"You just don't know your own strength," Josh said without accusation. Then he straddled Connor's lap and buried his face in Connor's neck. "I fucking loved it," Josh mumbled.

Connor held him tight and relished the feel of Josh's skin against his own. "I love you," he said gently.

"I love you, too," Josh murmured. "Don't ever get attacked in the forest again. Okay?"

Connor moved so that more of Josh's weight rested on him. The feeling of him was exquisite. Then he cuddled hard and made a mental promise to never go in amongst the trees again.

CHAPTER SEVEN

Josh was back at work the next day and Connor was signed off for another two so that gave him more than enough time to catalogue everything that had happened. He made notes—what he'd seen, what he'd done. He'd already done this once in the hospital for Sheriff Cross, who had visited with a fruit basket and a sadness about him that didn't leave.

He glanced down at what he'd written. Osborne's name in big letters and ringed in red. Was it quick? This dying thing? Had Osborne seen his attacker? Had he suffered? An urge to kill curled in the pit of Connor's stomach and he added a single word under Osborne's name. Wolf.

Not that anyone believed him about the wolf attack. Or rather, everyone heard him explain he was utterly sure it was a wolf that had attacked him. And everyone who heard that listened and nodded and said all the right things. Called in Wildlife services, called local zoos.

It was dark everyone ended up saying. Of course, the fact that what had at first appeared to be parallel and deep cuts into his chest from a wolf's claws now looked like nothing more than the scrape of a branch did nothing to back up his story.

Then how did Osborne get his throat torn?

It wasn't torn, Cross had told him in response. *It looked like he stumbled and hit his head, rolled awkwardly. The coroner says a broken neck.*

So what about all the blood? God, how many times had he asked this question?

There wasn't that much blood, Cross pointed out.

What about the dog the car hit? Was that maybe another wolf? A smaller one, maybe?

We don't have wolves in Vermont, Connor.

Should we get Josh to test blood type or something? He knows a lot.

Forensics have it covered. You just get well.

He felt like a damn dog having his head patted and being told to go sit in his bed until the owners sorted the problem. And yes, he was aware that was a very weird analogy to use.

Bored, he decided to make Josh lunch and wander over to the practice. Josh was lucky Edward was happy to cover when Connor had been in hospital, but Josh wanted desperately to be back and working and Connor desperately wanted him to go. Josh was probably tired of how many times Connor had jumped him over the last four days. Not that they weren't normally active, they were, but the sex between them had been intense and quick and rough. He owed Josh an apology and hoped his lover's favorite PB&J sandwiches might go some way to smoothing the waters. Josh wasn't unhappy, but he had sat Connor down this morning at the table and queried whether Connor was simply looking for life-affirming sex. In Connor's head that cheapened what they were doing to the point where he worried he was forcing himself on Josh.

He shook his head to clear the worries. He and Josh were solid and in love. He stuffed another sandwich in his mouth as he walked over. Hospital food sucked—it was like his body was making up for lost time. That, and the athletic sex, probably.

He grinned when he saw Josh through the window. He was sat at the desk in his office, scribbling furiously on notes, his back hunched and his hair looking like he had spent all morning twisting his fingers in it. Quietly, Connor let himself in the side door and made his way down the short corridor which ended in a T-junction. He didn't have to think where Josh was, he could smell the citrusy woodsy smell from here. He should really warn Josh that he was using too much of whatever he was using before he started killing the pets in here. Not everyone would appreciate the gorgeous sexy smell.

He knocked on the door and opened it when he heard the faint *come in*. Josh looked up from his paperwork and immediately grinned in welcome. He held out his hand in a gimmee gesture and Connor dropped the packed bread and filling on the table and a kiss on Josh's mouth.

"I need these." Josh fell on the provided meal with enthusiasm and in mid-mouthful grabbed two cold waters from a small fridge. He tossed one to Connor who caught it deftly.

"Busy morning?"

"Yeah." He swallowed a mouthful of water. "Two pet rabbits. I lost one, though. Not sure the kid who brought them in is going to be pleased."

"You tried your best," Connor insisted.

"How do you know that?" Josh teased. "For all you know, I could be a bunny murderer."

He laughed and the sound was familiar and welcome. "I love you," Connor blurted.

Josh had been leaning back in his chair, but at the quick words, he resumed sitting upright with his soles flat on the floor. He tilted his head in question and something about the way Josh sat, or maybe it was something he said, or hell, it could have been anything, but suddenly, Connor wanted Josh like he wanted his next breath.

Startled, he realized he needed to get out of the room before he literally jumped the bones of this man in front of anyone who happened by the window. He opened the door and a rush of cool air came in from the air conditioning unit in the hall. Bliss. It carried with it the scent of blood and Connor turned a little until he could smell less blood and more *Josh*.

"Show me the rabbit you didn't kill?" he deadpanned.

"Are you okay?" Josh asked seriously. "Are you in pain?"

Great. Now he looked like he was in pain? That was probably his must-not-have-sex face contorting weirdly and making it look like agony carved him deep.

"I'm fine." To emphasize the point, he raised himself up on the balls of his feet and bounced. He schooled his features into a smile even though his muscles burned and his joints ached. Seemed like the only time he didn't hurt was when he was buried inside Josh. Typical. He really needed to slow down with the sex before he did himself permanent damage.

Luckily Josh didn't notice anything and instead guided Connor down past the small reception manned by Jessie Flannigan, spinster of the parish and a stalwart of the clinic. They exchanged pleasantries, but there was something about Jessie that made Connor feel she could look right through him and to the pain inside. He didn't hang around and the two men went into the surgery wing and into the recovery unit. A wall full of cages, some with bedding and an animal inside, some empty and sterile, stretched along two walls. Larger cages at the bottom for bigger animals like dogs, he guessed, and smaller ones above for what he thought was the smaller animals like rabbits and such things.

"Look," Josh said softly. He stopped at a corner cage and tapped on the wire.

Connor crossed to peer inside. A brown rabbit lay on its side—its chest rising and falling in a regular rhythm, the only thing indicating it was alive. The name on the temporary cage title read *Flopsy* and carried details of the operation and the relevant family details.

Connor's heart quickened in his chest as he pictured the rabbit startled and scared, darting through the bushes as he chased it. He moved closer and pushed a finger through the wire. He just wanted to touch the soft fur. Feel the heartbeat. Press his hand around the rabbit's throat to feel its pulse.

That's all.

He didn't want to chase Flopsy, run it down, leap on it and tear into its flesh.

"No poking," Josh said firmly. He pulled Connor's finger away.

Irritation snapped and fizzled inside Connor. He wanted to . . . what? What did he want? He blinked at the sleeping rabbit. Fuck. His head was screwed. He was way too tired. Turning away from the injured pet deliberately, he couldn't help but notice the dark box on the far desk.

"Mopsy," Josh said sadly. "Whatever got to them didn't leave much for me to save there."

"Josh, can I borrow you? The Cyrills are on line one."

"Shit," Josh muttered. "Now I have to tell them Mopsy has moved on. Back in a minute."

Connor watched Josh leave. He loved the way his lover spoke about the animals he tried to save. That they had moved on. It was cute and a whole lot warmer than telling someone their pet bunny had died. Idly, he looked in other cages. A couple of smaller hamster type gerbil things, which looked particularly cute, huddled in a corner. Then a momma cat, pregnant and wide eyed, hissed at him and arched her back as he looked in.

Finally the box. He couldn't help himself. He just had to lift the corner and look inside. Poor Mopsy really hadn't stood a chance. The throat had been ripped and there was so much blood that the scent of it was all Connor could focus on. Idly he pushed a finger in and pressed the rabbit's side. There wasn't any give in it, and no pulse of course. Rigor mortis had set in and this kill wasn't fresh. In fact, decay had already taken this rabbit to a place where no one would want to eat it.

I wouldn't even want to taste it, he thought.

Startled, he dropped the lid. What the hell. As the lid, shut his finger caught and he swore. Backing away from the box, he left the room without taking his eyes off any of the animals. The cat stared at him in accusation, the hamster things still slept and Flopsy's chest rose and fell in a faster rhythm than his own heart. He left the room and shut the door of the recovery area behind him before leaning against the wood.

"You don't look so well, young man," Jessie commented.

He inhaled, hoping to get a whiff of Josh's citrus, or her rosewater and lavender, but all he had in his nostrils was blood and decay.

"Are you alright?" she asked, concerned.

No. I'm not. I'm losing my fucking mind. What the hell is going on?

"I'm fine," he lied. "Can you tell Josh I went home for a nap?"

Jessie nodded approvingly. "I will do."

Leaving the same way he came in so as to avoid Josh, he stumbled indoors and immediately stripped naked and took a freezing shower. Anything to cool down the heat that burned in his blood. He should get an appointment at the hospital. Maybe one of his wounds was infected. Under the water, he looked at the various places he had been injured. All that was left were faint pink marks. He was a lightweight, thinking his wounds had been violent. Everything in his head was screwed.

Shower finished, he wrapped himself in a towel and crawled into bed. The covers were too heavy and he ended up laying on top of the covers under the lazily moving fan and wishing for ice. He consciously relaxed each muscle until he was able to sleep.

The rabbit darted in a hopelessly random pattern in front of him. In and out and around trees until he felt dizzy with the chase. He looked down and saw his paws hitting the ground in a regular rhythm and the weight of his head moving forward had him tumbling ass over head into a bramble bush. Scrambling free, he shook himself, then rubbed off the worst of the prickles by rolling on his back. The sky above him was black velvet and stars hung in a celestial pattern that he loved. The moon was pregnant and full, high in the sky, and the only light he had to catch dinner. Rolling onto all fours, he shook from nose to tail, then lifted his snout and search for the distinct scent of fresh prey.

Darting right, he cut off the rabbit coming around another tree. He caught a glimpse of wide, frightened eyes as he grabbed the animal and shook it clean dead between his teeth. There was a scream and a struggle, then the prey had limply sacrificed itself for him and the blood that coursed out of it already slid down his throat. It was raw and hot and pulsed on his tongue until finally the blood stopped and he dropped he rabbit on the ground. Carefully, he ripped the meat away and devoured it. Finally full, he wiped his muzzle along the ground, then sat back on his haunches. Glancing once at the remains of the rabbit, he then raised his nose to the moon and felt the rush of her power inside him, until finally he howled his release to the sky.

When Connor woke up he realized two things—that he was crying, and that Josh was holding him tight and rocking him like a child.

Chapter Eight

Josh held Connor tight, rocking him and supporting him and wondering what the hell had just happened. Jessie told him Connor wasn't looking so well and that he'd gone home. Josh had used the break he had to jog to their house to check on him. What he'd found was a very naked Connor writhing on the bed in the throes of a terrible nightmare. Josh had gone into autopilot and climbed on the bed. He held Connor and promised him, in soft words, that everything would be okay.

He had watched Connor carefully over the last few days. Apart from the life-affirming sex, which he recalled after the last time he'd brought Connor home from hospital, nothing much had changed with Connor. Still, Josh worried. He'd seen PTSD before in a friend returning from war, he wasn't going to let Connor slide into something before getting treatment. Some of what they'd been told, that Osborne didn't have his throat torn, that there was no blood, that it had been nothing more than an accident up in the forest, didn't sit well with Josh.

But he wasn't the investigator. He was the lover, the partner, the one who sat at home waiting for their cop lover to come back safe. Connor looked up at him and his eyes were filled with pain. He looked confused and frustrated.

"What did you dream about?"

"A rabbit, chasing . . ." Connor said brokenly.

The rabbit? This was about the rabbit today? "You're awake now, babe. I got ya."

Connor hesitated and shook his head. "Fuck," he swore loudly. "I don't know what the hell I saw." With a determined effort, he pushed himself up and away from Josh. He snorted disbelievingly. "Jeez these meds must be good. I'm tripping out on them."

"I'll call Edward, see if he can cover for me."

Connor wriggled free. "I'm not a damn child, Josh."

"I'm not . . . I don't mean . . ."

Connor placed a finger on Josh's lips and his touch was so gentle it made Josh stop talking.

"Go back to work, I promise you, I am fine."

"You sure?"

"Honestly." He reached over and picked up the prescription bottle Josh had left next to the bed. In a quick motion, he threw them in a curve to the small bin by the closet. The pill bottle rattled to the bottom and Connor smiled. "I'm not taking any more of those damn things."

"What about the pain?"

Connor scooted higher in bed. "I'm feeling good." He pointed to his chest. This time last week he'd had four vertical cuts. Now all that was left were faint pink lines in his otherwise honey toned skin. "Fast healer. See?"

"Okay, more sleep, then go sit on the sofa and just veg out in front of *Law and Order* re-runs. I'm only over in the clinic and I'm working until eight."

"Then I'll see you at eight."

Josh hesitated momentarily and considered the evidence. He was used to Connor being the tough guy who didn't feel pain, but he'd never seen Connor in the throes of a nightmare. There was nothing he could do—Connor was a stubborn ass when he was set on something. Finally, he had to leave and he pulled the quilt off his side of the bed and pushed it over Connor. Then he kissed him on the forehead.

"I love you," he said quietly. Then he left.

The short walk between house and clinic wasn't long enough to worry about Connor—he would do that when he was working.

There was something subtly wrong with Connor that maybe only Josh, as his lover, partner and best friend, could notice. Tonight they needed to talk.

As soon as Josh was gone, Connor kicked the quilt away. He was so damn hot, although Josh hadn't commented that he had a temperature. Still, he couldn't bear the material on his skin. Too much. And he had a hard-on like he'd had iron injected into his damn cock—just because he could smell Josh. If he hadn't been feeling confused, he'd have taken his lover there and then. Again. Just like the myriad of times since he'd gotten out of hospital.

Hard. Fast. The urge to bite and mark and rub Josh's scent onto his own skin was overwhelming.

He pressed a hand to the disappearing marks on his chest, then gingerly touched the gouge on his arm. Trailing his fingers down to where his sleeve tattoo ended, he peered at the pattern and ran a thumb over it. The dark blue of waves smudged under the motion. He blinked. Checking his thumb, he couldn't see ink on the skin, but it had definitely moved on the tattoo itself. Or had it? He was still seeing things. Freaking meds.

I'm losing it.

His cell's ring tone for Proctor pulled him out of wondering what the hell was going on with him that he thought a fifteen-year-old tattoo was smudging. He contemplated ignoring the call because the phone was just out of his reach, then he decided he'd been lazy enough and hadn't spoken to his old cop-partner in weeks.

"So I hear you've been beaten up," Proctor led in immediately. His voice had that teasing tone that Connor recalled from every other time he had been on the receiving end of a fist or a gun. Josh had phoned him. Jeez, the last thing he wanted was Proctor's interfering ass anywhere near him.

"And who told you that, I wonder," he deadpanned.

"A little bird." Conner could hear Proctor's smirk. "And when I say bird, I mean sexy guy with dark hair, bedroom eyes and an ass I can—"

"Yeah, yeah, I get the point. Hands off my man, fucker." Connor rolled up and fully out of bed, padding naked into the bathroom. Standing in front of the mirror, he contemplated shaving and getting a shower, all the while listening to Proctor wax lyrical over Josh's chest and his arms and his lips. This was how they rolled. Proctor was actually the reason that Connor even knew Josh. Proctor had set them up together after one disastrous evening when Josh and Proctor had attempted a blind date. Given Josh was all about switching it up and Proctor was all big, bad, strong top, it was never going to work.

They weren't the ones for each other, but Proctor knew Josh would be perfect for Connor. That had been a few years back now.

"So anyway, I have three weeks owing and I'm coming to stay. Need to check out how soft small-town-middle-of-nowhere living has made you."

Connor flexed his muscles in the mirror. There was nothing soft about him.

"You staying here?" he asked.

"And listen to you two through the walls? Fuck no. I'm staying at a B&B in town, arriving on the thirteenth of next month."

Connor calculated the days in his head. That was three weeks or so.

"It'll be good to catch up," Connor offered carefully. They didn't really do the whole buddy-buddy movie hugging stuff, but nevertheless, he loved the guy who had been his friend since they were snot-nosed kids running riot in the suburbs.

"You're okay, right?" Proctor asked finally. So that was the real reason for the call. "When Josh called he was kinda freaked out. Said you thought it was a wolf attack."

Thought it was a wolf? I'm convinced it was a damn wolf, Connor thought, but didn't say. "What can I say? They gave me good meds."

Proctor was silent for a while. Then laughed. "Stay alive, homo."

"Back at ya, fairy."

The familiar teasing pulled Connor out of his introspection and he tossed the phone onto the bed. He needed another shower just to cool himself down. Running a hand over the thick stubble on his face, he also knew he needed to have a damn shave, otherwise there was no chance of getting anywhere near Josh, who liked him all smooth and baby soft. Touching his chest, which was darkening with hair, he shook his head. Seemed like some manscaping was in order as well.

The shower was too hot and he kept turning down the water until he realized it was mostly cool water. Seemed he was running a temperature. He probably needed to mention that to a doctor or something. His antibiotics were nearly done, so maybe they weren't working or weren't the right ones for whatever infection he had. The rush of water over his skin was bliss and in short order he was clean and blessedly cool. The benefit of a cool shower was that bathroom didn't steam up and he at least could see his face as he was shaving. Which was damn lucky because his electric razor got clogged with hair and he had to switch to a disposable BIC. When the blade caught his skin and dragged on his stubble, he swore and dropped it in to the sink. Damn thing was blunt. He watched as a single drop of blood shook from the blade and spread into the water.

Checking his face for evidence of a cut, he could see nothing. Well, nothing except various patches where he had missed stubble. Cursing, he rummaged in the vanity unit and pulled out a brand new disposable razor. A short time later, he had clean shaved skin and he rinsed the BIC and placed it on his side of the shelf. His chest would have to wait—he was suddenly feeling the need to get some air. In loose sweats, a baggy t-shirt and old sneakers, he stepped outside into the heat of the day and lifted his face to the sun.

He felt like a run, but probably a walk would be better. He knew he'd promised not to go into the forest, but the pull of the trees and earth was irresistible. He'd just walk a little way. He pressed on into the forest that their house backed on to and was soon under the cooling canopy of green. In here, the scents were of trees, leaves, and the loamy soil beneath his feet. At last his erection died down to nothing more than the prickle of awareness on his skin.

If I'm not careful, I'll hurt Josh, he thought. Not that Josh complained, but he had to be getting sore. Tonight he'd suggest Josh take the lead. A sensation of peace suddenly rolled over him. He loved it when he was under Josh. He loved Josh. Stopping at a fork in the path, he rolled his shoulders. To the right was a circular route back to the house, to the left was up towards the peak and the clearing where Osborne died. Resolutely, he turned right. He wasn't ready to go up there. Then he stopped. Resigned, he strode up to the path which took him higher up into the thickening forest. He wasn't a coward.

Chapter Nine

Connor's walk turned into a slow jog, which in turn became a steeplechase run over fallen logs and bushes and small creek beds that were dry in August. His speed increased as he lengthened his stride and his breathing settled into a familiar pattern. This was like heaven. He pushed on and up and was pleased his stamina hadn't been entirely lost in the *accident* up here. Finally, he slowed his pace and stretched out heated muscles until he was able to walk into the clearing feeling refreshed and able to meet whatever memories were grounded here.

The clearing was smaller than he remembered and innocent in the sunlight. There was nothing ominous in the trees around the space and there was no sign of what had happened here a week ago. A rustling in the bushes had him spinning on his heel and his hand reaching for a gun that wasn't even there.

"Who is it?" he called. Steadying himself to run if it was a big-ass wolf, he was surprised when it was a person who stepped into view. Tiber. He was barefoot and wore low-slung jeans that were unbuttoned at the top and loose. His chest was bare, and for a few seconds Connor was at a loss for what to say. When another person joined them—Donny, in a similar state of undress, Connor immediately put two and two together. Donny and Tiber, cousins twice removed or whatever, were an item? That blindsided him. Tiber, all growls and moodiness, against Donny with his twinky innocence, did not, in his head, make a good couple. In fact, seeing them together made him feel uneasy.

Not to mention how he felt inside at seeing the men at all. At the same time as feeling he should not be looking Tiber in the eyes, he felt like he wanted Donny's hands on his again.

"Hi, Connor," Tiber said. He hooked his thumbs in his jeans and looked at Connor steadily.

"Hey," Donny added.

Connor held up both hands. "Didn't mean to interrupt your outdoor sex session," he said. "Nice day for it," he added weakly.

Tiber and Donny exchanged looks. Then grinned at each other stupidly. "Us?" Donny snorted, then laughed.

Connor tensed, waiting for Tiber's reaction to Donny's comment. Was he going to be angry? Push Donny up against a wall and circle his hands around Donny's throat?

"We're not here for sex," Tiber said. He smiled at Connor, then turned to Donny. "You want to give us ten?"

"You're sure?" Donny asked immediately. He placed a hand on Tiber's arm, and for a second Tiber swayed towards him. Hell, Connor recalled that soft touch and how it made him feel.

"It was my fault. I'm sure. Go chase something."

Donny turned on his heel and disappeared back into the forest. Tiber took a couple of steps towards Connor and it took him by surprise. He stumbled back in reaction and nearly lost his footing. The only thing that stopped him from hitting the ground was Tiber grabbing his arm and holding tight.

The touch sent electricity through his body and he fell to his knees, breathless. Tiber immediately backed away and sat on the nearest tree trunk. He looked regretful and hard and sad all at the same time.

"Sorry," he said. "I can't always control it."

Connor scrambled to stand and while his brain told him to run, his body, his instinct, had him sitting on the tree trunk opposite. He couldn't look Tiber in the eye. Every time he tried he felt odd, lightheaded, out of control. Pushing his hand in his pocket, he pulled out his cell. He needed to call someone. Josh. He stared down at the cell. *Press the damn screen*, he told himself.

You don't need Josh here.

Startled Connor lost hold of the phone and it fell to the grass beside him. Glancing around the clearing, he couldn't see anyone else.

It's me. I'm thinking these words.

Connor sat rooted to the wood and stared in disbelief at Tiber.

"What the fuck?" he demanded.

"It's a long story," Tiber said. "I just want you to know, before I start, that I couldn't be more sorry for how everything got out of control. Do you understand that?"

Connor nodded mutely. He didn't even know about what he was saying he understood, but it seemed appropriate to nod.

"I was here when you were attacked. You and the young guy, Osborne."

"I don't . . . I didn't . . . did you see the wolf?"

"I did."

"Then it wasn't a figment of my imagination." Connor clumsily stood. "We need to call in animal welfare or something."

"Sit down," Tiber said simply.

Connor sat. He didn't question Tiber's instruction or even think to continue panicking. He just sat. And now he couldn't move, like his ass was stuck to the trunk or something.

"I saw the wolf that attacked you. I had been tracking it, but when Donny got hurt... look, I didn't even know the sheriff had sent up the two of you. He should have passed it by me, but he thought it would be safe because... jeez... look... if I'd..." He stopped, then shrugged. "I can't watch for everyone, I'm only one person, and Donny was hit."

"Why were you tracking... wait... there are wolves in Vermont?" Connor had so many questions he didn't know where to start.

"Osborne couldn't shift to save himself." Tiber ignored the statement and forged ahead. "He was too far gone, the wounds so bad I could see his spine." Tiber shuddered. "Who does that? Who treats a human like prey and rips them apart."

"A wolf," Connor said. "You said it was a wolf."

"Not just any wolf. A wolf shifter."

"A wolf shifter." Connor snorted a laugh, then looked around the clearing for the hidden cameras. "Is this some kind of Black Creek initiation or something? Nice one, guys, but I've seen worse in the city. Werewolves, my ass!"

"Be quiet," Tiber ordered. Connor stopped talking. "We don't like the term werewolves. Too many links to some really awful films. There are shifters in this forest. Humans with two sides and the abilities to change into wolf form at will."

"Howling at the full moon?" Connor asked quickly. Then he realized he'd asked a question that might make Tiber think he actually believed anything Tiber was saying.

Tiber looked at him pointedly. "We're strongest at a full moon."

"We? You're... you... you said we."

"Me. Donny. Some others. I'm the alpha of the Black Creek pack. Then there's whoever attacked you."

Connor laughed disbelievingly. What was Tiber taking? Meth? Something a little less glamorous? "Werewolves. Alphas. Is this some kind of kinky sex game or something?"

Tiber stood and pushed his jeans down over his hips. Connor tried to stand but suddenly his legs wouldn't move and help him into the upward position. In front of him, as nude as the day he was born, Tiber raised his face to the sky and extended his hands at either side of him. With a snarl from his lips and cracks in bones that sounded vicious, Tiber changed. Jerky, in a way that appeared to be painful, the man moved from upright to all fours. In seconds he was a wolf. Four paws pressed on the earth and the wolf had a long elongated snout and the most beautiful dark gray fur.

Connor's vision blurred and with a moan at the sudden blinding pain in his head, he fell off the tree trunk and his world turned to black.

"Connor? Connor?"

Connor groaned at the vise wrapping around his head and gingerly opened his eyes. That was one hell of a dream.

"You passed out," Donny said gently. He was cross-legged on the ground next to Connor and he had a hand laid on Connor's chest. The pain in his head lifted and he blinked up at the blue sky.

"So it wasn't a dream then," he murmured.

"Not a dream. I'm sorry." Donny's voice was thick with emotion. "He didn't want to do it. But the other wolf, the one who attacked you, had severed your femoral artery, and you were bleeding out. Only Tiber's bite was going to heal you."

Connor coughed. "Connor bit me."

Donny touched a hand to Connor's shoulder. "Just there," he said.

"And he saved me."

"You would have died otherwise."

"Then it's real."

"As real as it can be."

Connor closed his eyes again. Some thought pricked at him and he focused hard to make sense of the things in his head. He'd read paranormal books, seen enough TV shows, that he knew the various legends surrounding werewolves, or wolf shifters.

"Tiber is the alpha. And you're a shifter, too? What does that make you?"

"We're not sure," Donny said carefully. "Omega or something."

"Why don't you know?"

"This is new to us. We're—"

"He doesn't need to know it all right now," Tiber interrupted. "The rest of it can wait. Go home, Connor. I don't need to tell you not to talk about this with anyone. Meet us back here in a week at midnight—the full moon—and we'll show you how to shift. And most of all—stay safe. We'll be watching your back."

Connor was almost to the house before he realized he didn't even remember climbing down the path to home.

Chapter Ten

Time moved like treacle. The irritating stretching of it was made worse by the secret he was keeping. Connor knew he'd been dying. He'd been given a second chance to live, but at what cost? How was he going to explain to Josh what was wrong with him? If Connor believed what he was being told, that is. He didn't blame Tiber just because he couldn't wrap his head around any of it.

Josh had commented on how quiet Connor was, but everything had snapped at dinner. Sitting out on the decked area, they ate in silence.

"You need to tell me what's wrong," Josh said evenly. He pushed his plate to one side, then steepled his fingers in front of him on the table. "At least we tried. I can sell the practice and we can move back to the city tomorrow."

"What?" Connor was horrified at the thought. They were happy here, together...

"I don't have to be a mind reader to see how on edge you are. How unhappy. I get it was a big leap from there to here, and I know you only did it for me. Like I said. We tried and it didn't work. At least we know."

"First off, we didn't move here for you. I wanted a new start and we came here together. You're not selling up."

"It's mine, I can do what I want with it," Josh said. His eyes filled with emotion, and Connor pushed down his need to be angry at the defeat in Josh's voice.

"No, you're not selling."

"I won't let this break us up. You don't smile. You're quiet, irritable, angry, I think maybe you have PTSD. We should get you to a specialist."

Connor's blood heated and he pushed up and away from the table. "PTSD is the least of my concerns," he snapped. He didn't want to be angry, but he ached and the heat inside him was burning him up.

Josh launched to his feet at the same time and his hazel eyes glittered dangerously. He pushed around the table and jabbed Connor in the chest. "Admit you hate it here." Josh forced Connor backwards until he was forced up the stairs and his back was against the exterior of the house.

"I don't hate it here," Connor snapped. "I love it here. I love you."

"Then what is it? You can't lie to me, Con, I know you're upset. What have you done?"

"Nothing," Connor shouted back.

"If you're fucking leaving me, I want to know why. What did I do? Who did you sleep with!" Josh said with a shove.

The heat inside Connor became intolerable. Was that what Josh thought? That Connor was cheating on him?

"We fuck every night," Connor said, disbelieving of what Josh was saying. "How can you think I'm having an affair?"

"That's it though, we fuck." Josh spat the last word like it was vile. "You grab me and push me around and you fuck me 'til I scream, but you never say anything. We don't make love. We don't kiss. You stopped saying you love me, you hurt me."

"I didn't mean—"

"Then you leave the bed or the kitchen or wherever you fuck me, and you go. What the hell is wrong with you—"

Connor cut Josh off by dragging him in for a noisy, messy, hard kiss. In an instant Connor had Josh inside the house and into the bedroom. They didn't stop kissing frantically, and the heat inside Connor seemed to wrap both of them in a blanket of lust. Stripping, they tumbled onto the bed and Connor counted back from ten to relax himself. His drive wanted Josh pinned to the bed, whimpering under him, but the man who had control in him wanted love.

How did this make any sense?

"Make love to me," Connor pleaded between kisses. "Remind me . . ."

Josh's hold loosened and Connor whined low in his throat. Why was Josh going? The beast inside him whimpered. *Fuck. Go away.*

Josh didn't go far, simply grabbed at lube and rolled Connor on his front, pulling at Connor's legs until he was on all fours. The prep was quick and Josh was inside with a burn that made Connor's eyes water.

"Is this what you want?" Josh demanded. "You want me to fuck you like this and bite you, then walk away?"

"No," Connor pleaded. "Love me."

Josh pistoned into him for three, four, five pushes and Connor resigned himself to the revenge that Josh was inflicting. Then Josh stilled, balls deep.

"I do," Josh said softly. "I love you." Carefully he eased them both back so he was supporting Connor's weight on his thighs.

Connor did his best to hold himself still and nearly lost it when Josh reached around and closed his hand around Connor's needy cock. Then he set a rhythm that would send them both wild. Josh was the one with the skills, the moves, the ability to make Connor forget his own name. The heat inside Connor receded as Josh rocked into him. The growing anger and restlessness that drove him this last week began to slow and subside. Was it this easy? Was the beast inside him suppressed with Josh's love?

"Please tell me," Josh pleaded in his ear, over and over in time with his thrusts.

Connor cried as his orgasm grew. Tears rolled down at his face as some nameless emotion gripped him and took him to orgasm. "I love you. Josh, I love you," he breathed. Turning his face for a kiss, he tasted Josh and the scent of his lover surrounded them. Connor felt centered. In control and finally, everything stilled. Until he was coming over Josh's hand. "I'm sorry. I'm sorry. I love you. I love you."

Josh yelled at his release and held Connor tight. They were breathing heavily, then they tumbled to lie absolutely still on the bed. After a few minutes, Josh spooned him from behind and Connor nestled back. He was thankful that Josh couldn't see his tear-stained face. Peace stole upon him and suddenly he felt he could sleep.

When he woke, moonlight flooded the room through the still-open drapes. Connor looked at the alarm clock and saw it was just after 11 PM. He debated just laying there, but if he was to tell Josh the truth about what he was being told had happened, then he needed to hear the whole story.

Carefully, he eased out from Josh's hold and winced at the flaky evidence of their lovemaking on his chest and thighs. Quickly he wiped a wet washcloth over the areas, then pulled on what he been wearing before.

Josh mumbled in his sleep and turned over in bed, but didn't wake.

"I love you more than you will ever know," Connor whispered at his lover. He pressed a kiss to Josh's short hair and in less than ten minutes, he was at the door. With a final thought about Josh and what the man meant to him, he went out to the small garage where he picked up the bag he'd hidden behind the lawnmower. He'd seen the films and he knew he needed spare clothes and maybe chains so he didn't tear someone to death. Finally he was on the trail and heading up to the clearing. The scent of Josh followed him and he smiled at the thought that this smell was the one thing that calmed him inside. He didn't run this time, he took his time and it was nearly midnight before he reached the clearing.

True to their word, Donny and Tiber stood waiting, along with the sheriff.

The sheriff? What the hell? Was this some kind of take down? Nothing was making sense.

Sheriff Cross stepped forward and extended a hand. "I'm sorry," he said soberly.

Connor shook his hand and Cross moved away.

He continued, "You have to know that we had no idea what was going to happen. We'd tracked the rogue twenty miles away—we thought we had cleared the area. None of us knew." He sounded a little desperate, as if he was looking for forgiveness. *Cross was a shifter as well?*

Connor said nothing and the sheriff finally continued.

"When Donny was hit by the car, we had taken our eyes off what was happening. We had to get Donny to safety."

"Who was driving the car?" Connor asked.

"The scent is the rogue's," Tiber said.

"Wait. Are you saying this wolf that attacked me and Osborne was also a shifter, and that he was the one who drove the car deliberately at Donny?"

Sheriff Cross shrugged and turned helplessly to Tiber, who in turn frowned. "We can't be sure."

"If you can't be sure then tell me what other theories you have."

"That isn't what we're here to do," Tiber stopped him. "We're here to get you to shift and get your head around what you are now."

"What I am?" Connor said immediately. "I'll tell you what I am, I'm confused as to what the hell happened." He sat on the nearest trunk. "I'm trying nothing until someone tells me what the hell happened to get me here."

"A rogue wolf shifter. One of us who just wants to kill. We've been tracking it for weeks," Donny said quietly. "It slipped past me."

Tiber held up a hand to stop Donny, "Enough talking. Connor, we need to get you to shift, otherwise the pain in your muscles will be too much for even the strongest shifters to bear."

"If I shift the pain will go?"

"The need to give in builds between shifts, like a heat inside you," Tiber explained.

A heat? Like the trickling, burning pain that had him feeling so weak? "So what do I do?" *To stop the pain. I want to stop this pain.* "I brought chains and clothes."

Donny spat out a laugh and Connor frowned at him.

"You don't need chains," he said.

"I've seen the movies. I'm not shifting, then killing the first person I see."

"You won't," Tiber interjected. "The human that you are will still have a say in what your wolf does."

"Really?" Connor couldn't help sounding so doubtful.

"Strip," Tiber said.

That was easy enough. That he could do.

"There's two sides to you now, your human side and the part of yourself that is wolf. Take off your clothes and you won't need replacements."

"Seriously?"

"You're not the incredible hulk," Donny laughed.

Connor stripped. He felt awkward and embarrassed in front of Tiber and Donny.

"Now, close your eyes," Tiber said. "Can you see your wolf?"

Connor did as he was told. Shutting his eyes tight, he tried to focus on something, anything. He didn't even know what he was looking for. Was he looking for something in his brain? Or his body? Or something in the forest?

"I can't see a damn thing," he finally said, exasperated. "I think this is one huge wind up." Connor opened his eyes to see Tiber staring right at him with a determined expression on his face.

"Close your eyes and call your wolf," Tiber instructed.

Connor did as he was told and immediately felt stupid when he began calling his wolf. *Here, wolfy... here, wolfy...* He wasn't entirely sure that is what Tiber meant and he only did it in his head. He laughed internally at the stupidity of what he was doing. Then, when the bubble of laughter subsided, Connor felt something—a sense that there was part of him that was separate from his own thoughts, yet intrinsically connected. He didn't see anything, but something... there... a strength building and asking to be released.

Tiber's voice was softly encouraging. "Can you see him? Feel him. Just let him in, imagine yourself as a wolf..."

Connor wondered how he was going to do that. How did you imagine you were a wolf? Did you think that you were actually on four paws? Or that you could howl to the moon? Instead, he forced himself to relax and the other self inside him was suddenly breaking free.

The pain was excruciating and he felt himself fall to the ground, the scent of the forest damp and thick at this level.

He crouched on all fours and every muscle spasmed as bone cracked and reformed. He wanted it to stop.

How do I make it stop? Help me make it end. I can't take this.

Abruptly the pain ended, as sharply as it started, and he whimpered in his throat at the loss of it. He ached. Every part of him was tender and bruised.

"Open your eyes, Connor," Tiber instructed firmly.

I can't.

"Open your eyes," Tiber repeated.

Connor cracked his eyes open a little and saw nothing but the forest floor in a blur of dark colors. He shook his head and something felt wrong. Focusing on his hands, he saw furry paws, and with absolute certainty knew he had shifted. He waited to freak out—for the overwhelming horror of what had just happened to sweep over him. But nothing happened. In actuality he was calm, centered.

Something, or someone, pressed at his side and he glanced at it. A wolf. Large and dark, it was bigger than him and the scent of him was intoxicating. He immediately lay down and rolled on his side. The perspective of the forest shifted until all he could see was the trees.

The big, black wolf huffed at him and nosed him with his snout. This was Tiber. *How do I know that?*

A smaller wolf with lighter fur nuzzled his snout—Donny.

Connor rolled to stand on all four paws. He felt excited, apprehensive, free, trapped... so many confusing emotions flooded his brain. The other two moved to the forest edge outside the clearing, then turned and waited. Connor knew what this meant—they wanted him to follow. Walking on four paws was awkward for the first few steps. He hadn't realized that in being a wolf he would retain so much of his human self. Instinctively, he knew he had to push that side of him away, to stop his human brain from overanalyzing what was going on.

As soon as he did that, he felt able to walk and finally he was at their side. Tiber raised his snout to the sky and howled. As a group, they dove into the forest.

At first, Connor fell behind as they jumped and ran through the trees. His clumsiness had him rolling to a stop every so often. Tiber and Donny didn't go too far and were always there to help him up, and Cross appeared to be covering their rear. After some time he was in his stride—this was running and sprinting with no limitations. The air was thick with the scents of night, of prey, and the loamy earth beneath his paws. This was freedom.

How long they ran for Connor wasn't sure—the moon was still high and was hidden most of the time behind clouds, and the darkness became all consuming. But he recognized the clearing by the scent of it when they returned. Tiber shifted in a smooth motion, Donny immediately after.

"Connor, your turn," Tiber said formally. "Listen to Donny's voice."

Connor needed to know how to shift back. Evidently Donny was going to show him. Donny crouched next to him, crooning instructions to relax and imagine his human self. Donny scratched him behind his ears and he pressed against the young man's side. The warmth and scent of Donny was heady and Connor-Wolf shut his eyes tight and allowed himself to focus on the words.

The pain was just as intense as bones reformed, but it was quicker. He was left panting, laying naked on his back in the dirt.

"Amazing" was all he could manage to force out. He was exhausted and exhilarated and he had one overwhelming thought—he wanted to tell Josh.

Chapter Eleven

"We have a problem."

The familiar voice came from behind Connor. He spun to face the newcomer and couldn't believe who was stood there. Edward. What was he doing here? They should all hide; what if he found out what they all were?

Edward moved into the clearing and nodded his head to Tiber. "Alpha," he said carefully.

"Edward. Why are you here?"

"To pay for my sins," Edward said softly.

"You shouldn't be here," Tiber protested.

"Your rogue is my responsibility. I was the one who turned him." The previous owner of the veterinarian clinic and Josh's Gramps's lover was a wolf shifter? *What the hell?*

Silence. Deadly silence that Connor could see spiraling into noisy accusation and shouting.

"Start from the beginning," Connor said. The heat was building inside him and that insidious voice was in his thoughts telling him about the night and the moon and the freedom of running. He glanced at Tiber, but it wasn't him talking inside Connor's head. It was Connor's beast. The wolf that was the other half of him.

Edward sighed heavily. "I thought it was over." His voice dripped with sadness and the scent of despair grew stronger.

Connor turned his face a little and waited for Edward to continue. When he didn't, Connor prompted him. "Thought what was over?"

"Oscar. The rogue's name is Oscar. He and I were part of a dark time for wolf shifters." He shook his head sadly. "There used to be two packs of wolf shifters in the forest here. Many hundreds of years ago. We lived in a constant state of battle—we killed each other, we were never a pack, not in the real sense of the word. There was no community. It was last wolf standing. Until only one shifter lived. Me." He paused and pressed a hand over where his heart was. "I was alone, and lonely, that was when I found Oscar on the side of the road, bleeding out, he'd been hit by a car and fallen into the ditch. I saved him. I turned him because I selfishly wanted another like me." He huffed. "I had this grand idea that I was going to do it right this time. Make a pack. Be the alpha. The whole enchilada." He stopped talking.

Impatient for more, Connor encouraged him. "So what went wrong?" He still couldn't get over the shock of what Edward was, on top of the questions of what was happening to himself.

"He was a vagrant, a murderer. I should never have saved him. Myself, I was lucky to have Zachary come into my life. His granddad centered me and gave me humanity. The other one, Oscar, he disappeared and I never knew where he went. I should have cared—he was my responsibility. But now I think he's here."

Tiber interjected. "Why is he in Black Creek? How do you know it's him?"

"I know the scent of him." Then he turned and faced the wall of the forest. "He's out there somewhere."

"Last trail I had was ten miles north," Tiber said quickly.

Something stumbled into the clearing and Connor was eye to eye with a wolf. The wolf shifted and Connor immediately recognized Deputy Bryant. He was bleeding.

"He's here," Bryant gasped, then fell to his knees.

"Shift back," Tiber ordered. "Heal. Find us. Edward, stay with Bryant. Cross, Donny, you're with me." Donny, Sheriff Cross and Tiber shifted and left the clearing.

Connor turned to Edward—the older man looked resigned and grief carved his face. "What do we do?" He tensed to run into the forest, his cop instincts pushing to the fore. Edward grabbed his arm to still him.

"There is nothing we can do now," he said.

"I can shift."

"You're exhausted, boy. We need to get you home."

Josh. Home to Josh. I have to tell Josh what was happening. Let him make a decision on whether he stays or goes.

He wasn't sure how long it took to get down the path and back to the house. He only knew that every step hurt like a bitch and that he was fighting his instinct to fight all the way down. He and Edward didn't talk, and Edward concentrated on getting Bryant, unsteady on his four paws, down the hill. Even with that, Connor saw Edward was on alert, so he wasn't going to be the one to start a conversation. When they reached the bottom Bryant shifted back to human and he already looked better. With a sad shake of his head and no words, he walked in the direction of town.

"Will he be okay?"

Edward nodded. "He'll be fine."

Connor managed to climb the four steps to the deck, then slumped into the nearest garden chair. He heard howling in the distance and it scared him at the same time as sending a frisson of excitement through his body. Edward settled into the chair opposite.

"Do you have any questions?" Edward asked gently.

Connor didn't know where to start. Who made Edward a wolf shifter? Why did wolf shifters even exist? Was there a way to be healed? Could shifters die?

"I was born a shifter," Edward answered.

Connor looked up startled. Had Edward read his mind?

"To shifter parents, long gone. I don't know why shifters exist, we just do. And as to dying, any shifter can die the same as a human. Look at Adam Osborne, he didn't even have the chance to shift before he was dead.

"Osborne was a wolf?" Connor said incredulously. "Of course he was. Next thing you'll tell me is that Jessie Flannigan is a shifter." Images of Josh's receptionist as a wolf scared the hell out of Connor. She would make a fearsome wolf.

Edward huffed a laugh. "No, she's not. She's just ornery and bossy," he said.

Connor sat forward in his chair. "I was turned by being bitten. Which bite—Oscar's or Tiber's?" He felt that was a reasonable question to ask. Was it Oscar with his psycho tendencies, or Tiber with his heroic personality? If a new wolf took on the biter's personalities, he would rather it was the heroic side and not the mentally deranged side.

"Oscar wanted to kill you. There was no thought to turning you. His bites were to murder you. To turn someone takes care and patience, and it would be Tiber who is your sire."

"So, I'm a wolf shifter and I have to learn to live with it—have a normal life—tell Josh." Connor buried his face in his hands. How the hell was he going to explain this to Josh?

"You'll tell him the truth and he will love you despite what has happened."

"I should have told him when I first began to smell things, feel things. I hurt him, was too rough with him, my instinct was to bite."

"The hardest thing is to tell the man you love." Edward said sadly. Then he looked into the darkness of the house behind him and smiled sadly. "You can come out now, Josh," he said firmly.

Chapter Twelve

Connor couldn't believe his eyes when Josh stepped out from the shadows. How much had he heard? Connor stumbled to stand and grabbed hold of the table when his legs cramped. Josh wasn't looking at him—he was staring at Edward with a look of horror on his face.

"Did Gramps know?" Josh asked.

Connor's heart sunk. What was Josh doing awake? They'd talked quietly, but then Connor realized a part of him had wanted Josh to overhear them. Then he wouldn't have to face having to tell Josh directly. He took a step towards his lover, but Josh was resolutely staring at Edward with accusation on his face.

"How much did you hear?" Edward asked.

"Enough," Josh said with no hesitation. He was still staring at Edward.

"Your grandfather was the one who saved me," Edward said sadly. "I kept my secret all through college and he never knew. When he arrived in town, I knew that I had to tell him before he thought we could take it further. I was smitten from day one, but how could he love an aberration, a monster?"

Connor inhaled sharply. He'd never thought of the word monster to describe this new life he had, but in reality, no truer word had been spoken. Josh glanced at him, but his expression was dead. Connor's heart began to crack.

"Zachary turned up on my doorstep and made me see I could be something else," Edward continued. "I had fifteen years with him. He knew every day that I fought the darker side of my nature, yet still he loved me for every single one of those days."

"Then why didn't he tell me what you were?"

Connor's gut twisted. Josh sounded destroyed. He'd stumbled on this knowledge and heard enough to make Connor a stranger to him. Suddenly, Connor knew he'd done nothing but betray Josh.

Edward carried on, his voice filled with sadness. "He said it was my secret to share. After all, he reasoned I was hurting no one by being here and living my life in peace. He kept my secret until the grave and I was going to as well."

"Not even when he was dying? I was his grandson. You should have told me. I went into partnership with you, brought the damn clinic."

"Would knowing about me have made you change your mind?"

"I don't—fuck—before ten minutes ago I didn't think werewolves were real."

Edward took a step closer to Josh and touched his arm. Josh jerked away and stalked towards the back door.

"Josh, we need to talk," Connor said quickly

Josh spun on his heel and temper carved across his face. "Fuck you, Connor."

"Josh?" Connor pleaded.

"Now you want to talk?" Josh stalked over to Connor. "I knew something was wrong. You think I'm stupid. When were you going to tell me the truth?"

"Would you have believed me?" Connor asked wearily. "Until tonight, I didn't even believe me. You were so focused on PTSD, and I knew it had to be more."

For a second Josh looked mutinous, then inch by inch he relaxed. Finally, he sighed. "No, I wouldn't have believed the wolf shit."

Connor stepped closer as he sensed Edward leaving the porch. He reached out a hand. "Can we talk, Josh?" he asked again. "Can you help me?"

Josh's expression softened. They were so close and Josh reached for his hand. He was smiling, then suddenly his eyes widened in fear.

"Connor—"

The world shook and Connor was bodily lifted into the air before slamming against one of the uprights on the deck. Winded, he lay absolutely still for a second. But Josh's shout of fear had him rolling on all fours. A huge, jet black wolf had an unconscious Josh pinned to the ground, his jaws wide, his teeth coated with blood.

Connor concentrated on the wolf inside him and tried to change, but every sinew screamed at the attempt. Scrambling to stand, he ran and used his body weight to force the huge wolf to stumble sideways, but he was ineffective—until the wolf turned his attention to Connor. In a swift move, Connor was on his back, pinned to the deck, and he could hear himself screaming for help. He had to shift, he had to.

A howl from his left and a new wolf entered the fray, knocking the attacker off him. The two wolves battled and he crawled over to Josh, covering his lover's body with his own. The attacking wolf would have to go through his cold, dead body to get to Josh.

Howls grew closer and the fight on the deck stopped as suddenly as it began. Connor dared to look and saw the black wolf leave the deck and sprint into the forest. The other wolf lay surrounded by blood and when he looked closer, he saw Edward's eyes. Torn between what he should do, he checked

Josh for wounds. Nothing obvious—it appeared that the black wolf had knocked him unconscious but nothing worse.

He stumbled to the unconscious wolf and watched in horror as it shifted back to human. Edward. The gaping wound in his neck, the blood on the deck . . . was Edward too far gone?

"I was wrong," Edward gasped.

Connor thought he knew what Edward meant. Was that black wolf Oscar? Was Edward saying he should never have turned Oscar?

"It's okay," Connor said uselessly. He pressed his hands over the wound in the neck, but blood was pumping.

"I wanted to change Zachary. I loved him." Edward coughed.

"Stop talking," Connor instructed.

"Stop . . ." Edward said weakly. His eyes rolled back in his head.

"Stay with me," Connor snapped.

Hands pulled him away and he looked up to see Tiber and the sheriff pulling him away. He fought against the hold, but finally he ceased struggling.

Connor allowed himself to be led back to Josh and silently he slid down the wall, then pulled Josh's body so his head was in Connor's lap.

"He's gone, Connor," Tiber said gently.

"We need to find the wolf who attacked," Connor murmured. "Black. Huge. He hurt Josh. But we lost Edward."

"I'm leaving Donny and Bryant here, but I'm going to find him." Tiber sounded determined. "Whatever it takes, I will find him. Okay?"

Connor nodded. He was in shock, he knew it, but couldn't stop it.

"Okay," he said simply.

Josh moved under Connor's caresses then a few seconds later he was scrambling to sit up. Hope filled Connor—Josh looked confused but he wasn't angry. Then abruptly his expression of confusion lifted and he pushed himself up and away from Connor with horror carved into his features.

"Josh . . ." Connor said.

Josh didn't answer. He looked at the dead wolf near him, then up at the night sky, and finally he leaned back against a wooden support and closed his eyes.

"Josh, please—"

"No."

Evidently talking wasn't on the agenda.

Chapter Thirteen

"When does Proctor get in?" Josh asked formally.

That was how it had been since that night. Stiff and awkward, with the two of them skirting each other. They had buried Edward today in the same plot as Zachary, and Josh said some very kind words. The pack was there in full. Connor didn't question how easy it was to group Tiber, Donny, Bryant, and Sheriff Cross as a *pack* which he guessed now included himself.

"Tomorrow. He's getting a cab here," Connor answered immediately. He paused and waited for the next sentence. Maybe he should start the conversation. He'd been in that place where he didn't know whether to let Josh have time to grieve or to ask him how he was feeling.

"You'd better show me today then," Josh offered carefully.

"Show you?"

"Your wolf. I heard Edward saying, on the deck, that you were exhausted. From changing, I assume?"

Connor nodded.

"You look healthy and awake to me. So shift."

"What?"

"Just do it now, so I know what to expect. Shift." Josh waved at the ground. His expression and his voice were all wrong. He spoke so matter of fact, like it didn't matter. Like he didn't care what he would see.

"I don't know if I can," Connor said quickly.

"What kind of a wolf shifter can't shift?" Josh folded his arms over his chest with a casual expression.

"What about us?" Connor said. "We need to talk about us."

A flicker of emotion passed over Josh's face. Regret, anger? Connor couldn't tell.

"Us?" Josh mocked.

Connor snapped. "Don't do that."

"Do what?" The same temper that curled inside Connor was evident in Josh. In the way he uncrossed his arms and balled his hands into fists at his side. "What exactly am I doing?"

"Acting so cold."

"Cold? I'm not cold, I'm lost. My gramps was partnered with a wolf shifter. You're a wolf shifter." Josh stepped forward and gripped Connor's arms. "Not to mention there are fucking wolf shifters." He shook Connor.

Connor's wolf self snarled at the action. The sound in his head took him by surprise and he tore himself away from Josh's grip.

"Shift so I can see your dog."

This time the snarl was verbal and Josh took an unsteady step backwards. Immediately Connor felt contrite. He didn't want to scare Josh.

"I'm sorry," he said gently. "So sorry. But I didn't ask for this and I love you, and I want to work on who I am *with* you. Please . . . please don't stop loving me."

Josh slumped. "I could never stop loving you, Con, it's just so much to take in."

Connor nodded. He stepped closer and kissed Josh gently. When Josh returned the kiss, it seemed like the world of worries lifted from Connor's shoulders. Filled with confidence, he took a few steps back into their front room, then deliberately pulled the drapes shut.

Turning to face Josh was the hardest thing he'd ever had to do. Speedily he stripped naked. Suddenly he felt vulnerable in front of the man who had seen him like this so many times it was impossible to count.

"I won't hurt you," Connor said softly at the apprehension in Josh's expression. "When you shift you still know . . . you have a sense of self."

Josh nodded. He stood at the threshold to the sitting room and smiled weakly.

The transformation looked painful. Connor grimaced as he changed and all Josh wanted to do was run over and tell his lover to stop. Determination to see this through had him staying his hand.

He realized he was in shock, that he had all the clinical signs of shock, yet under it all, he loved Connor and he needed to know more. He wasn't walking away, he simply had to understand how this changed things. Their dynamic had been so equal, and suddenly it was Connor who was guiding everything. Could Josh come to terms with that? Not only that, but what did it mean for Connor? Would he become more wolf than man? He needed to talk to Tiber and get his head around all of this.

A groan of pain left Connor's mouth and Josh stepped forward. His heart cracked as his lover bent double in pain. He wasn't sure how he was going to watch this if it hurt Connor.

Then, in a blink of an eye, where Connor had stood there was a beautiful gray wolf. The wolf padded over to Josh and Josh reversed until he was backed up against the wall, which wasn't far, but it obviously gave off a message to Connor-Wolf who sat and tilted his head. There were Connor's green eyes and a question in his expression. Connor-Wolf whined and Josh's compassion flooded him. In seconds, he was on the floor, on his knees, eye to eye with the shifter.

"Hey," he said. He had to fight using his fixing-dogs-up voice and focus on just being Josh. Reaching out, he sunk his fingers into thick fur and leaned forward to press his forehead to Connor-Wolf's wet nose. He scruffed Connor-Wolf's fur and smiled at the small huff of contentment from the large animal.

Josh had so many questions. Connor was a tall guy, but how did his body weight as a human equate to the body weight of a fully grown wolf? Did it hurt when he shifted? What colors did he see? What could he smell?

"Come back now," Josh said quietly. Connor-Wolf almost immediately became Connor again and Josh couldn't be happier to see him.

They sat opposite each other in silence. Connor looked wary.

Finally Josh asked the first question. "Do you hate Tiber? For what he did to you?"

Connor shook his head and scooted around so they were next to each other with their backs against the wall.

"I was dying, bleeding out, lucky to not have my neck broken, but what Tiber did . . ." He paused. Then he gripped Josh's hand tight. "It meant I got so many more years back with you. How can I be angry? He saved my life."

"We'll be okay, won't we," Josh said.

"You make that sound like a question," Connor replied. He squeezed Josh's hand, then released it.

"I don't mean to. I don't doubt us at all." Josh wanted to reassure his lover of what he felt. How could he do that?

What could he say that wouldn't have Connor questioning him?

"Even with fur and teeth?" Connor asked. His voice was flat.

Josh turned to sit at an angle and kissed Connor soundly. "The fur and teeth are something we'll both have to get used to." He smirked. Then he was more serious. "This isn't going to be easy, I don't even have my head wrapped around what is going on with you. Or us."

"But there is still an us?"

"Yes," Josh answered simply. Then he huffed a laugh. "Just give me time and for fuck's sake don't get too toppy."

They kissed again and this time it was Connor that pulled back. "I can't help it, you know. When we're making love it's as if a new part of me emerges. Like . . . when you were inside me, my wolf wanted that. Tiber explained that the wolf is the human, and the human is the wolf . . ." He paused. "What I mean is that the kind of person you are is the kind of wolf you are. Does that make sense?"

"Yes. Perfect sense," Josh lied. He'd see how that worked after they'd talked.

"We can make this work, at the core of everything, it doesn't change us," Connor said.

"No, you're right. It doesn't change that I love you." Josh decided there and then that this was the absolute truth. Life without Connor was something he had already faced once. He wasn't going to do it again.

Connor gathered him in for a hug. "And I love you so much."

Josh relaxed into the embrace. Abruptly the future seemed less black and confused and full of new things to discover.

"Just one thing . . ." Josh began.

"What?"

"Are there vampires out there as well?"

Connor laughed loudly. "Nah," he said. "They're just stories."

About the Author

I am a writer of male/male novels and short stories.

From cowboys to bodyguards, and firemen to billionaires I write dramatic and romantic stories of love and passion between men. My first real love will always be the world of romance and my goal is to write stories with a heart of romance, a troubled road to reach happiness, and more than a hint of happily ever after.

I am the author of the award winning books, The Christmas Throwaway and Oracle. I am known for both my Texas series charting the lives of Riley and Jack, and also my Sanctuary series following the work of the Sanctuary Foundation and the people it protects.

One Bratty Omega
Building the Pack Two

By

Stephani Hecht

To Amber and RJ. You gals rock!

Chapter One

Lies... lies... all of it was lies. Well, maybe all of them hadn't been exactly lies, but they had been omissions of the truth. Which in Donny's book were the same thing. Donny let out an aggravated huff as he idly trailed his fingers along the surface of the river. He was on his stomach, his cheek pressed against the soft grass. The distant sounds of laughter from the pack's few children drifted through the forest. The air was crisp with the smells of fresh flowers and newly ripened apples. It was everything a wolf shifter could ask for and more. So by all rights, he should be at peace with the world, happy, calm, but he wasn't... and it was all thanks to those damn lies.

Deep down, Donny knew that they had told the lies in order to protect the pack. That Connor and Josh were new to this world and virtual strangers, thus making them untrustworthy. Yet Donny had still felt bad for all the lies they'd told the couple. After all, the pair had just been looking for answers because Connor had been bitten and made into a wolf shifter. So didn't he deserve to know some of the truth?

But Tiber had wanted to err on the side of caution. And after everything they'd gone through, who could blame him? Their childhood pack's parting had been less than pleasant. Ever since then, Tiber had shut down part of himself.

Donny blamed himself for that. Even though he knew Tiber would say differently, it was thanks to Donny that they were in their current situation.

"If only I hadn't been born an Omega," Donny whispered to himself.

He rolled over and looked at his reflection in the mirror-like surface of the water, grimacing at what he saw. He was way too thin, too blond, his eyes were too blue, his features too delicate. Damn it all, he might as well give it up and get a job as a shot boy at some gay club. He'd rake in a fortune, they always went for the twink type there, and he had that look down in spades. That's all he'd be good for, anyway. He sure as hell wasn't a fighter like the few Betas they'd managed to pick up, and he'd never ever be an Alpha.

Unable to stand the sight of himself anymore, Donny brought his hand down and splashed the water, obliterating his reflection. He then sat up and drew his knees up to his chin.

They should have brought Connor and Josh back with them. Donny didn't care what Tiber said. Leaving them out there to flounder on their own wasn't a good idea. It was just calling for trouble. They needed to get Connor to the pack lands where he could be protected, watched over, and, most importantly, learn the ways of their people. All they had to do was consider Adam. He'd been a loner, and look at what had happened to him. Now he was dead, and there was no bringing him back.

But Connor doesn't know anything about this new, tiny pack you have. You never told him about it, remember? A small voice mocked in his head. Donny briefly closed his eyes. How he wished that inner monologue would shut its yap once in a while. It had gotten him into trouble more than a time or two.

That had been one of the omissions of truth. Although to be fair, it had been a recent development. A small pack had come to Tiber, asking to join him. They had just recently lost their Alpha, and none of the Betas had wanted to step up and take the position.

Since Tiber was so desperate to build up his pack, he had accepted them. So now they had themselves five Betas, a handful of mates, some elders, and a group of children to take care of. While Donny was happy for Tiber, it was a hard adjustment to make since he wasn't used to there being so many people around them. It hadn't been like that since they had left their childhood pack, and just thinking about that brought back all kinds of bad memories for Donny.

"Donny! There you are!" a feminine voice called out.

Donny groaned. He recognized that tone anywhere. It was Kelly, the one female in the new pack that hadn't gotten it through her thick skull that Donny was gay and would always be gay, no matter how hard she wished otherwise.

Not to say that Kelly wasn't pretty. She was really cute, with a short brown ponytail, slim waist, big breasts, and infectious smile. She just didn't do it for Donny. And she never would.

She had a blanket draped around one arm and a basket around the other. She spread out the blanket, sat down on it, made herself nice and comfortable, then began to rummage around the basket. Donny's alarm began to sound with each motion she made. This couldn't be good at all.

"What are you doing?" he asked.

She peeked up at him, then giggled. "Setting up a picnic lunch, silly. What does it look like?"

"Why?" Donny asked, genuinely perplexed.

While he hadn't gone through the pack lands and waved a rainbow flag, it was common knowledge that Donny liked dick. So why Kelly continued to try to pursue Donny confused him. Especially since he was a lowly Omega. Now if it had been Tiber she had been going after, that would have made more sense.

An Alpha would have been a real catch. Donny was just a nobody, the lowest one on the pecking order of the pack.

Kelly reached over and playfully ruffled Donny's hair. "Because you're cute. That's why."

"Kelly . . . I'm gay."

"I know, but I can still try. You may change your mind."

"It's not a light switch that can be turned on and off. Either you're gay, or you're not. I can assure you, I most certainly am and will always be. Now if you want to be friends, I would love to do that, but that's all it's ever going to be."

Kelly picked up a pickle spear and took a big bite of it. "I can accept that."

Donny let out a deep sigh of relief.

"For now," she continued.

Donny fell onto his back and threw his hand over his face.

"I get it now. You were sent as my punishment for lying to Connor and Josh. That has to be it. There is no other explanation."

"Who are Josh and Connor?" she asked.

"A couple we met. Tiber had to change one of them into a wolf shifter in order to save his life."

"Then why aren't they living here in the pack with the rest of us?"

Ah, now if that wasn't the million dollar question. Especially given the fact that there is still some unknown hostile wolf out there.

Donny frowned as he thought over what to say very carefully. While he might not always agree with Tiber, his cousin had literally given up everything for him, so Donny idolized the guy.

"Tiber didn't think it would be a good idea to bring a strange shifter into the group until we knew more about him," Donny finally said carefully.

"Well, hopefully Tiber gets to know this guy soon. We only have five betas, plus you and your cousin for protection. So we are pretty vulnerable for attack right now," she said with a sigh.

"Yeah, your last Alpha left you pretty fucked up."

"Which is why we were so happy when he took off one day and never came back."

"You must have been a bit bummed though when you found out that your new Alpha came packaged with an Omega."

Kelly tilted her head to the side. "You really need to stop cutting yourself down that way. It's not so bad being an Omega."

"You just say that because you're not an Omega," Donny drawled.

"I'm serious. Hasn't anybody ever told you that Omegas are what keeps the other wolves less aggressive and stable?"

Donny slowly shook his head. No, he'd never heard that. But then again, his father was always too busy yelling how disappointed in Donny he was to pause to point out the good.

"I've heard of whole packs going feral just because they don't have an Omega," Kelly informed him.

Donny gave her a dismissive gesture. "You're just saying that to make me feel better about myself."

"No, it's the truth. I saw it starting to happen with my pack. Ever since our last Omega died a few years ago, the male wolves were getting antsy and angry. Now that they're around you, they're back to normal."

Donny gave Kelly an are-you-kidding-me look. "Don't bullshit me. I saw Wheezer trying to hump a tree yesterday."

"See! He hasn't done that in ages. You got his mojo back."

Donny gave her a sideways glance. "So Wheezer molesting a tree is a good thing?"

"Yes, it shows that he's feeling like his old self again."

"That poor tree," Donny muttered.

"So what lies did you tell Connor and Josh?" Kelly asked, bringing them back to the conversation.

Donny had to blink a few times before he could get back on topic. "Yeah, well, we told them that there were only a few of our kind in the area besides the one who attacked Connor."

"You were doing that to protect us. There is no harm in that."

"We also acted like we didn't know if I was an Omega or not."

"Again, you did that to protect us. So you didn't really lie, you fibbed."

Donny cocked a brow. "Aren't they the same thing?"

"No, a lie is when you make up a story to get away with something. A fib is something you say in order to protect others." She reached out and pinched his cheek.

Donny batted her hand away. "But in the end, aren't they both wrong?"

"Not if it means keeping the pack safe. We have children and pregnant woman to think about. They are the future of the pack, and we need to protect them at all cost." Kelly let out a sigh, then put her hands in her lap. "You're not always going to agree with the decisions Tiber makes, but I know he has the pack's best interests at heart. So you need to trust him."

"Of course, I trust him. He's my cousin, and he gave up everything to keep me safe. My last pack didn't want an Omega, so Tiber took me and ran away. He never looked back once. That doesn't mean that Tiber can't make a mistake here or there, though."

"You sure don't talk like any Omega I ever met," Kelly mumbled, her disappointment obvious.

"What did you want? Some boyfriend that you could lead around on a leash or something?" Donny asked with outrage.

When Kelly just looked down at her hands and gave a shrug, he knew he'd busted her.

"I still think that you're cute, though," Kelly said.

"Great, puppies are cute, kittens are cute, babies are cute, full-grown men aren't supposed to be cute."

"I can't help it, but you are. You're even cuter than the guys in *One Direction.*"

"That is a compliment I will take," Donny said. "Even if it's a bit on the creepy side."

Kelly held out a wrapped package. "Will you at least eat a sandwich? It's roast beef. Your favorite."

Donny took it from her. "Just so you know. If I weren't gay, you would be the first girl I would go after. Not very many people would take the time out to remember the Omega's favorite sandwich."

Kelly beamed at him. "Can we at least be friends? In case you haven't noticed, there aren't that many people our age around here."

Yeah, that was something Donny had noticed. The place also lacked a number of gay guys his age. The only ones were two Betas by the names on Aslan and Beau, but Donny had been too intimidated to approach either one of them. As a result, Donny had been jacking off so much lately he was going to get calluses on his hands soon.

"Sure, we can be friends. Especially if you keep bringing these fantastic sandwiches to my worksite."

She frowned in confusion. "You're supposed to be working?"

"Yeah, you see that dam over there?" He pointed to a small manmade dam.

"Sure, I do."

"It has a hole in it somewhere. I'm supposed to find out where it is and patch it up."

"Then why aren't you doing it?"

"I just haven't felt like it yet."

Her brown eyes grew huge with horror. "But you have to do it. The Alpha ordered you to."

Donny unwrapped his sandwich and took a great big bite. Yum. Kelly did know how to make a mean roast beef. Chewing, then swallowing, Donny said, "I'll get to it eventually."

"But what if you don't have time?"

Donny gave her a *please* look. "Why do you think Tiber gave me such an easy job in the first place? It's because he knew I'd fuck around and take my damn time getting it done. It's just the way I've always been."

"Have you ever thought of... oh, I don't know... changing?" she said with a heavy dose of sarcasm.

"This is no way to get a second date." Donny pointed at her with a chip.

"We aren't on a date. Remember?"

"You would pick this time to finally realize that," Donny sighed.

"Just eat up so you can get to work."

They ate in comfortable silence until all the food was gone. After his stomach couldn't take another bite, Donny got up and brushed off his hands.

"That was great, Kelly, thanks."

"Anytime."

When she made no move to leave, he said, "You're going to stay here to make sure that I do the job, aren't you?"

She wrapped her arms around her knees and nodded up at him. "Yep, consider me your foreman for the day."

"You really are pressing the limits of this friendship," Donny teased.

Kelly let out a sigh. "And here I was, going to set up an appointment for us to get matching BFF tattoos, too. Oh well, guess that will have to wait."

Donny ignored her and went over to the dam. As soon as he got near it, he could tell the problem already. Whoever had built it had done such a half-ass job... and he should know since he was the king of half-ass... the thing looked ready to fall over. Donny let out a muttered curse when he realized that they were going to have to tear down the whole thing and rebuild it again.

He was just coming out of the water when Tiber came up. As always, Donny tried to figure out how they could be related. Where Donny was blond, thin, and had blue eyes, Tiber had dark eyes and hair and was built like a tank. They were about as opposite as opposite could get.

"The whole dam is for shit. It needs to be rebuilt," Donny said as he joined his cousin.

Donny noticed that Kelly had made herself scarce. Most likely because the last Alpha had been less than welcoming to the pack members. Donny made a mental note to tell her that Tiber was friendlier, and he was open to talking to his pack. The last thing Donny wanted was for everybody to be afraid of Tiber. Tiber had enough to overcome as it was.

"You don't need to worry about the dam right now. I'll give it to one of the Betas to handle. Right now, I need you for a more important assignment."

Oh boy, those words never boded well for Donny. It usually meant he was about to have to work his ass off.

"What do I have to do?" he asked.

"Connor's old work partner is coming into town."

That got Donny's attention. "Work as in police?"

"Exactly. I need you to hang around there and make sure they don't talk too much and expose our secret. Can you do that without causing too much trouble?"

Donny gave a dismissive gesture. "Of course, I can. Piece of cake. You can count on me."

Tiber let out a sigh. "Why do I get the feeling that you are going to cause trouble one way or another?"

"I won't. I promise."

"Yeah, we'll see," Tiber said. "Just make sure they don't see you. Got it?"

"Got it. I'll be as stealthy as a ninja."

Tiber pinched the bridge of his nose. "How do I already know that I'm going to regret this?"

Donny patted Tiber on the arm. "Don't worry. I've got this covered. There is no way that they are going to catch me. I'm too good at what I do."

Chapter Two

Proctor drove his car down the winding streets that lead into the city of Black Creek. He had originally planned on getting a cab, but when he'd seen this sweet ride in the car rental lot, he couldn't pass it up. He knew that he was sure to get some ribbing from Connor about how he was a car whore, and Proctor knew he was, but oh well. He just couldn't help himself.

Proctor was doing his best to enjoy his ride, but he couldn't shake the hinky feeling that kept getting worse the closer he got to Black Creek. He looked at the surrounding forest, and a sense of foreboding slithered its way down his spine. Which was odd. It looked pretty enough, the foliage was thick and lush, the many shades of green making for a beautiful view. But Proctor felt like it was hiding something sinister.

While he knew he should be happy to see his old work partner, Connor, again. Proctor couldn't shake the feeling that something was off about the whole situation. As a cop, he'd learned long ago to go with his gut instinct, too, and right now, it was screaming at him to get as far away from this place as possible.

As he drove into the town, the feeling grew even worse. Proctor didn't know why. It looked simple enough. Some would even say rustic. It had several antique stores and a few bars and restaurants. There was one movie theater, but it was small and played older movies. So the town itself looked innocent enough. All that was missing were the damn poodle skirts and flat tops.

That didn't explain why Proctor was getting a bad vibe from the place. Proctor didn't like it when he got that kind of feeling because it always spelled trouble. Never once had it been wrong. Not in all his years as a cop.

Since the town was the size of a dime, it didn't take him long to find the veterinary practice that Connor's partner, Josh, owned. Getting out of his car, Proctor went inside to greet him first before going to see Connor. Proctor always loved to razz Josh while he was at his job. It was fun to see Josh fighting with the animals.

After getting past the hard-ass receptionist, Proctor found Josh taking care of a spitfire of a kitten who didn't want to have his shots. Yes! Just what Proctor had been hoping for.

Never one to be helpful, Proctor yelled out, "That's it, kitty, don't take it lying down. Make them work for it. After all, it's your body, and you have your rights."

Josh gave him an annoyed look. "You're really not helping here."

Proctor held up both of his hands. "Hey, somebody has to stand up for kitty rights. I figured I may as well do it. After all, I do have a three week vacation with nothing to do but annoy you."

Josh rolled his eyes. "Lucky me."

Josh finally managed to stick the cat with the needle. He plunged in the syringe before handing it off to the tech. Proctor sadly shook his head. "Kitty, I am so disappointed in you. I thought you had more fight in you. You should have hissed and scratched for at least five more minutes."

"Are you going to rile up all my patients?" Josh asked with a laugh.

"Only the ones who are being treated unfairly."

"Oh, come on. I was just giving kitty Sophia her yearly vaccines. She needs it to keep healthy."

"But Sophia didn't want them."

Josh just shook his head. "Come on. Let's go to the house. Connor is waiting for you."

They went back to a nice house. Proctor had to admit to himself that if he ever were to meet the right type of guy and settle down, he wouldn't mind it being at a place like this. Of course, he would pick it in a town that didn't freak the hell out of him.

Looking down the street, Proctor caught a glimpse of a tall, thin blond man. He was dressed in tight worn jeans and a red hoodie, and damn if those pants didn't fit his body to per-fect-tion. Proctor found himself wishing the guy would turn around so he could get a good look at the stranger's ass. Proctor just knew it would be a dream come true.

"Who's that?" Proctor asked.

"Who are you talking about?" Josh asked.

But when Proctor went to point, the blond had vanished as if he had never been there at all. Proctor looked up and down the street, but there was no sign of the hottie anywhere. Proctor shook his head. Had he just imagined the guy or something? Or maybe the town was messing with his head more than he thought and was giving him hallucinations of the sexy kind.

"Never mind," Proctor mumbled.

He'd finally found something worthwhile in this boring town, and it had upped and disappeared on him. Proctor was beginning to feel as if he'd just walked smack dab into an episode of the *Twilight Zone*. Only everything was in color, and there was no Alfred Hitchcock or Rod Sterling to be found.

They went inside and found Connor working on dinner. Proctor's bad mood immediately vanished at the sight of his friend cooking.

"How did you get roped into making dinner?" Proctor asked as he gave Connor a hug.

"Josh was backed up at the clinic, and since I had the day off at work, I said I would do it," Connor said, squeezing Proctor back.

As Connor stepped back, Proctor couldn't help but notice that there was something different about his friend. He couldn't quite put his finger on it, but Connor wasn't the same. There was a haunted look in his gaze that hadn't been there before, and Proctor was determined to get to the bottom of it.

"Hey, I hope you guys don't mind, but I cancelled my reservations at the B&B and decided to take you up on your offer to stay here. I thought it would give us more time to spend with each other," Proctor said.

He expected Connor to be happy, so when Josh and Connor exchanged uneasy glances, Proctor was a bit surprised. Proctor began to wonder if maybe he had made a mistake and overstepped his welcome.

"I'm sorry, if you want I can call them back and see if they still have some vacancies," Proctor said, feeling more awkward than ever.

"No, you don't need to do that. We're more than happy to have you," Connor rushed out. "We were just caught off guard that's all."

"Yeah, we're excited that you're staying with us," Josh added.

"Okay, great to hear it," Proctor said.

A part of him couldn't help but feel that there was still some tension there, though. But then he pushed it aside. He and Connor went way back. They were best friends. So of course Connor wanted him. Although, there still was something going on, and Proctor was still determined to figure out what it was.

"Why don't I take you up to your room and show you where you'll he staying while Josh watches the food?" Connor suggested.

"That sounds like a great idea." Proctor agreed. It would also give him some one-on-one time with Connor. Something that looked as if it was long overdue.

They went up the stairs, and Connor showed Proctor to the guest bedroom. It was bigger than his regular bedroom back at the city. But then again, his bedroom back home didn't look like it had been decorated by an old lady. It was obvious that Connor and Josh hadn't got around to adding their own touches to their new house. The wallpaper in the room was all floral and pink, and the carpet was a horrible mauve color. The only thing missing were the doilies and the china dolls, and the image would be complete.

As soon as they were alone, Proctor crossed his arms over his chest and said, "Okay, what's going on here?"

"What do you mean?" Connor said.

"You can give it up with that fake smile of yours. I can see right through it."

Proctor could, too. It was the one reason why they could never play cards with each other. Proctor could always tell when Connor was hiding something. It never failed, maybe it was because they'd known each other since they'd been kids.

"There's nothing going on," Connor repeated, looking away.

Now there were all kinds of alarm bells ringing in Proctor's head. Not only because the town gave off a creepy ass vibe, but the fact that Connor was blatantly lying to him.

Proctor thought about pressing Connor about it but decided to let it go for now. After all, Proctor was going to be there for three weeks. That would give him plenty of time to get to the good out of Conner.

Proctor dumped his bags by the bed, and they went downstairs. As they were walking down the steps, Proctor could have sworn he caught a glimpse of the blond peeking in through the living room window. But when Proctor looked closer, the man was gone. Shaking his head, Proctor decided that he was letting the craziness of the town get to him. Maybe once he ate, he'd stop having the weird hallucinations.

Proctor walked into the kitchen and rubbed his hands together. "Okay, how can I help? You know how I hate to stand around and do nothing."

Josh nodded to the left. "You can cut the veggies for the salad."

Connor wrinkled his nose. "We're having salad again?"

Proctor gave his friend a strange look. "Since when don't you like salads? You used to eat them all the time when we worked together."

Josh and Connor exchanged uneasy looks again before Connor cleared his throat and said, "I . . . uh . . . just got sick of them is all. You know how that goes."

Not buying it for one second, Proctor still nodded. "Sure."

Proctor caught another glimpse of the blond, this time through the side kitchen window.

"Did you see that?" he asked.

"See what?" Connor asked.

Of course, when Connor looked over, the blond was gone. Nothing could be simple in this whack-a-doodle town. It would be too easy on Proctor if they were.

He let out a sigh and continued to cut up the vegetables in nice even rows. He had a bit . . . okay, he had a lot of OCD in him, and he liked to make sure that everything matched up. Which is exactly why they had given him this job. It was to take his mind off all the questions they didn't want him to be asking. He finished with a cucumber and reached for a tomato.

At that same moment, he caught another glimpse of the blond man peeking in the back kitchen window. Proctor finally had enough.

Setting down the knife, he said, "Okay, you don't have to tell me what has you two acting all hinky. But you at least have to tell me about the twink who's stalking you two."

"What twink?" Connor asked.

By way of answer, Proctor opened up the back door, grabbed the blond by the back of his hoodie and dragged him inside. Damn if he didn't look all the better close up, too. Now that Proctor got a better look at the blond, he could make out the man's rounded cheekbones, how full his lips were and the way there were darker flecks of blue in his eyes.

"Hi?" the blond said.

"Donny? What are you doing here?" Connor asked, his hands clenching the edge of the counter so tightly that his knuckles were turning white.

Why did Proctor get the feeling that Donny had something to do with the reason why Connor and Josh were acting so strangely? And why did Proctor all of sudden not give a damn? All that mattered to him was getting to know the little brat a bit better.

"Tiber asked me to stop by and see how you two were getting along," Donny said.

"If Tiber was that curious, why didn't he come and ask us himself?" Josh asked.

"More importantly, why didn't you come up to the door and check up on them personally, instead of stalking them?" Proctor asked.

Donny opened and closed his mouth several times as he seemed to be trying to work up a proper answer. "I didn't want to disturb them."

Proctor still had a firm grip on Donny and gave him a few shakes. "Do you want to try again?"

"It's kind of hard to think with you shaking me up like a martini," Donny grumbled.

"Are you even old enough to drink a martini?" Proctor countered.

"Of course, I'm twenty-two."

Proctor let out a sigh. Why did he think that being around this kid was going to lead to all kinds of headaches? "Why were you stalking Connor and Josh?"

"I told you. To make sure they were getting along okay."

Josh stepped forward. "I believe him, Proctor. We saved a pet dog of his last week, and Donny has become very protective of us ever since. Haven't you, Donny?"

Donny gave them a sardonic smile and said, "Woof. Woof."

"So you see he means us no harm," Connor added. "He's just a bit overzealous."

Proctor knew they weren't telling the whole truth, but he was game to play along. "Well then, by all means, why don't you invite Donny to have dinner with us?"

Donny's eyes grew wide with terror as he slowly shook his head. "I have to eat with my pa . . . cousin."

"I'm sure he won't mind you missing this one meal. I'm only going to be here for three weeks, and I want to meet some of the locals. Especially cute ones like you."

The way Donny blushed, then ducked his head told Connor everything he needed to know. One, Donny was gay, and two, he was very available. Maybe this trip wouldn't be so bad after all.

"What's for dinner?" Donny asked.

"Well, I was helping out with the salad, so I know that we're having at least that" Proctor said.

Donny got the same look of disgust on his face that Connor had when that particular course had been brought up. What was it with men and salad in this city? One would think that they thought it was poisonous or something.

"Don't worry, we're having steak with it, too," Josh said.

"Will it be rare?" Donny asked, an eager look on his face.

"For you and Connor, yes."

Donny looked so excited that he was practically bouncing around the place. He even grinned, and damn if it wasn't the most adorable thing that Proctor had ever seen. Proctor shook his head at himself. He shouldn't be looking at Donny at all. The guy was six years younger than him. The last thing Donny was probably interested in was some old man like him.

Donny gazed at him, and Proctor was shocked to see some genuine interest in the younger man's eyes. Damn, he must be really hard up for some action if he was already putting the moves on Proctor. There must not be too many available gay men in the area.

"So you're a friend of Connor's?" Donny asked.

"Yeah, we grew up together and then were partners on the force."

Donny shoved his hands in the pockets of his hoodie. "It must be cool to be a cop."

"It is. If you're ever interested, I could show you how to sign up for the academy."

Donny laughed. "I'm not the fighting kind. In fact, you could say I was born not to get into scuffles."

"More of a lover, huh?"

Proctor wanted that loser of a line back as soon as he said it, but it was already out. He cringed as he wondered how

Donny would react. But Donny just grinned, showing off one dimple on his right cheek, and gave a slight shrug.

"Yeah, I guess you could say something like that."

"So you've gotten pretty close to Josh and Connor since they've moved here then?" Proctor asked.

"Yeah, they helped me when I had... trouble with my dog."

"Why do I have the feeling that nobody in this town is telling me the truth?" Proctor asked, his frustration growing by the second, first his own best friend was lying to him and now this brat.

He put one hand against the wall above Donny's head, so Donny was halfway pinned in. Donny made no move to get away, but he did suck in a breath. Proctor let himself smile. He'd finally gotten somewhere with somebody. While Josh and Connor might not crack, Donny would—with enough squeezing.

Donny looked up from under his lashes. "Sometimes, the truth is a lot scarier than you want it to be."

"What's that's supposed to mean?" Proctor asked, more confused and angry than ever.

"Well, I'm trying to tell you that it may be better to be kept in the dark about certain things because the reality is just too much to handle."

Before Proctor could even begin to ask what in the hell that meant, Donny ducked under his arm and walked away. Proctor stood there feeling more aggravated than ever before. He did know two things for certain, he wanted the truth, and he wanted Donny.

Chapter Three

Donny was trying his best to concentrate on the meal in front of him, but it was so hard when he was sitting across from what had to be the sexiest man in creation.

Be it Proctor's short dark hair, or maybe it was his warm, brown eyes. Perhaps it was his high cheekbones and a set of muscles that looked like they were sculpted from marble. All Donny knew was he liked what he saw, and he wanted to lick every inch of it.

Oh sure, Donny knew that Tiber would have a fit if he even knew that Donny was sniffing in this guy's direction, much less considering mounting him like a riding bull. Donny could almost hear their argument in his head.

He's too old for you, Tiber would say.

Age is just a number. Plus you always say I need to grow up. What better way than to have a mate who is older than me? Donny would counter.

He's human, Tiber would warn.

We could always swear him to secrecy or turn him into one of us, Donny would argue.

It's too dangerous, Tiber would scold.

What part of our lives isn't? Donny would ask.

And that would be the point where he would have Tiber. Even as Donny sat there, all cozy and warm in Josh and Connor's kitchen some feral wolf shifter was on the loose doing God knows what. The sad thing was Tiber's pack, which normally would have taken care of such an issue, was too small and weak to do jack shit about it. So to say that their lives currently sucked would be an understatement.

Donny knew that Tiber needed more Betas in his pack, but short of Donny going out and biting every well-built male human, there was little he could do. And since that kind of activity was generally frowned upon, he couldn't even do that.

"How's the steak?" Josh asked Donny.

Donny snapped out of his musings and gave a tiny smile. "It's perfect. Thank you."

"You seemed to be thinking about something very hard there for a moment. Care to share?" Proctor asked.

That was the one fault of Proctor. While he might be perfect in every other way, he asked too many damn questions. As it was, Donny was already getting a headache from having to think so hard to come up with so many different answers.

"I was just thinking about a project that has to be done back home," Donny lied.

He was getting so good at lying that even he didn't know the truth half the time anymore. God, how he hated living like this, but it was for the good of the pack he reminded himself.

"Donny lives with a group of other survivalists that live in log cabins deep in the woods and try to live mainly off the land," Josh explained to Proctor.

Proctor studied Donny carefully. "You never would have struck me as the tree-hugger type. I thought all you guys were vegetarians, too."

Donny shook his head. "Nope, we just mainly hunt and kill what we eat."

Ha! He'd managed to tell one true thing for the day. It was the pack's job to track and hunt enough meat for the winter. It was one of the few excursions an Omega was allowed to go on. It was the one event that Donny always looked forward to each year, even when he'd been with his childhood pack.

Proctor pushed his plate away, then crossed his hands over chest. "So do you live there with your parents?"

"As if," Donny scoffed.

Donny realized he revealed too much when Proctor raised a brow at him. Shit! Shit! Shit! Why did Tiber have to send him on this damn mission in the first place? He knew better than anybody what a fuck-up Donny was. In fact, if one looked up fuck-up in the dictionary, Donny was pretty certain his picture was going to be there as an example.

"What I meant is I'm estranged from my parents. My cousin Tiber has been taking care of me ever since," Donny said with a coolness he was nowhere near feeling.

"Why are you estranged from your parents?"

"Why are you asking so many questions?"

"I'm a cop. It's my job."

Donny cocked his head to the side. "But I'm not under arrest."

"Maybe not, but I do have the right to make sure that my friends aren't associating with the wrong kind of people," Proctor pointed out.

Donny tossed out what he hoped was a flirtatious smile. "Really? Do I look dangerous?"

"Yes, but in a completely different way," Proctor said.

"Okay," Josh said loudly, bringing everybody's attention his way. "Who wants some dessert? Proctor, can you help me?"

As soon as Proctor and Josh were out of sight, Connor turned on Donny. "What in the hell do you think you're doing?"

"Tiber told me to come here and make sure that you didn't blab too much to your friend."

"Ha!" Connor ran a hand through his hair. "Like Proctor would believe me even if I did. Most likely he'd have me committed. Do you honestly think that I'm going to run around and tell people that I can now shift into a wolf? I may be crazy, but I'm not stupid."

Donny held his hand out. "Hey, I'm just following orders."

"And did the orders also include you salivating and flirting with Proctor?"

Donny looked up at the ceiling and began to whistle. He was sooooooo busted. He'd be damned if he'd roll over and admit it to Connor, though.

"I don't know what you're talking about. I'm just being friendly to your guest," Donny said with all the innocence he could muster.

"If you were any friendlier, you would be humping his leg."

"Is that a dog joke? Because if it is, that's not cool, dude. Us wolf shifters are sensitive to that kind of shit."

"*Us wolf shifters?* I thought you didn't know that many others of our kind." Connor pinned Donny with a narrowed-eyed stare.

Damn! This was not going down like it was supposed to. To make things even worse, Donny's cellphone started to vibrate. Since only Tiber had the number, it had to be him. The shit was hitting the fan from all different directions.

Donny pulled his knees up to his chin and said, "Can I just go home and forget that this night ever happened?"

"Just answer me one question, and I want you to do it truthfully. You're an Omega, aren't you?" Connor asked.

Not able to meet Connor's eyes, Donny gave a nod. He just couldn't go on with the lies, even if it did make Tiber mad.

Donny tensed up as he waited for Connor to start yelling at him.

Instead, Connor touched the back of his neck. "You're okay, Donny. You were just following your Alpha's orders. You're a good wolf."

"Yeah, tell Tiber that when he finds out I told you," Donny retorted, relieved that Connor wasn't angry at him but still terrified of how Tiber was going to react.

"It didn't take us long to figure it out on our own. All we had to do was a little research. You would be amazed at what you can find on the internet," Connor said with a laugh. "I'm sure there is a lot more that you haven't told us. Like for example, those people in the cabins—they're not survivalists, are they? They're other pack members."

"Yes, but the pack is small and vulnerable to attack. We have to build it up and hunt down that rogue wolf who attacked you before it harms any other innocent humans. Plus, we need to rebuild numbers and make it stronger for generations to come. The last Alpha wasn't a good one, and he ran the pack into the ground. A lot of them left out of disgust and are still refusing to come back."

Connor ran his hands over the stubble on his cheek. "Hmmm... I wonder if you build up the pack some and show that Tiber has some real leadership skills, some of those old members might have a change of heart and come back. Maybe they're just waiting for him to prove himself."

"You think?" Donny asked hopefully.

It would be wonderful to get even a handful of the old pack members back. Then they would have a stable foundation they could work with. They would be well on their way to having themselves a pack.

"Why didn't you tell us any of this sooner?" Connor asked.

"Because we've just met you. We didn't know how much we could trust you," Donny admitted, a heat coming over his face.

"That's okay, don't be embarrassed. I know you have others to protect. I can see where you guys were coming from. I just wish that we could have known some of this stuff sooner, we may have been able to help each other out more."

"Sorry," Donny, mumbled, feeling ten times the fool.

"So you and Proctor . . . huh?"

Donny could feel the heat on his face grow. "Ah . . . it's nothing. He probably just looks at me and sees some geeky kid."

His cell went off again, reminding him that Tiber was still waiting for an update. Getting up, Donny shot Connor an apologetic look. "Sorry, I have to take this call."

"Let me guess, it's Tiber."

Donny nodded, his stomach sinking at the thought of being caught between his cousin and his new friends. Connor, Josh, and Proctor weren't bad at all once you took the time to get to know them.

"Tell Tiber we're keeping low but we have decorated the whole house in a werewolf theme," Connor said.

Donny chuckled as he stepped outside to take the call. As soon as he answered, Tiber asked, "What's taking you so long?"

"They kind of caught me spying on them," Donny ventured.

"God, Donny."

Donny could almost visualize Tiber pinching the bridge of his nose. He did that a lot whenever he was annoyed with Donny. Which happened to be most of the time they were around each other. Donny couldn't help it. He tried to be a good wolf, he really, really did. But sometimes it was just so much easier and fun to be bad.

"Hey, if you had wanted somebody who was stealthy, then you should have sent one of your Betas, not an Omega. I was peeking into the windows when Proctor caught me," Donny defended himself.

"And Proctor would be Connor's friend?"

"Yes, he's really nice."

"Shit! You have the hots for him. Don't you?"

"Why would you say that?"

"The only time you say a guy is really nice is when you want to screw him six ways to Sunday. You forget. I know you better than you know yourself. So I'm only going to say this once—hands off the human."

Donny gave a little stomp of his foot. Maybe it was childish, but there was nobody there to see so he could vent a bit. "Can't I at least have a little taste? No harm can come from it."

"Plenty of harm can come from it since he's so close to Connor. You want some action, go to the local gay bar a couple of towns over."

"But none of those guys are even half as cute as Proctor," Donny grumbled.

"Mind over dick, little cousin," Tiber said in a tight voice.

Donny let out a huff of irritation. "Fine, but shouldn't I at least make friends with him? That way somebody can keep an eye on him while he's in town."

"That is the first good idea you had all day. Yes, go and become his friend, but that's it, nothing more."

Donny felt like banging his head against the wall. It was so unfair. He was going to get to spend all this time with Proctor, but they were going to have to do it with their clothes on. Blue balls were going to take on a whole new meaning by the time Proctor went home.

"Fine, I'll be good," Donny said. "I have to go now. They're getting ready to serve dessert, and if I stay out here too long, they'll get suspicious of me."

"Yeah, I can see them missing you when you're not there for the sweet stuff," Tiber teased lightly.

"Oh, and one more thing, Josh and Connor aren't nearly as dumb as you think they are."

"Meaning?"

"They've already figured out that I'm an Omega. They also figured out that it isn't a bunch of survivalists living in the log cabins and that we have a pack. By the way, what are we going to do if a real survivalist shows up and tries to live with us?"

"Donny," Tiber breathed out irritably.

"I guess we could find some way to scare him off. But what if he proves to be stubborn? I guess we could always sic Kelly on him. She could scare the pants off any guy with her tenacity."

"Go in and have dessert. Tell Josh and Connor that I'll be there tomorrow to talk to them."

"Do you think you'll be able to get them to move into one of the cabins and join the pack? We could use another Beta."

"I don't know, but I'll try my best."

"That would be awesome. The Betas we have there now are all kind of grumpy."

"That's because you're always pulling pranks on them."

Donny shrugged. "I have to get my entertainment somehow, and since you won't get internet, how else am I going to get it?"

Donny caught sight of Connor bringing a pie to the table. "Gotta go, Tiber. Just saw a pie with my name written all over it."

"Be good, Donny."

"Aren't I always?"

"No, you never are. In fact, I can't think of one day when you didn't get in some kind of trouble."

"You should thank me," Donny said. "Without me, think of how dull your life would be."

Before Tiber could come up with an argument to that one, Donny hung up on him. Sure, Tiber would get him for it later, but the satisfaction Donny felt at the moment made it well worth it.

He walked back inside and smiled. "That looks so good. What kind is it?"

"Strawberry. I know you would have liked meat better, but you'll have to suffer through it," Josh teased.

"Strawberry is perfect," Donny said with a laugh.

He sat down and began to dig in. He moaned at the first bite. "Who made this?"

"I did," Josh said.

"You heal animals and bake? How did Connor get so lucky?" Donny asked.

"I ask myself that same question every day," Connor countered.

Donny turned to Proctor. "So I was wondering, what are you doing while they're both at work tomorrow?"

Proctor seemed surprised by the question. He quickly glanced at Connor and Josh before saying, "Nothing, actually. I was just planning on hanging out here and watching boring daytime TV. Why do you ask?"

"I have some free time tomorrow and was wondering if you wanted me to take you around and show you some of the more interesting places in town. It would just be as friends, I swear I'm not trying to make any moves on you or anything," Donny assured him.

Although, I would love nothing more than to be making all kinds of moves on that hot body of yours.

Proctor finally gave a shrug. "I don't see why not. It sounds like fun. Sure."

Donny smiled to himself. Mission accomplished.

Chapter Four

The next morning, Proctor went to the diner where he'd agreed to meet Donny. Entering, he didn't see the cute blond anywhere. Which wasn't too surprising since Proctor was ten minutes early, and Donny didn't seem to be the punctual type.

Sure enough, fifteen minutes later, Donny came rushing into the place. His cheeks were flushed like he'd been running, and his clothes looked wrinkled as if he'd just pulled them out of his drawer or the backpack he had on his shoulder.

"Sorry, I'm late. Got distracted by a rabbit," Donny said as he took a seat.

"A what?" Proctor said.

"A ra... bbit..." Donny flushed even more as if he realized he'd just flubbed up. "Okay, you caught me. One of the girls down the street was showing me her little bunnies, and I got so caught up in looking at them I lost track of time."

Proctor didn't buy the story for one moment, but he decided to let it go for the time being. He had plenty of time yet to get to the bottom of things. He knew one thing for certain: there was no way he was leaving this town until he had all his questions answered. Even if that meant tying Donny down on the bed and not letting him up until he spilled everything.

"So what's good to eat here?" Proctor asked.

"Just about anything," Donny replied. "I eat here all the time."

"Funny, I thought you hunted and killed all the food you ate."

Donny tilted his head to the side and gave a flirtatious smile. "Are you going to tell on me? I can't help it that I'm not that good of a hunter. It's just not in my blood. My father was always so disappointed in me because of that."

The last sentence was laced with such venom that Proctor actually backed up a bit. Okay, well now he did know one thing for sure, Donny had some serious daddy issues.

"So I take it you and your father don't get along?" Proctor asked.

"The only reason I'm happy is because my cousin Tiber took me away with him when he left. Otherwise, who knows what my old man would have done to me. He didn't like the fact that I was born small and weak," Donny said.

"You don't look small or weak to me," Proctor said.

Sure, Donny might be on the short side, but he wasn't tiny or frail by any means. By the way he talked, one would think that he was nearly a child or an invalid. Just because Tiber was big didn't mean Donny had to be.

The waitress came up, and they placed their orders. When he heard how much food Donny was ordering, Proctor's eyes grew wide. How the guy managed to stay so thin and eat that much was amazing. He must have the metabolism that would make a supermodel green with envy.

After the waitress left, Proctor asked, "You're really going to eat all of that?"

Donny shrugged as he poured some creamer into his coffee. "I burned off a lot of calories on my run over here."

"You ran all the way here?" Proctor asked.

How was that possible? Donny didn't look sweaty at all. Sure, he looked a little flushed, but that was it. If he had run all the way from where the cabins supposedly were, he should have been drenched. Yet Donny looked as fresh as ever. His hair was even perfectly styled.

"Yeah, the town isn't that big." Donny smiled. "Plus I'm in good shape. You would be amazed at what kind of stamina I have."

Proctor nearly choked on the drink of water he'd just taken in. He wasn't dumb, and he knew a come-on when it smacked him in the face. So he hadn't been imagining things last night. Donny had been flirting with him. Now the question remained. What was Proctor going to do about it?

Part of him wanted to take full advantage of the situation. Not only was Donny hot as hell and obviously interested, but it had been a long time since Proctor had seen some real action. Yet there was another part of Proctor that felt like it would wrong to start anything with Donny when Proctor would be leaving in three weeks. The last thing he wanted was to leave behind a brokenhearted brat. That was sure to make Proctor a candidate for asshole of the year.

"Do you talk to all guys this way?" Proctor asked as he wiped his face.

Donny gave an impish grin. "Only the good looking ones."

"How many of those do you run into?"

"Not too many. You'd be amazed at how lacking this town is in handsome gay men," Donny said as he fiddled with his spoon.

"You do know that I'm older than you?" Proctor pointed out.

Although, the more they talked, the less important the age gap became to Proctor. Usually, he wouldn't even consider hooking up with a guy Donny's age, much less starting a relationship with one. But with Donny, it was different. Donny might be bratty at times, but he had a certain maturity level that other guys his age didn't. It was as if he'd seen things beyond his years.

"Yeah, but that doesn't matter to me," Donny said. "I've always liked older men. Guys my age just don't seem to get me. They always think that I'm this weak thing that they can push around, and me being the human rug that I am, I let them."

"And older men don't try to do that to you?" Proctor challenged.

Donny frowned. "Well, yeah, they boss me around and stuff, but they don't bully me about it. Does that make sense?"

"Yeah, it does."

What Donny wanted was somebody to lead him in life, not push him around. There was a huge difference. A difference that maybe not even Donny was aware of, yet.

The food arrived, and Donny attacked it like a man who was half starved. Proctor watched him with fascination. If he hadn't seen Donny eat a whole meal the day before, he would have sworn it had been weeks since Donny had last eaten.

"Slow down. The food isn't going anywhere," Proctor teased.

Donny looked up from under his lashes and gave that impish grin of his. "Sorry, I'm used to having to eat fast. When I lived at home, the less time I spent at the dinner table, the better."

Proctor frowned. That didn't sound good. "Why's that?"

"Because it gave more time for my dad to nitpick at me. So I learned real quickly to eat fast and get the hell out of there before he could get started."

"Your dad sounds like a real asshole."

"Yeah, well, I wasn't the son he wanted, so it was my fault for letting him down," Donny said softly.

Proctor swore silently to himself that if he ever met Donny's father, he would give him a piece of his mind. That was after he put his fist through the man's face. No father should ever make their son feel so little about themselves. Especially somebody as sweet as Donny.

They ate the rest of their meal in silence. When it came time to pay the bill, Proctor insisted on paying. "If you're going to be giving me a guided tour of the town, the least I can do is pay for your meal."

Donny nipped on his bottom lip. "Yeah, but I kind of pigged out on you."

"That's okay, I can afford your eating habits."

They walked outside, and Donny spun around in a slow circle as he looked up around, as if he were trying to decide where they should go first. It gave Proctor a chance to get a good look at the younger man. Donny had on a pair of skinny jeans that left nothing to the imagination and a t-shirt that clung to his thin frame. His blond hair was spiked up a bit, making it look like he'd just gotten out of bed. Which led Proctor to think of all kinds of naughty thoughts. Ones that he knew he shouldn't be having, but damn if he could help himself.

"So what do you want to see first?" Donny asked. "The old cider mill or one of the antique shops?"

What I really want to see is you naked and under me, Proctor thought. But since that could never be, he said, "Take me to the cider mill. Are they open this time of year?"

Donny nodded. "They just opened so everything will be fresh. I'll bet the doughnuts are still warm."

Proctor laughed. "How can you even think about eating after that huge breakfast?"

Donny gave him a wide-eyed stare. "It's fresh cider mill donuts. There's always room for those."

Well, when Donny put it that way, who was Proctor to argue? With a laugh, he followed Donny down a short dirt road. It led to an old ramshackle building that looked as if it were on its last legs. It had a brightly painted red roof and matching door. Donny opened it and gestured for Proctor to come inside.

As soon as Proctor entered, he was assailed with the scents of apples, cinnamon, butter, and nuts. He inhaled deeply, knowing already that he was going to love this place.

Donny went around the corner and leaned against the metal railing. "Look, they're making some donuts right now."

They sure were. It was a huge machine that took up a good portion of the back part of the building. Proctor had to bite the inside of his cheek when he noted that Donny was just as fascinated by the process as the small group of children who had formed around him.

They ordered a half dozen of the sugared ones and some cider, then found a picnic bench outside to sit down. Donny devoured his half, even going so far as to lick his fingers clean. As Proctor watched Donny's pink tongue darting out to caress his digits, he had to fight back a groan of desire. Just the thought of that tongue doing all kinds of dirty things to Proctor made him hard and needy.

Remember, he said this was just an outing as friends.

Yeah, but he has been flirting non-stop with you.

Of course, he could just be friendly. He may act that way with everybody.

Dear God, this brat is going to be the end of me.

"Do you want to go for a walk in the woods?" Donny asked. "We can work off all this junk we ate, and I can show you some of the neat stuff we have back there."

Proctor cleared his throat and tried to clear his head of his lewd thoughts. "Yeah, that sounds like a great idea. Just make sure you go easy on this city boy."

"Ah, something tells me you can handle anything I throw your way." Donny hopped down from the picnic table. "Do you have to be home by a certain time?"

"Not really. Why?"

Donny gave a wicked grin. "I was just wondering how long I get to keep you."

See, there he went again with the flirting. Proctor just wished he knew where he stood with Donny. That way he would know if it was safe for him to make a move or not. That was if Proctor even wanted to make a move, he still wasn't even for sure if he wanted to or not. Agh! He was so confused he wanted to find the nearest tree and bang his head against it.

Donny walked a couple of steps before he stopped, then turned around. "Are you coming or not?"

Proctor shook his head as he realized he'd been standing there like some kind of idiot. "Sorry, I'm coming."

As they walked through the woods, Proctor couldn't help but admire how Donny moved around them so easily. It was as if he knew them so intimately that he was almost at one with them. Proctor decided that it must be all part of the whole survivalist thing. Donny probably spent a good part of his time hunting out here. Although, from the way he talked, he didn't catch much game.

"There's a creek over here that's so clear you can see the fish in it," Donny called.

Proctor followed, stumbling a couple of times because he was more used to sidewalks than hiking trails. When he arrived there, he saw that all the hard work had been worth it, though; the creek really was a thing of beauty.

It looked to be only a few feet deep, and the bottom was all rock, but it was full of fish in an array of colors and sizes. It was like they were looking into a giant fish aquarium, but it was real life.

"Wow, Donny. You were right. This is amazing," Proctor said.

"I'm glad you think so," Donny said.

Proctor turned his head and realized that his lips were inches from Donny's. Proctor froze, still unsure of what would be the best thing to do. He wanted to taste Donny so damn bad it hurt, yet he didn't want to end up hurting the younger man either.

"Please?" Donny rasped.

That single word shredded away the last of Proctor's self-control. Cupping the back of Donny's head, he brought him in for a deep kiss. When Donny immediately went pliant in Proctor's hold and let him take over, the dominate side of Proctor roared its approval.

Things were just starting to get good when a growling sound broke the mood. Pulling apart, Proctor gazed into the woods. "What in the hell was that?"

Donny gave a nervous laugh. "It was nothing. These woods are completely safe."

"Are you sure it wasn't a wolf or something?"

The last thing Proctor wanted was to have a run-in with some wild creature. He didn't even have his gun on him for protection. Which made him feel vulnerable as hell.

Donny gave another laugh and shook his head. "Don't be ridiculous. Everybody knows that there aren't wolves around here anymore. They've been extinct here for a long time."

"Then what was that growling sound?" Proctor asked.

"It was probably some kid gunning off a four-wheeler or something. They do that all the time in these woods. We hate it because it drives away our game."

"It didn't sound like a machine."

Donny rolled his eyes. "Well, maybe then it was some dog that got loose and is just trying to find its way home, and we spooked it. If you want, we can get out of here."

"Yeah, that sounds like a good idea to me," Proctor said.

As a cop, he'd learned to go with his gut instinct, and right then, it was telling him that those woods were a very dangerous place to be.

Chapter Five

As soon as his day with Proctor was over, Donny ducked behind a tree. Taking off his clothes, he stuffed them into his backpack, then shifted into his wolf form. After making sure that nobody was watching, he took off to the pack lands as fast as his four legs could carry him.

He had already called Tiber and told him about seeing the black wolf shifter in the woods. It was the very same one who had attacked them not too long ago. During the attack, Connor had almost died—in fact, he would have were it not for Tiber intervening and transforming Connor into a wolf shifter, so he could heal.

Donny had no doubt that Tiber and the Betas were already out hunting down the black wolf. But maybe if Donny was fast enough, he could catch up with them and help them out. Then he could show them all that he wasn't just some helpless Omega, and he could carry his own weight in the pack.

When Donny got back, he shifted back into his human form and quickly dressed again. Going into the main house, he was pleased to see that Tiber and the Betas had come in to restock. How perfect! Donny could go out with them instead of having to search for them.

"Just give me a couple of minutes, and I'll get changed," Donny said.

Tiber frowned. "For what?"

Donny gave a half smile. That hadn't been the reaction he'd been expecting. "To go out with you guys to hunt down the black wolf. What else would it be for?"

"You're not going out with us. Your place is back here with the others," Tiber said firmly.

Donny's heart stuttered a bit, and he felt like he'd been kicked in the gut. It was like listening to all the cruel words his father had tossed his way all over again—*useless, weak, no good, not a real man, a pansy, a mistake, a freak, an embarrassment.*

"Why would I stay back with the mates and children? I'm a man, so I should be out fighting like one," Donny argued, trying hard to keep his voice from wavering.

He'd expected this from the others but never from Tiber. Tiber had always had his back. It was Tiber who had always stood up for him. Who had given up everything for him. Who had always believed in him. To have Tiber now tell Donny that he didn't measure up was a crushing blow.

"You may be a male, but you're an Omega. The Omega's job is to stay behind and soothe the mates and children," Tiber said.

"Fuck that. If they need soothing, give them some *Haagen-Dazs* and a chick flick. They don't need me for anything."

Tiber came up and grabbed Donny by the back of the neck. "I know what you're thinking right now."

"Oh, really? What's that?" Donny spat back angrily.

"That I'm no better than your father. That I think you're less than a man because you're an Omega. But nothing could be further from the truth. The reason I'm leaving you behind is because your Omega skills are needed here. These people are terrified, and you're the only one who can calm them down. Whether you like it or not, that's the hand that life dealt you, and you have to play it. If you won't do it for you, then do it for the good of the pack."

Donny's shoulders sagged. Damn it, when Tiber put it that way, there was no way Donny could argue without coming off like a huge asshole. It didn't mean that Donny had to like it, though.

"Fine, I'll stay here and be the pack's security blanket."

Tiber ruffled Donny's hair. "Thank you. You have no idea how much this means to me."

Donny took a seat at the main dining table and gloomily watched as all the other able-bodied men left. Meanwhile, Donny was left with the old, the young, and the mates. Never before had he felt so humiliated or so useless.

An elderly lady came up and sat across from him. She looked to be of Native American descent. Her long, gray hair was done up in one long braid, and she wore a pink, striped housecoat. She took one look at Donny and started laughing.

"What's so funny?" he asked, trying his hardest to keep his voice respectful despite the fact she thought he was just frigging hilarious.

"You still don't get it, do you?" she asked.

"Get what?"

"That you are the one."

Donny was really getting sick of these riddles. He wondered when she would just get down to business and tell him what in the hell she meant.

"The one who does what?" Donny asked.

"You're the most important member of this pack."

Donny gave her a droll stare. "Yeah, try telling that to my father. He was always looking for a way to tell me what a disappointment I was to him because I was born an Omega."

"Well, then your father was a fool," she exclaimed.

Donny gave a slight nod. She wasn't going to get any argument from him there. Donny couldn't stand his father, and if he never saw the man again, it would be too soon. The old lady reached across the table and grabbed Donny's hand, her touch icy cold.

"The Omega is the glue that keeps a pack together. A good Omega is hard to find. Alphas may come and go, but it's hard to find an Omega who is strong enough to hold the weight of the pack on his shoulders."

Donny shook his head. Clearly the lady had no idea what she was talking about. "I'm just a nobody. You saw how Tiber treated me."

"Tiber didn't take you out because you are too valuable to lose. Plus, you are needed here to comfort the rest of the pack."

"If all this is true, then why did my father hate having an Omega as a son? You would have thought he would have been proud of the fact," Donny pointed out.

The old lady made a dismissive wave of her hand. "Bah! Who knows how some men think? Sometimes they believe muscles and strength are all that matters in this world, but we know better."

Donny cocked a brow at her. "We do? Because I've been in a lot of situations where if I'd had a little more muscles, it would have come in handy."

"Yet you managed to get out, and that's because you used your mind. I've seen how you act. You like to pretend that you're nothing more than a brat, but underneath all that, your brain is always working."

"I don't act like a brat," Donny argued.

"Of course you do. You shirk the jobs Tiber gives you because you know they're menial. You're always late for things. And don't even get me started about that mouth of yours. You're angry at the world, and you want everybody around you to know it."

"Well, maybe that's true, but you would act the same way if you were in my place."

The old woman let out a soft laugh. "You sound just like my son used to."

"*Used*," Donny echoed, not missing the way she referred to him in the past tense.

"Yes, my son was the pack Omega years ago before we came here. He died when the old Alpha took him along on a raid. The Alpha was low on men, and since he needed more bodies, he took my Ralphie even though I begged him not to. I told the Alpha that the Omega has no place on the battlefield."

"Because Omegas are weak," Donny said sadly.

"No, because Omegas are strong but just in other areas. My Ralphie never came home from that raid. The pack grew even weaker without an Omega to hold it together, and members gradually drifted away. We were down to the handful you see now before we found out about your cousin and came to him to join his pack. We were so excited, too, not just because we needed a better Alpha but because we needed an Omega again. You see, Donny, we need you just as much as we need an Alpha, perhaps even more."

Wow, while Donny wanted to believe her—he really, really did—all those years of being belittled by his father still rang in his ears and made him doubt himself. If an Omega really was that important, then why wasn't his father proud to have one in his family? It all didn't make sense to him.

Something tugged on Donny's shirt. Looking down, he saw it was one of the pack children. A boy that looked to be about five years old, dressed in his jammies, thumb in mouth looked up at him with a huge brown-eyed gaze.

"Hey, little guy. What do you want?" Donny asked.

By way of answer, the boy scrambled up into Donny's lap. After some maneuvering that involved a lot of elbows and knees digging into Donny, the kid made himself comfortable. Snuggling into Donny's chest, the kid let out a happy sigh.

"See? He feels safe with you," the elderly lady said.

"Either that, or he knows a sucker when he sees one," Donny grumbled.

Pretty soon another child came up and after that, another one. Soon Donny had to get up and sit on the ground, then stretch out his legs so he could accommodate all the kids who wanted his comfort. After a while, his back began to ache from sitting in such an awkward position, but it was worth it because there were no more tears or sniffles.

One by one, the children drifted off to sleep until only the adults remained awake. They all spoke in hushed tones as they kept glancing at the door, looking for signs of Tiber and the Betas. Donny knew they were worried, just as he was that they might not make it back. Sure, Tiber and the others might have the numbers on their side, but the black wolf was a fierce opponent. There's no saying that he couldn't take out Tiber and the Betas.

Finally, after what seemed like to be forever, the front door opened, and Tiber and all the Betas came in. Donny quickly scanned them all for injuries. When he saw none, he let out a sigh of relief.

"Did you find him?" Donny asked.

"No, we followed his tracks for miles until they led to a road and vanished. He must have had a car parked there and shifted, then drove away," Tiber said in disgust.

Donny let out a grunt of disappointment. They had been so close this time, too. He was so damn sick and tired of having to look over his shoulder all the time, worried that the black wolf might be lurking there. Donny just wished the thing would either die already or move on to different pack lands.

Tiber cocked a brow when he saw that Donny was covered in sleeping kids. "Did you make some new friends while I was away?"

"Something like that. They needed comforting, and of course, they had to gravitate to the nearest Omega. They were all so cute, I just couldn't say no."

The children began to stir. When they saw their fathers, they all got up and ran to them. Free of his buddies, Donny got up, then stretched the kinks out of his back. He wanted to get back to his cabin and take a nice, long hot bath. He might even go all out and add some bubbles. Kelly had bought him some strawberry scented ones, and he wasn't too ashamed to use them. Hell, he would even take a trashy, gossip magazine with him to read.

"If you're done with me, I'm going to go back to my cabin. It's been a long day for me, and I just want to wash up and crash," Donny said.

Tiber patted him on the shoulder. "Sure, we can catch up tomorrow. We need to talk about that dam."

"Ohhh... boy. Can't wait," Donny drawled out sarcastically.

He ducked to avoid getting swatted in the back of the head, then left the main cabin. Making his way to his much smaller cabin, Donny drew a bath, making the water as hot as possible. He added some of Kelly's bubbles, then undressed and got in.

He was just settling down for a good soak when his cell went off. Donny wondered who in the hell could be calling him. Usually only Tiber rang him, and Donny had just got done talking to him. Picking up the phone, Donny was shocked to see that it was Proctor.

Well, wasn't that a pleasant ending to his day. Answering the phone, Donny said, "Miss me already?"

"How did you guess?"

"It happens all the time with me when I hang out with people. It's my winning personality."

Proctor's warm chuckle filled Donny's ear. "I see low self-esteem isn't a problem with you."

Oh, if he only knew. Low self-esteem and I are best friends.

"I must admit I didn't expect to hear back from you so soon," Donny said.

"I didn't expect to be calling you so soon," Proctor countered. "I should be doing everything to keep my distance from you. Not only are you way too young for me, but I'm leaving in three weeks. I have no business starting anything with you."

"What if I want you to start something anyway?" Donny countered.

"And what if I'm afraid of hurting you?"

"I'm a big boy. I don't break that easily."

There was a long pause before Proctor said, "Damn it, why do you have to be so irresistible?"

"I don't know. I just can't help myself. Somebody told me today it was in my blood, and I was born that way," Donny replied, thinking back to his conversation with the elderly lady.

"Are you free tomorrow?"

"I have some work I need to do during the day, but I can be free for dinner. Would that work for you?"

Donny held his breath while he waited for Proctor's answer. He so wanted to see the man again. More than anything that Donny ever wanted in his entire life. There was just something about the detective that called to Donny like no other ever had.

Finally, Proctor said, "Sure, I'll pick you up about five-thirty. Would that work for you?"

"That would be perfect." Donny did a little happy dance, making the water splash.

"I can't wait to see you again."

"I can't wait to see you, either. I'll be counting the hours," Donny replied.

Chapter Six

Proctor was excited. After a week of seeing Donny every day, they were finally going to have a chance to have some real alone time. Josh and Connor were leaving for the evening, and they had given Proctor permission to have Donny over for dinner.

Proctor was in the kitchen getting the ingredients together for the meal when his friends came downstairs. They were both dressed in their best. Proctor noticed how they often touched each other and the way they often glanced at each other with love in their eyes. Before, he'd never been envious of that, but now he found himself wanting to have a piece of that in his life. While being a bachelor was fun, lately it'd gotten dull and a bit lonely.

"We're getting ready to go. You sure you don't want to join us?" Connor asked for what had to be the tenth time.

"No, I'm looking forward to having Donny to myself. Every time we've been out, it's been in public. I feel like we haven't had a chance to really get to know each other," Proctor replied.

Connor and Josh exchanged uneasy glances. Proctor paused in what he was doing to stare at them. He was really getting sick of them doing that. It seemed it was becoming a common theme between them.

"Is there something you guys aren't telling me?" Proctor asked.

Connor hedged a bit before he said, "Isn't Donny a bit young for you?"

"Sure, he's not as old as the guys I usually date, but we just clicked. Is that a problem for you?" Proctor asked, somewhat surprised by Connor's question.

He would have thought that Connor would be the last one to have an issue with something like an age gap. His buddy was usually laid back about that kind of thing. Plus, since when in the hell had Connor cared who Proctor dated?

"I just don't want to see you get hurt," Connor said.

"Don't worry about me. I'm a big boy." Proctor laughed.

"Just be careful around Donny. He has . . . uh . . . family issues. I would hate for you to get mixed up in them," Connor persisted.

Proctor was beginning to get a little ticked on Donny's behalf. Like he could help who his family was. As far as Proctor was concerned, Donny was a great guy, and he deserved a fair shot. Nobody should be judged on who they came from. Sure, Donny's dad might be an asshole, but that didn't mean that Donny should be painted with the same brush.

"I'm dating Donny. Not his family," Proctor said a little harshly.

"Yeah, well, sometimes the two get mixed up even though Donny might not want them to be."

Proctor crossed his arms over his chest. "Do you have something against Donny?"

Connor held up his hands. "No, I like him. He's a great guy. But you're my friend, and I have to look out for your best interests, too. I just want you to be careful is all."

"I will be. Thanks," Proctor replied tightly. "Have fun tonight."

What Proctor didn't add was that he'd already fallen hard for Donny and that it was going to hurt like a bitch to leave him once his vacation was over. If Connor were to find that out, he'd probably blow a gasket. That was after he picked his jaw off the ground. Proctor was Mr. Non-Commitment to a T, and here he was going all ga-ga over a man he'd just met. It was the cruelest irony ever.

"Okay then, I guess we'll be going. We'll see you tomorrow," Connor said.

He still didn't look happy, but that was too bad. Proctor didn't know what Connor had against Donny, but he would just have to get over it. Besides, Proctor would be leaving soon, and Connor wouldn't have to worry about it anymore.

Five minutes after Connor and Josh left, there was a knock on the door. Connor rushed to answer it, his heart skipping a beat when he saw how gorgeous Donny looked. He only had on a pair of worn jeans and a t-shirt, but he could have been a model from a magazine he looked so good in them. His blond hair was slightly wet, like he'd just finished showering not too long ago. As always, his cheeks were slightly flushed as if he'd just been running, and he smelled of the woods.

"You look good enough to eat," Proctor blurted.

"Well, if you want to put off dinner for a while, I don't mind being the first course," Donny replied.

That was all the invitation Proctor needed. With a growl, he grabbed Donny by the waist of his jeans and pulled him inside, then kicked the door closed behind them. Still keeping a grip on Donny, Proctor began to lead him upstairs.

"Well, I was just kidding, but if you want to start off with the fun stuff, I'm all game," Donny said.

"I've been wanting you for so long. You should have known better than to tease me," Proctor said as he began to tug Donny down the hallway to the guest bedroom.

"We could have done it out in the woods if you were that eager. I know of some great secluded spots."

"Our first time is going to be more special than that. Besides, I want to take my time with you and not have to worry about somebody stumbling across us."

Proctor opened the door to his room, then all but tossed Donny on the bed. Yessssss... that's exactly where he'd wanted the man for so long. Proctor nearly came on the spot just from the sight of Donny all spread out and waiting for him, and they hadn't even gotten undressed yet.

Donny crooked a finger at him. "You gonna join me, or do I have to take care of things myself?"

Damn! Donny was going to be the death of Proctor. Just the thought of Donny stroking himself off had Proctor aching with need. If Proctor weren't already so jacked up, he might have ordered Donny to do so right then and there.

Instead, Proctor began to peel off his clothes, all the while keeping his gaze on Donny. Donny stared back, licking his lips before letting out a low growling sound. It seemed so out of place from the usual carefree man that Proctor almost laughed.

Once Proctor had all his clothes off, he pounced. Getting on the bed, he began to tear at Donny's shirt and jeans. Proctor was in a near frenzy to get some skin-on-skin action. Lucky for him, Donny seemed just as excited for the same thing, and he eagerly helped with the process.

After what seemed like a lifetime, he finally had Donny nude. Proctor sat back on his knees, so he could take a moment to admire the view. Donny might be a bit on the thinner side, but he still had an impressive set of muscles. Proctor took the time to outline them with his fingers, making Donny's breath hitch.

"I have a feeling this is going to be the best first course I'm ever going to have," Proctor declared.

"I don't know. You've probably been with a ton of more guys than I have. I hope I can measure up to them," Donny replied with a nervous chuckle.

Proctor reached down and wrapped his fingers around Donny's thick cock. "You already have. Even before we got undressed."

Donny let out a moan as Proctor began to pump his hand up and down. The entire time, Proctor kept his gaze on Donny's face, taking in the look of pure bliss that washed over the man's expression. It gave Proctor a feeling of power to know that he put that expression on Donny's face.

Dear God, what I would do to be able to keep him forever.

Now where had that come from? He had only known Donny for a week. Proctor was the last one to run headfirst into rash decisions or to be led by his heart. Yet here he was letting this blond menace worm his way into his heart.

Shoving those thoughts ruthlessly aside, Proctor continued to stroke Donny off, pausing only long enough to reach under the pillow to grab the lube and condom. Proctor had stashed them there earlier with great hopes that he would be using them.

Cracking opening the lube, Proctor dribbled some on his fingers and spread it over his hands. He then went back to stroking Donny. Leaning down, Proctor slanted his mouth over Donny's and kissed him.

Donny let out a small sound of surprise before he began kissing Proctor back in earnest. He even cupped the back of Proctor's head and brought him in closer, clinging on so tight that it was like Donny was afraid that Proctor was going to leave him. Which was crazy. There was no way in hell that Proctor was going to leave just when things were getting good.

Using his free slicked hand, Proctor reached under and found Donny's hole. Rimming it a few times, he then slowly slid the digit inside. Donny gasped into Proctor's mouth, but he then let out a groan of desire.

Proctor worked the finger in and out several times before he added a second one. By then, Donny was panting and letting out soft cries of pleasure. Proctor was about to add a third finger when Donny shook his head. Hooking his arms behind his knees, Donny opened himself up to Proctor.

"Fuck me now. I need you inside me," Donny pleaded.

Well, Proctor wasn't going to argue with that. He got back on his knees and grabbed the condom. Opening the package, he slicked the latex on his dick and added some extra lube to it. He then lined the head of his cock to Donny's hole.

"If I hurt you, just let me know. We can stop and take a break," Proctor said.

For some reason, Donny found that comment funny. "Don't worry. I'm a lot tougher than I look. I don't break easily. Just give it to me hard. That's how I like it."

Well, if that's what he wanted, then that's what he would get. Grabbing onto Donny's hips for support, Proctor slammed into Donny in one brutal thrust. Donny let out a loud cry.

"That's what I'm talking about! Give me some more."

Whoa! It would seem that Donny was full of all kinds of fun surprises. Not that Proctor minded. He always liked things a little rough in bed, too. Leaning down so he had Donny almost bent in half, Proctor gave Donny a hard, all-consuming kiss before he began to pound the fuck out of him.

Soon the room filled with the sounds of the headboard slamming into the wall, of flesh hitting flesh, of grunts, groans of pleasures, and the occasional curse word.

Donny didn't just lay there and take it either. He kept thrusting his hips up as best he could, given his position, to meet Proctor halfway. Donny even wrapped his arms around Proctor's back and dug his nails into the skin, which was odd since Proctor didn't recall Donny having long nails. Shit, they almost felt like claws. But instead of hurting, it added a whole erotic mix to the scene.

Then Donny started with the little growling thing again, and Proctor knew he wasn't going to last much longer. He didn't know what it was about it, but for some reason, it was the biggest turn-on ever. Proctor gritted his teeth as he picked up his pace even more, determined that he would not be the first one to come. It was bad enough to be the old man in the relationship, but to be shown up by your younger lover was quite another thing.

Then just as Proctor was about to give up all hope, Donny cried out Proctor's name and came, hot ropes of spunk covering both of their stomachs. Silently singing the *Hallelujah* chorus in his head, Proctor let go and had his own orgasm.

Afterward, he collapsed, falling to the side of Donny. It gave Proctor some satisfaction to see that Donny was breathing just as hard as he was. So Proctor hadn't done so badly for being the elder of the two.

Proctor reached over and brushed away a tendril of sweaty hair that was stuck to Donny's forehead. "That was so worth the wait."

"Yeah, but now you really have to feed me because I'm starving."

"When aren't you hungry?" Proctor teased. "Fine, let's get cleaned up, and I'll feed you before you waste away to nothing."

They took a quick shower together, got dressed, then went downstairs. Donny helped Proctor finish making dinner.

During the entire time, Proctor couldn't help but think how at ease he was with Donny. He never had to force the conversation or pretend to be somebody he wasn't, like he had with other guys. With Donny, he could just be himself. It was so refreshing.

They were just sitting down to eat when Proctor asked, "Why don't you stay the night with me?"

Donny gave a slight frown. "Won't Connor and Josh mind?"

"No, they're not coming in until late."

Donny gave a slight shrug. "Okay, I just have to call Tiber first and let him know where I'll be."

That seemed odd. "You have to call and okay it with your cousin? You're an adult."

"I know, but there's been some wild dog attacks, and he worries about me when I'm out and alone by myself at night." Donny got up and went to the back door. "Just give me a minute to call him, and I'll be right back inside."

Donny went outside and shut the door behind him. He was out there for several minutes. While Proctor couldn't hear the conversation, it must have gotten heated a few times going by Donny's body language. Finally, Donny hung up and came back inside. He gave Proctor a grin and sat down again.

"Sorry about that. My family can be a bit of a handful sometimes," Donny said.

Thinking back to what Connor had hinted at earlier, Proctor said, "I understand."

"It's no biggie, though. I'll be staying. He was just worried about me being away from the others. We always watch each other's backs. They tend to baby me a lot."

"Are you the youngest?" Proctor asked.

"Something like that," Donny mumbled.

Well, if that wasn't cryptic enough. Sometimes Proctor felt like he knew Donny better than anybody, yet there were other times when he felt like Donny was holding back something big from him. This was one of those times.

"You know, Donny, if there's something that you need to tell me, you can go ahead and share. I've been a cop for a while. I've pretty much seen just about everything there is to be seen."

Donny gazed right into Proctor's eyes, and Proctor was taken aback by the haunted look in the younger man's gaze. "No, Proctor. You haven't seen everything. There's a whole world out there that would still shock the shit out of you."

CHAPTER SEVEN

Early the next morning, Proctor was walking outside in front of the house with Donny. Proctor couldn't remember a time when he'd been happier. He was tired was hell, that was sure, since he and Donny had spent most of the night making love or talking. But for the first time in forever, Proctor felt at peace with the world. So much so that, as crazy as it seemed, he was even beginning to entertain ideas of possibly coming back for a very extended visit, one that might become permanent.

"Are you sure you have to go home?" Proctor said.

"Yeah, if I don't get back and help out with the dam, Aslan and Beau are going to be pissed at me for leaving them with all the work," Donny replied. "I'll come back tonight, though. Maybe you'll be adventurous enough to try out one of those secluded areas in the woods I was telling you about."

Proctor grabbed Donny and gave him a deep kiss. "Who knows, maybe I will be. You do tempt me to do all kinds of crazy things."

They had just reached the end of the drive when Proctor first spotted a man in a police uniform walking their way. Donny frowned and said, "Hey, Sheriff, what brings you all the way out here? If you're looking for Connor, he's still in bed."

The sheriff shook his head. "No, it's family business. Not official police business, if you know what I mean."

While that made no sense to Proctor, understanding dawned on Donny's face. Proctor couldn't help but feel a little frustrated. He was getting sick of feeling like he was being left out of some big secret that everybody was privy to but him. This town seemed to have more secrets than the damn CIA.

"Is anybody ever going to tell me what's going on here? I'm getting sick of everybody always talking in riddles around me," Proctor asked in exasperation.

Donny put a comforting hand on Proctor's shoulder. "The sheriff is just talking about the wild dog attacks I was telling you about last night. Weren't you, Sheriff?"

A confused look crossed the sheriff's gray eyes for a moment before he blinked a couple of times and said, "Yes, yes, the wild dog attacks. That's right. I was just tracking them down this way. I picked up their scent . . . I mean their tracks and was following them this way."

Proctor let out a sigh. He didn't have to be a police detective to know that story was a bunch of bullshit. What in the hell were they hiding from him? What's worse was Donny and Connor were both in on it. To know that both of them were keeping information from him and lying to his face felt like a punch to his gut.

Proctor glanced up at the sheriff to call him out on his story when a dark shadow came out of the woods. Before Proctor could call out a warning, a tall, muscular man dressed head-to-toe in black came up behind the sheriff. Moving quickly, the man sliced the sheriff's throat with a long, wicked-looking blade, the wound going so deep it nearly decapitated the man. Blood spurted out, covering the dirt road. The sheriff let out a gurgling sound as all the color left his face.

Donny gasped and took a step forward, but Proctor put out a hand to stay him. The man in black let go of the sheriff, who fell to the ground. The sheriff let out one more gurgle, then stopped breathing altogether. The murderer looked down with an impassive expression on his face. Everything about him screamed thug. His long, dark, slightly curly hair was is a dirty ponytail that went all the way down his back. He wore a long black trench coat that looked to be heavily weighed down with weapons. His pitted, pale face was marred with a long scar that went from his temple to his cheek. The worst thing about him, though, had to be his eyes, they were such a dark brown that they were almost black, and they were devoid of any emotion, making him look slightly wild. He was the type of guy you didn't want to run into at a bar or a dark alley or anywhere for that matter.

"Oscar?" Donny whispered. "You're one of us. Why would you attack and kill other shifters? It doesn't make any sense. We're supposed to work together. Not against one another."

Oscar? Who in the hell is Oscar, and how in the hell did Donny know him? What's more, why in the hell did he just kill the sheriff? And how in the hell am I going to get Donny and me away from this madman?

"I have my reasons for doing this," the man in black answered as he used the end of his black trench coat to wipe his blade clean. "I don't like shifters and I never will, they are an abomination that needs to be cleansed from the world."

Donny shook his head. "We don't need to do this here. Not here. Not now. This isn't the place to do our business."

"What? You don't want your boyfriend to know that he's been fucking a dog?"

Proctor didn't know what in the hell the insane conversation meant. He just knew that he needed to get some help ASAP. He didn't have his gun on him, but if he could get Connor's attention somehow, then his friend could come out and take care of this freak. Proctor glanced up at the house to see if maybe Connor had heard all the commotion and was coming out. Right then, that seemed to be Proctor and Donny's only hope. Because while Proctor might be able to take on the guy in a physical fight, Proctor had no doubt the guy was packing some serious heat in his trench coat.

The man in black must have caught Proctor glancing at the house because he made a tsking noise. "Don't even think about screaming for help, or I'll just kill blondie outright instead of giving him a chance to fight for his life."

"It won't be a fair fight, and you know it," Donny said. "There is no way an Omega can take on an Alpha."

The man in black laughed. "Too fucking bad, because that's the way it's going to be. I should have never been made into a disgusting shifter to begin with and my way of getting back is I'm going to eradicate every pack I run into, starting with yours. Tiber is too strong for me to take on now, but if I take out his Omega, then he'll be weaker. That's when I'll be able to strike and take him out and the rest of his pack will fall after him. So, I'm sorry, Omega, but that's just the way it's going to have to be."

Proctor shook his head in confusion. What in the hell were they talking about? Alpha? Omega? None of it made any sense to him. But he knew it was pretty damn important, and at least Donny's life depended on Proctor figuring it out quickly.

"What honor is there in killing me?" Donny asked. "I'm just the Omega. I'm nothing."

The man let loose with that grating laugh of his again. *Just the Omega.* Oh, isn't that rich. Either you're stupid or too young to realize how powerful you really are. It's the Omega that keeps the pack together. Without the Omega, there is no pack. When I kill you, I'll cut the feet off the pack."

"And what makes you so sure that I'll fight you?" Donny countered.

The man cocked his head to the side. "Because if you don't. I'll kill your human. Besides, I've been watching you for a while. You're cocky and just dying for a chance to prove to the others that you're as strong as them. What better way to prove it to them than by taking me out? Plus, think of how much you'll impress your boyfriend when you save the day."

And in that moment, Proctor knew that Donny would accept the challenge. He'd seen the way Donny had looked at him. The utter devotion in the Donny's gaze when he stared at Proctor. He'd do anything to protect Proctor.

Proctor lunged for Donny, at the same time, yelling, "No!"

He was already too late. Donny was off and running at the man. The man started charging Donny at the same time. Halfway there they both jumped into the air. Right before Proctor's eyes, they both morphed into wolves. Donny into a gray one, the other man into a black one.

The two animals crashed together in a clash of teeth and claws. The wolves landed on the ground with a loud thud, then began to roll around as they fought for dominance, the sounds of their snarls and growls filling the air.

Proctor could already tell that there was no way Donny could win the battle. He was so much smaller than the other wolf. Yet he had gone into the fight anyway. Just to save Proctor. It made Proctor feel angry and humble at the same time.

Proctor took a couple of steps back. This had to be a dream . . . no, a nightmare. This kind of stuff happened in books or movies. They sure as hell didn't happen in real life. Yet the snarls of the animals sounded real enough. The smell of blood when the black wolf bit into the haunch of the gray one was pungent enough. The bitter cold of the wind biting into his skin seemed cruel enough.

"Holy shit! Is that Donny?" Connor said as he came running up.

"I think so. I mean it was, and then it wasn't," Proctor said.

"Josh, take the car and go get Tiber and the others," Connor ordered.

"Okay, but only if you promise not to do anything rash, like shift and try to help," Josh said.

"To hell with that. I know I can't take him on in my wolf form. I'm going to shoot the fucker. Now go!" Connor said.

Josh got in the car and took off, his wheels skidding on the gravel road. Proctor couldn't take his eyes of the wolves. The black wolf started to pin the gray one down. When it looked like it was about to go for Donny's throat, Connor shot above the animals' heads. It worked. The black wolf looked up, distracted by the sound, and Donny was able to wiggle out from under him and crawl away, his movements slow and jerky.

By that point, Donny's fur was a matted, bloody mess. Proctor let out a sob when he realized that they were probably already too late and that Donny wasn't going to survive. Everywhere Proctor looked at on Donny there were gouges, bite marks, and scratches on his gray fur.

Proctor could see the trench coat on the ground where it had fallen when the black wolf had shifted. If he could only get to it, then maybe he could get a gun, too, and help Connor. But the fighting wolves blocked his path. So all Proctor could do was stand there and watch as the man he'd grown to care so much for got mauled to death.

The black wolf let out a snarl, almost like it was laughing at them. It then lunged at Proctor. Connor fired a couple of shots, but the wolf was too quick. It bit Proctor in the neck. Connor let out a scream of anger and shot again, this time hitting the black wolf in the flank. The wolf let out a yelp of pain, then took off, running into the woods.

Proctor fell to the ground, his hands going to the wound in his neck. Blood gushed out between his fingers, the liquid warm and sticky. Shit, he and Donny were both going to die if help didn't get there quickly.

Connor took off his shirt and pressed it to Proctor's wound. "Don't die on me. I don't know how to bite and save you."

Proctor didn't know what in the hell his friend was talking about. But then again, he didn't know what in the hell was going on, period. His boyfriend, if you can even call a guy you've only known a week that, was in the form of wolf and dying a few feet from him. Proctor had just seen not one, but two, men turn into wolves. And now Connor supposedly could turn into one, too. It was as if the whole world had gone mad, and he was the only sane one left.

The sounds of howling ripped through the air and soon a handful of gray wolves came into view, followed by Josh's car. Connor gave Proctor a little shake. "Stay with me, buddy. Help is on the way."

Proctor rolled his head so he could look over at Donny. The wolf just lay there, panting but otherwise, not moving. While Proctor knew he should be mad at Donny for not telling him about the whole wolf thing, Proctor was too busy trying not to die to worry about it. Plus he was more worried about Donny living, too. If they both made it out of this mess okay, then he could give Donny hell.

The biggest gray wolf led the group, it stopped at Donny, sniffed him, then lifted its head to the air and let out a loud howl. The rest of the wolves in the small pack followed suit.

"Hey, Tiber, I'll make you a deal," Josh called. "I'll take care of Donny if you take care of Proctor."

Proctor had no frigging idea what Josh meant, but the wolf obviously did because it let out a snuffing noise and came trotting over. Before Proctor could react, the wolf bit him. Proctor let out a scream, both from pain and outrage.

"What the fuck was that for?" Proctor asked.

"He just saved your life," Connor said. "Oh, and welcome to the pack."

"Are you saying what I think you're saying?" Proctor asked as horror filled him. He wasn't bleeding as badly as before.

"Yeah, you're one of us now," Josh said. "It was either that or you were going to die. Now I have to go and save Donny before he dies. If you want to get pissed at me, you can do it later."

One by one the wolves shifted into men. Josh opened up the trunk of his car and handed out clothes. They quickly got dressed and then carefully picked up Donny. Even though they treated him gingerly, Donny still yelped in pain several times. Each time he did, it felt like a dagger in Proctor's heart.

A couple more men went over to the sheriff and started to take care of his body. Proctor turned away and followed Connor and Josh into the veterinary clinic. He didn't want to be far away from Donny.

"Why doesn't he shift back to his human form?" Proctor asked.

"Because he's too injured," Tiber said.

Or at least Proctor assumed it was Tiber since he seemed to be the one in charge and he looked like the guy Donny had once showed Proctor on his cellphone.

"Why in the hell would Donny take on the black wolf in the first place?" one of the wolves asked.

"He did it to protect me," Proctor said hoarsely.

Proctor thought about telling Tiber all the other things that the black wolf had said but he held back. It wasn't his place to divulge such things to Tiber. He would let Donny explain it all to Tiber. That was if Donny lived.

"That sounds like something Donny would do," Tiber said as he ran his hand lovingly over Donny's fur.

"Why isn't Donny healing like I did?" Proctor asked.

"You just had one bite. Donny was mauled. There is only so much even our enhanced healing skills can cope with," Connor said.

"Will he be okay?" Proctor bit his bottom lip.

"He will if I have anything to say about it," Josh said. "Now everybody back up, so I can have some room to work."

They all stepped back, but nobody left the room as they watched Josh work frantically to save Donny's life. Time seemed to tick by at a slow pace, and Proctor was on edge so intensely he felt ready to snap.

Finally, Josh stepped back and said, "Well, I've done all I can do. Now we just have to wait and see if he will get better."

"How soon before we know if he'll live or die?" Tiber asked.

Josh shrugged. "I don't know. This is the first time I treated a shifter. Only time will tell. Now come here, Proctor, so I can stitch up your neck wound. It should heal pretty quick, thanks to Tiber's bite. You were lucky. If the black wolf had bit you to change you, instead of killing you, then you would have been evil like him. Since Tiber bit you to transform you, you will pick up his traits and be good."

"What's that supposed to mean?" Proctor asked.

"Just be happy that Tiber is your sire instead of Oscar, otherwise you would be batshit crazy. You were very lucky."

Looking down at Donny, Proctor didn't feel lucky. If anything, he felt like he might have just lost the thing that mattered the most to him in his life.

CHAPTER EIGHT

Donny's whole world had become nothing but pain. It hurt to move. It hurt to breathe. It even hurt to frigging blink.

He lay in his wolf form on a metal table, the smell of his own blood pungent and strong, mixing in with the scents of antiseptic and other medicinal stank. But there was another smell there, one that kept him from giving in to the darkness. One that kept him fighting to live. The one that gave him the strength to go on. It was the scent of Proctor.

Donny could also detect that Proctor was now a wolf shifter. It broke his heart that the kindhearted detective had been pulled into their world. That Donny had been careless and dragged Proctor unwillingly into their life. He'd never wanted that. In fact, he'd done everything he could to protect Proctor from that side of his life. And in the end, Donny had failed miserably.

Maybe it would be better off if he did die. Proctor probably hated him. Tiber was no doubt angry as hell at him. Connor would likely never forgive him. Donny had let down the pack by letting the black wolf get away. So what good was he anyway? He might as well just die and let everybody out of their misery. Then they would never have to put up with his sorry ass anymore.

He tried to get himself in a more comfortable position and whined when pain shot through his body. A hand ran down his body, the touch soothing and soft.

"Shhh . . . just stay still and let the drugs take effect. You need lots of rest if you want to get better and show me those secluded spots you keep talking about."

Donny would have recognized that voice anywhere. It was Proctor. He hadn't taken off and left. Nor had he turned his back on Donny in revulsion. He was still there.

Donny opened his eyes and saw a red mark on Proctor's neck. It was then that he remembered that the black wolf had bitten him there. Donny let out a whimper of distress. He'd let Proctor down. He was supposed to protect Proctor. Keep him away from the world of shifters and Donny had let him down in so many ways.

Tiber came into view. "Hey, look who's awake."

Donny averted his gaze. He couldn't look at his Alpha. Not when he'd failed him in so many ways. Donny had fucked up so badly he wouldn't be surprised if Tiber banished him from the pack. Donny knew he sure as hell deserved it.

"Donny, look at me," Tiber demanded in a strong voice.

Even though he wanted to refuse, Donny was powerless to ignore his Alpha's command. So he turned his gaze over to Tiber. Donny let out a soft, submissive sound as his heart sank to his paws.

"Nobody is upset with you. Proctor told us what happened. You had no choice in the situation. The black wolf would have attacked you either way. At least you fought with some honor."

How Donny wanted to bask in that praise, but a small part of him felt guilty. For the black wolf had been right about one thing. Donny had been cocky and wanted to prove himself to be a real fighter. He had wanted to be able to boast to the rest of the pack that he had been the one to take down the enemy. So while Donny had been fighting to protect Proctor, he had also been battling because of his overinflated ego. And because of it, Proctor had almost died. For that, Donny would never be able to forgive himself.

"When will he be able to shift back to his human form?" Proctor asked.

"It should be pretty soon. He was injured pretty badly, but he's healing quickly. He's going to have some lasting injuries, though. Josh said Donny's leg may never be the same again. He may walk with a limp for the rest of his life."

Well, if that didn't just suck. Now not only was Donny a lowly Omega, but he was damaged goods as well. If his old man ever caught wind of that one, he would be laughing his ass off.

"Shit, the poor kid. That's going to kill him," Proctor said. "Speaking of shifting, how long before I have my first shift?"

Donny's ears perked up. *First shift?* So, obviously Proctor now was a shifter. What in the hell had happened? Donny had been in and out of consciousness near the end of the attack. Had he missed something important?

"You can shift whenever you feel ready to. When you want to, come to me, and I'll talk you through it," Tiber said. "It's the least I can do since I'm your sire."

Okay, that did it. Donny needed to be in his human form, so he could do some talking. He needed some damn answers, and he needed them now. Closing his eyes, he willed the change to come over him.

It hurt . . . oh, God, did it hurt like nothing had ever hurt in his life. It felt like every bone in his body was being broke and reset. But he gritted his teeth and pushed on. Through the haze of agony, he could hear Tiber and Proctor yelling at him to stop, but Donny ignored them. He just continued to fight the pain, and soon he was in his human form.

Sweat covered Donny, and he shook all over. He tried to speak, but he was too out of breath. When he tried to sit up, he fell back on the metal table with a loud thud. Proctor let out a curse as he grabbed a nearby blanket and covered Donny with it.

"What in the hell were you thinking?" Tiber demanded.

"Wanted... to... talk... to... you," Donny finally managed to pant out, his voice raspy and barely above a whisper.

"It was way too soon for you to try and shift back," Tiber admonished. "You could have really hurt yourself."

"Since when do I ever follow the rules?" Donny asked.

He clenched his teeth together as a wave of pain washed over him. Whatever dose of pain medication Josh was giving him might be good for a small wolf, but it obviously wasn't sufficient for a full-grown man.

"It could have waited. Nobody is going anywhere," Proctor said.

"I have to know what happened to you... oh God, it hurts. Can somebody get Josh?"

Tiber nodded. "I'll go fetch him right now."

As soon as Tiber was out of the room, Donny asked Proctor, "Did they turn you?"

"This really isn't the time to worry about this. You need to be more concerned about you right now."

"Tell me," Donny demanded harshly.

Proctor let out a sigh as he ran a hand through his short hair. "Yeah, Tiber had to do it to save my life. The black wolf bit me, and I was going to die."

Donny rested his forehead against the cool metal table as despair crashed through him. Because of him, Proctor's life was never going to be the same anymore. Because of Donny's one reckless act, Proctor was now going to have to pay a huge price. Donny had never before felt like a bigger failure than he did at that moment.

"I am so sorry," Donny said.

Before Proctor could reply, Tiber came in, Josh in tow. When Josh saw that Donny was in his human form, he let out a gasp. "What in sam hill was he thinking about?"

"I asked him the same thing," Tiber said, his voice tight with anger.

"Tiber, you need to know something," Donny bit out through the pain. "Oscar is angry about being turned and is determined to wipe out all shifters."

"But why would he attack you? That doesn't make any sense," Josh said.

"He wants to take out Tiber first and thinks that if he takes out his Omega first it will make him weak enough to attack," Donny said.

Donny looked up through his haze of pain to see how his cousin would take the news. But Tiber remained as stoic as ever. He just gave a nod and said, "Okay, well, at least we know who we're battling now. That's more than we knew before. Let's just focus on getting you better first, and we can worry about the other later."

"Speaking of which. Why did you shift? Do you realize that you could have done permanent damage to your body?" Josh asked angrily. "Not only that, but I have patients that are going to be coming in, and my receptionist is right out front. How am I going to explain to her why I have a naked man in one of my exam rooms?"

Donny didn't care. He had let Proctor down, the one person in his life that mattered the most to him. He could curl up into a ball and die at that moment, and he'd be okay with it.

Josh came over and put a new IV into Donny. Donny was so caught up in his grief that he barely noticed the pinprick of pain. Soon, he felt the warm rush of pain meds washing over his body. Donny relaxed against the hard metal table and allowed his mind to go numb.

As he closed his eyes, he was painfully aware that Proctor never did say anything when Donny had said he was sorry. Which could only mean one thing: Proctor was mad and didn't want him anymore. The man in black had been right, Proctor really didn't want to be fucking a dog, and in the end, that's all Donny really was.

"We need to move him to the house. He'll be more comfortable in a real bed, and then I won't have to worry about somebody seeing him," Josh said.

"It's going to hurt like hell to move him," Tiber argued.

"I know, but I knocked him out pretty hard with the pain meds, so that should help some. We just need to move him to the second guest room in our house. He can stay there until he's healed. That way I can keep an eye on him. I may not be a human medical doctor, but I'm the closest thing we can get."

"You're right," Tiber agreed. "It's not like we can take him to a hospital anyway."

No, they couldn't, Donny agreed silently. Then there would be all kinds of questions they didn't want to have to answer when they ran Donny's blood work. So it looked like he was stuck staying at Josh and Connor's, which meant he would have to be around Proctor. Not the best of situations since Proctor probably hated him.

Somebody gently picked him up, and Donny was shocked when he recognized it as the scent of Proctor. He would have thought that Proctor would have been too sickened by Donny to even want to touch him, much less carry him all the way to the house.

Donny decided not to dwell on that. Instead, he allowed his head to fall onto Proctor's chest. It felt so nice, even though it hurt like hell to be jostled around. Just being in Proctor's embrace made all the pain worth it.

Proctor carried Donny out of the back door of the clinic and up to the house. The trip was agony on Donny's sore body, and he couldn't stop a whimper or two from slipping from his mouth.

"It's okay. I have you. We're almost there," Proctor soothed.

How could Proctor be so nice after everything Donny had done to him? It was a mystery that Donny couldn't even begin to wrap his mind around, especially since he was loopy from all the drugs in his system.

So instead, he just let it go. He'd think about it later when his mind was clearer. Soon they were at the house, and Proctor was carrying him up the stairs. As they walked by the first guest bedroom, Donny couldn't help but think about how happy they'd been in there. It had only been mere hours ago, too. How fast Donny's world had crashed down upon him.

Proctor went into the second bedroom and gently laid Donny down on the bed, then pulled the covers over him. It wasn't until he had Donny tucked in and as comfortable as possible that Donny finally found the courage to talk.

"Are you mad at me?"

Proctor shook his head. "No, I am disappointed that you lied to me so many times, though. I thought I knew you, and now I'm finding out that I never really did at all."

Those words hurt worse than any amount of physical pain that Donny was feeling at the moment. He took in a shuddering breath as it felt like his heart was being ripped into pieces.

"I didn't want to lie to you. I just had to protect the pack," Donny said.

"I can understand that, but in the process of you lying, both of us almost died. Had I known that there was a dangerous wolf out there, I would have been better prepared to protect us. Instead, I was caught with my pants down, and now we're both going to be paying the price for the rest of our lives."

Donny threw an arm over his eyes, hissing in pain from the motion. "I never wanted to drag you into this world, you have to know that. I did everything in my power to protect you from it."

"Yeah, but by doing that, you ended up exposing me to it in the worst way possible. Now I'm a part of it whether or not I like it. I'm a wolf shifter now. How is that going to affect the rest of my life? I don't even know if I can go back to my old home or job. My whole world if fucked up."

Donny squeezed his eyes shut. God, this was exactly what he had not wanted to happen. It was his worst nightmare come to life. All he had wanted was a little piece of happiness, and he had ended up ruining everything for Proctor. Plus Donny didn't even want to think of the poor sheriff. He couldn't get the image of the man's dead body out of his mind.

"I was stupid, okay? I'll admit it. I thought that I could protect you. But I should have realized that I couldn't. I'm nothing but a weak Omega. That's all I am, and that's all I'll ever be. The pack would be better off without me," Donny said.

"It's funny you should say that, considering that nearly the whole pack is here and is refusing to leave. They're worried about you. It's like you're royalty or something to them."

"Are you serious?" Donny asked.

Never in his wildest dreams would he have believed that the pack cared that much. By way of answer, Proctor scooped Donny up and carried him to the window. What Donny saw amazed him. In the backyard were almost all the wolves from the pack. They were in their animal forms, and they were all lying down in the grass, gazing up at his window.

"They've been here ever since they found out that you were wounded," Proctor said. "They've been a mess without you. Tiber said it has something to do with you being the Omega and how you hold the pack together."

"Yeah, but I never really believed it until now," Donny said in an awed voice.

He raised a hand at the wolves. The wolves all responded by howling. Donny cringed slightly. "They're not exactly being discreet, are they?"

Proctor laughed. "We're pretty far out. So I think we're pretty safe."

Donny gave one last wave before Proctor carried him back to bed and tucked him in. By then Donny was so tired and sore that all he wanted to do was sleep. But he was afraid that if he did, he would wake up and find that Proctor had left for good.

Unable to handle the stress anymore, Donny asked, "What are you going to do now? Are you going back home?"

Proctor gave a shrug. "I haven't decided yet. I still have a couple of weeks to sort things out. I just don't know."

"Would it help if you knew that I wanted you to stay?" Donny asked.

"Maybe. Right now, I'm so confused about us I don't know where we stand."

Donny closed his eyes. He knew he should have expected that kind of answer after all he had done to Proctor. But it still didn't make the pain any less.

Chapter Nine

The next day when Proctor went to go into Donny's room, he was shocked to find it empty. Walking farther inside, he went to the window and saw that the backyard was devoid of any wolves, too.

Heart beating wildly, Proctor ran down the steps and went into the kitchen, hoping that maybe he would find his lover there. But all he saw was Connor and Josh. Disappointment crashed over him as he realized Donny had left, and he hadn't even bothered to say goodbye.

Well, why should he after the way I treated him, Proctor thought to himself.

He knew he had been harsh on Donny. But to be fair, Proctor had been adjusting to a lot of things that had been thrust at him. It's not every day that somebody finds out that they've been dating a wolf shifter and then has to see said wolf shifter almost die in a battle. Don't forget the part where Proctor was turned into a shifter himself. Can't leave that important part out.

"He left, didn't he?" Proctor still asked, even though it was obvious.

Connor gave Proctor a sad look. "Yeah, they took him back to pack lands early this morning. Josh cleared him since Donny was healed enough. Shifters recover much quicker than humans, so Donny is doing much better already."

"Did he say anything before he left?" Proctor asked.

He knew he sounded desperate and more than a little pathetic, but at that point, he was beyond caring. He hadn't truly realized up until that point how much Donny had come to mean to him. Which was amazing since they'd only known each other a week. Had somebody told Proctor a month ago that he'd be this lost over some brat that he'd only known for a mere seven days, he would have laughed in their faces. Yet here he was, completely lost and empty feeling.

Connor shook his head. "No, in fact, he looked a lot like you do right now. I don't know what you said to him last night, but it must have been bad because it tore him up. He wasn't talking to anybody."

Guilt like none that he'd ever felt before hit Proctor like a punch to the gut. He sank down into the nearest chair and put his hands in his face. "I was all messed up. I had just found out about all this shit, and my reaction wasn't the best it could have been. I kind of left him hanging about how our relationship would be going."

"Shit, Proctor. That kid thinks you hang the moon. He nearly fought to the death for you. I don't know how much more you need to know how much he cares about you," Connor said. "I know how hard it is to face all this. I was in your place not too long ago, so I understand. But to take it out on Donny, especially after what he's done for you, that's rough."

"Wow, you aren't holding back at all. Talk about rubbing salt on an open wound," Proctor shot back.

Connor leaned against the counter and crossed his arms over his chest. "We've known each other for way too long for me to hold back on you. When you fuck up, I'm going to tell you. I know you were a bit shocked yesterday, and I can understand your reaction, but you gotta realize all that Donny was going through too. Now my big question to you is how are you going to fix it? Or do you even *want* to fix it? You could just leave and never come back. That is, if you don't care about Donny."

Proctor put a hand to his chest. Never see Donny again? Just thinking about it made his stomach churn. To never see that sweet smile again. To never hear that infectious laugh. To never feel those soft lips pressed against his again. No, that was something that Proctor couldn't live without.

"I can't live without him," Proctor admitted.

"I had a feeling you would say that. So my next question is what are you going to do to get him back? It's not going to be easy. The whole pack knows that you hurt him, so they are going to close ranks and try to keep you away from him," Connor said.

"And you saw how protective of him they are," Josh added. "I wouldn't be surprised if they didn't go for your throat the second they see you."

"They won't because they know Donny cares for him. But they will do their best to keep Donny away from him. They'll think that they're doing it for Donny's best interests," Connor said.

"What do you suggest we do?" Proctor asked.

"We'll have to talk to Tiber and convince him to give you a second chance. That's our only way," Connor said. He ran a hand through his hair. "That's not going to be easy."

"So does this mean that you'll be moving to this town permanently?" Josh asked.

Proctor blinked. He hadn't even thought of that. But he guessed he would have to. Could he give up the big city for a small town life? He didn't have to think for long. He would do anything if it meant he could have Donny.

"Sure, you think I could get a job at the local PD?" he asked Connor.

"Yeah, since we've had two recent deaths, we have openings," Connor grimaced. "So they're looking for experienced cops. They'd hire you in a second."

"I would just have to find a place to live. Right now, I don't think I would be welcome on the pack lands," Proctor said.

Although the idea of living in one of the cabins with Donny did hold a certain appeal to Proctor. Just the thought of the two of them so far separated from the rest of the world, cuddling together in front of fire, made Proctor want to smile.

But first he had to get to Donny, and then he had to get Donny to forgive him and take him back. Both of which were two great big hurdles. But if there was anything that Proctor was, it was determined. He cared deeply for Donny, and he hadn't gone through all this just to let the man slip through his fingers.

"Call Tiber and see if he'll meet us at the diner," Proctor suggested. "Maybe I can beg my case to him there."

Connor nodded his head, but he let out a sigh. "Okay, but I'll warn you now, he's very protective of his cousin. It's not going to be easy for you."

"I don't expect that it will be. But I'm willing to do anything to get Donny back. Even if that means I have to beg every pack member for mercy."

They met Tiber at the diner two hours later. The Alpha was already there, sitting at a booth. Connor and Proctor took the seat opposite of him, both of them bowing their heads, respectfully to him.

"Alpha," Proctor said.

Tiber gave what could have been called a half smile were it not for the angry glint in his eyes. "I see that Connor has taught you some of the pack rules and manners."

"Yes, I'm the first to admit that I don't know shit about this stuff, but I'm trying my best to learn," Proctor admitted.

"Yeah, well you still have a long way to go," Tiber said harshly.

Okay, so things weren't off to a smooth start, but then Proctor hadn't been expecting an open-armed welcome after what he'd done to Donny. He cleared his throat nervously and prayed that the rest of the meeting went better. It sure as hell couldn't go any worse.

"Why did you want to meet with me?" Tiber asked.

Proctor took a deep breath. "I want to see Donny."

Tiber lifted his upper lip in a snarl. "Why? So you can break his heart a little more? I think you've already done a good enough job of that already."

"No, it's so I can make things up to him. I know I fucked up big time. Donny means the world to me, and I want to be with him more than anything. So much so that I'm willing to give up my old life in the city and relocate here so I can be with him," Proctor said, hoping that Tiber would believe he was sincere.

Tiber stared at him for several moments. "And why should I believe you? You already betrayed him once. How do I know you won't do it again?"

Shit, how was Proctor supposed to answer that one? He scrambled his mind, trying to think of an answer that would be suitable.

Finally, Proctor said, "There has been a lot that has happened to me in the past couple of days. Things that I never thought were possible. I still haven't been able to wrap my mind around some of them. I don't even know if I ever will be able. But there is one thing I am positive of, and that's my feelings for Donny. I care for him more than anything in this world. I know you may not believe that since I've only known him a week, but he's somehow managed to wiggle his way under my skin, and there's no way that he's ever going to get out. Donny is it for me. I know that as certain as I know that I'm sitting here. I'm not going to stop fighting until I have him back, either. I don't care how long it takes to win back his trust. I won't ever give up. He's worth the wait."

Tiber gave a slight nod. "Wow, those are some impressive words. I have to admit that I didn't expect to hear that from you. But you have to realize how important my cousin is to me. I don't want to see him hurt more than he already has been."

"He won't be. Just give me five minutes with him. That's all I'm asking for."

Tiber let out a long sigh. "Fine, but don't make me regret this. Trust me, you don't want to see the angry side of me."

Proctor had no doubt of that. He'd seen Tiber in his wolf form, and he was huge. Proctor did not want to go against that ever.

"You won't. I promise," Proctor said, hoping that he was right.

"Okay, I'll take you to Donny right now."

As soon as they entered the gates of the pack lands, Proctor could feel all the hostility directed at him. It would seem that word had spread that he had been the one that had broken their Omega's heart, and the wolves weren't happy with him at all. In fact, if he didn't have Tiber by his side, Proctor wasn't so sure he wouldn't have been attacked on the spot.

"Back off," Tiber said to the pack. "He's here to try to make things better."

The pack members moved along, but Proctor could still feel the dirty looks being tossed his way. He wouldn't be winning any popularity contests anytime soon with this bunch, that was for sure. Oh well, it wasn't them that he had to make amends with, it was Donny. That's what he needed to focus on.

Tiber led him to a cabin and said, "This is Donny's. Good luck getting him to talk. He hasn't said a word since we left Connor's."

With that parting bit of advice, Tiber turned and left. Connor shoved his hands in his pockets and said, "I'll stay out here and wait to give you some privacy."

"What if he doesn't forgive me?" Proctor said, finally voicing his biggest fear.

"The guy nearly died for you. I would say that he has some pretty strong feelings for you. That has to say something for your chances."

Taking a deep breath, he tried to steady his nerves, but it wasn't until Connor gave him a pat on the back that Proctor worked up the nerve to knock on the door. When there was no answer, Proctor tried the knob and found that it was unlocked. Taking a chance, he opened the door and walked inside.

He entered the cabin. It was simply decorated. There was a dresser off to one side. A futon pushed against the wall, a large screen TV—which didn't say much for Donny being a survivalist—and a bed.

Donny was huddled on the bed, his back to Proctor. If he had scented Proctor, he gave no indication. In fact, he didn't move at all. He just continued to stare at the wall, the blankets pulled up so high only the tip of his head was visible.

Not one to be daunted, Proctor went over to the bed and sat down on the edge of it. He wanted so badly to reach out for Donny, but he knew that the moment wasn't right just yet.

"I've been looking for you," Proctor said.

When Donny didn't answer, Proctor decided to keep speaking, hoping that he could get through somehow. "Look, I know I fucked up. I should have handled the situation between us better. I never meant to break your heart. I was just scared and messed up by all the shit that had been thrown my way, and I didn't react well to it. But when I went to find you this morning and realized that you had left me, it made me realize something. None of that mattered. All that I care about is you. I know it may seem crazy since we've only known each other a week, but you've come to mean to the world to me, Donny, and I would do anything for you."

Donny turned around and looked at Proctor, but he still didn't speak. Donny's eyes were red and circled with dark rings. It killed Proctor to know that he'd made his lover look that way. Desperate to make things right, Proctor kept talking.

"When I saw you fighting that black wolf, and I thought that you were going to die, a piece of me was dying along with you. To know that you would make such a sacrifice for me was so humbling. No one has ever done anything like that for me before."

"I should be the one apologizing to you," Donny rasped.

"Why?" Proctor asked.

"Because of me, now you're stuck being a wolf forever. I took away your old life, and now you'll never get it back."

"Who says I want my old life back?" Proctor asked.

Donny shook his head. "What are you trying to say?"

"I don't want to go home. I want to stay here with you. That is if you'll have me after all I've done to you."

"You still want me even after all the lies I told you?" Donny sat up in the bed so they were facing each other.

"Yes, I do. More than anything. I think I'm falling in love with you, and damned if I'm going to go back to the city and give up any chance of being with you."

Donny put a hand to his mouth. "I thought that you hated me."

"Nothing could be further from the truth." Proctor took Donny's hand down so he could cup his cheek. "You are everything to me."

"You're everything to me, too."

Proctor felt a rush of relief pour over him with those words. "So does that mean I get to stay?"

"Yeah, it does," Donny said. "We need you in the pack, and I need by my side."

Proctor pulled Donny close to him and gave him a deep kiss. "I would be happy to do both. Now that you have me, you're never going to get rid of me."

Donny let out a laugh. "I like the sounds of that. There's just one thing I need to do."

Donny got out of bed and went to the door. He walked outside and began to walk amongst the pack members. As he reached out and slowly touched them, just a slight caress on the arm here or there, Proctor could feel the hostility leave the pack. Soon the members all had smiles on their faces, and the mood was much brighter.

Tiber came up to Proctor. "So I see you made things right with Donny."

"Yeah, you got room for one more Beta in your pack?"

"Always. You're more than welcome here. Just so long as you treat him right. He's really important to us."

As Proctor watched Donny do his Omega thing, he had to agree. Donny truly was the one who kept the pack grounded. "He's important to me, too. More than you'll ever know."

Chapter Ten

It was late at night. Proctor lay with Donny in bed. Proctor was tired. He had just completed his first shift and run with the rest of the pack on a hunt. He'd even been successful and caught a few rabbits. Donny, as usual, had caught nothing, but he hadn't minded. Proctor was beginning to think that Donny wasn't taking down any prey on purpose. He was just too kindhearted to kill anything. But that was a secret that Proctor would never share with anybody else. He would let Donny keep that little tidbit to himself.

They'd just finished making love, and Donny lay on his stomach, the moon shone through a crack in the curtains, the light hitting the small of Donny's back. He had a nice sheen of sweat on his body, and his hair was slightly messed up. Never before had he looked sexier.

"So what time do we leave in the morning?" Donny asked.

Donny was going with Proctor to help him pack up his old apartment and set up things in the city, so he could make the move back to the pack. At first, Proctor had insisted that he could do it all on his own, but Donny had be adamant about going along. Now that they were back together, they didn't like to spend any length of time apart. The only time that they were away from each other was when Proctor went to work at his new job with the sheriff's department.

Proctor hadn't wanted to go back at all, but it had been a month since he'd left, and it was foolish of him to continue to pay rent on an empty apartment. Plus, he had to turn in his gun and badge at his old job. He'd put it off as long as he could. Like it or not, he had to return to the city, if only for a week to set matters in order.

"I was thinking about eight, so we have plenty of time to catch the flight," Proctor said as he reached over to smooth some of Donny's hair back. "Are you sure the pack is going to be okay with you being away for a whole week?"

"Yeah, they have Tiber to keep them in line, and I'll be back soon enough." Donny responded. "I think they can go Omega-less for seven days without going into complete despair."

"You do realize how important you are to the pack?"

Donny nodded. "I do now. I didn't before, I thought that I was useless and the bottom of the pack because I listened to my dad for all those years. But now I realize that the pack needs me just as much as they need the Alpha and the Betas. It's good to know that I'm an important part of the pack. It makes me feel useful for the first time in my life. I may never be able to bring down game or fight in any battles, but I have another role that I play, which is just as important, and I'm okay with that."

Proctor gave Donny a long, lingering kiss. "To tell you the truth, I'm proud to be the Omega's mate. You're the glue that holds this pack together. I think that makes you the most important member of this pack."

Donny let out a soft chuckle. "You may be a little biased."

"It's true, I do love you. So I may be blinded by that."

"I love you, too," Donny said. "Which is why I think you're the best Beta ever."

"You're just saying that because I made the most kills tonight," Proctor said.

"Yeah, and you're first time out. That's pretty amazing. Just think of what you'll do once you have a little more practice. You're going to put all the other Betas to shame. Everybody is going to be jealous that you're my mate."

"I don't know. I see the way Aslan and Beau look at you. I think that if I hadn't come along, one of them would have snatched you up," Proctor said.

Donny wrinkled up his nose. "Really? They never even talked to me."

"I think they were too shy to approach you. But I can tell by the way they stare at you that they have the hots for you. I almost ripped their arms off today. But I decided why bother since I was the one that you were going home with at the end of the night. Let them look all they want. They were never going to get to have you."

"And they never will. I'm addicted to Proctor, and that's never going to change," Donny declared.

Proctor gave Donny another kiss. "And I'm addicted to Donny, and that's never going to change."

Proctor meant it, too. He had his bratty Omega, and he wouldn't trade him for anything in the world.

About the Author

STEPHANI HECHT is a happily married mother of two. Born and raised in Michigan, she loves all things about the state, from the frigid winters to the Detroit Red Wings hockey team. Go Wings! You can usually find her snuggled up to her laptop, creating her next book.

Contact her at:

Email Address:
stephani@stephanihecht.com

Twitter:
http://twitter.com/StephaniHecht

FaceBook:
ttp://www.facebook.com/profile.php?ref=profile&id=110935385

tumblr:
http://rainbowsandmish-mash.tumblr.com

The Alpha's Only
Building the Pack Three

By

Amber Kell

*For Stephanie Hecht and RJ Scott
who agreed to write this trilogy with me*

Chapter One

Tiberius examined the footsteps in the soft earth. Following the trail for a few yards revealed a progression from bare feet to paw prints—large paw prints.

"These could be Oscar's, they are certainly large enough," Connor, the new sheriff of Black Creek, said.

"Could be." The faint, familiar smell of the black wolf still wafted in the air, but not strongly enough to indicate the shifter had lingered in the area. A slight breeze brought the strong smell of blood from the same direction.

"Why would he return? He has to know we're hunting him. He might be a bigger wolf, but he can still be taken down by a pack. Not to mention you shot him last time."

The sheriff crouched over the marks in the ground. "He's after something. If we figure out what, maybe we can determine where he might have gone and where he'll be later."

Tiber inhaled deeply, trying to pick up the wolf's scent. He expected to smell Oscar's distinct stench of fury and filth. Instead a deeper, richer fragrance greeted him. Delicious.

"Someone besides Oscar went this way."

As if under a compulsion, Tiber headed after the scent. He didn't bother following the tracks. He didn't need them. Instead, he followed the amazing scent. It called to him stronger than a siren's call and twice as alluring.

"Wait up, Tiber!"

Connor's footsteps followed him, but he didn't care. His entire focus, his entire world narrowed to the aroma beckoning him forward.

Focused on the smell instead of the ground, he tripped on a branch. Tiber stumbled forward a few steps only to come to a stop at the sight of an enormous red wolf lying in the shade. Tiber frowned at the blood on the beast's muzzle and the wide bloody scratch bisecting the strange wolf's side.

"Wow, he's huge," Connor whispered behind him.

"Yeah." Tiber breathed in deeply. The amazing smell emitted from the wolf. "Why does he smell so good?"

"Good? I don't smell anything. I mean he smells like a wolf, nothing special."

Connor stepped forward. Tiber growled. "Don't get close."

"What's wrong with you? Let me go first. He might attack."

Tiber frowned at the Beta. "I think your shiny new sheriff badge is going to your head."

"You're too valuable to lose because you're too stubborn to take precautions. If this were an Alpha fight I'd step aside, but this is police work."

Tiber opened his mouth to argue, but hated that Connor might be right. Before he could object, the sheriff stepped forward, cutting in front of Tiber to examine the wolf first.

The animal's eyes snapped open. It bared his teeth at Connor, an unfriendly curl of the lip. Tiber moved Connor out of the way, then dropped to his knees beside the growling beast.

"Shh, you're scaring him," Tiber scolded.

"Scaring *him*. He's going to bite your face off and then I'll have to tell the pack I let you get killed. That's not a discussion I want to have with them."

Tiber ignored the ranting sheriff and held out his hand, palm up toward the injured animal. The wolf sniffed at Tiber. Its growl turned to a low whine, all aggression gone.

"Do you think you can change back now? I need to talk to you as human." He couldn't exactly interview the wolf over why he had entered Tiber's territory without following the proper channels. The human lurking inside the beast peered out at him.

The wolf struggled to get closer to Tiber as if it couldn't handle the separation between them. Tiber rewarded it with a scratch behind the ears. "Hey, it's all right. I just need you to shift so I can talk to you. You want to talk to me, don't you?"

Tiber could've forced the shifter to change, but with the cut on the wolf's side he couldn't determine if it would be dangerous for him to turn human or not.

"I think we should take him to Josh. Your mate can let us know if it's safe for him to change."

"How do you think we can get him there?"

"I'll carry him."

Connor snorted. "He's massive. You sure you don't want me to help?"

The wolf snapped at Connor, its sharp white teeth aggressively displayed.

"I'm pretty sure he won't let you help. Come on, boy." Tiber hefted the injured wolf up in his arms and followed Connor slowly. He let out a sigh of relief when he spotted Connor's extended cab truck at the end of the trail. Although the wolf wasn't too heavy for him, he worried about causing more damage with his awkward carrying.

Tiber hardened his heart against the soft whimpers. He had to get the wolf to Josh to check out his wounds.

"Wait a second I'll get the blanket." Connor dragged a blanket out of the back of the truck and laid it across the upholstery.

Tiber set the wolf down, careful of the injury. "Try to stay as still as possible."

After warning the wolf, he slammed the back door shut, before climbing into the passenger seat. He tapped his fingers along his thigh, silently urging Connor to speed up his driving.

"Hey, everything will be fine. The damage didn't look that severe. We can have Josh patch him up, then we'll question what he's doing here. Don't you guys have territory laws or something?"

"Yeah, he should've let me know he was coming through my pack lands. A common courtesy to whatever wolf owns the territory you are traveling through. He might have been on his way to see me when he ran into trouble, too. No point in assigning blame before we talk to him."

Tiber hoped the wolf had come to join them. He was oddly reluctant to discipline the red wolf. He didn't know if the shifter's scent had muddled his thoughts, but he wanted only good things for the unknown shifter.

"You're right, no point in speculating when he can tell us soon enough."

Still, Tiber couldn't stop the thoughts going through his head as he tried to decide what might have happened. "I wonder if he ran into Oscar. Any of my wolves would've come and informed me of a strange wolf in my territory, especially if they had a fight."

"Unless he attacked first."

"No." Everything in Tiber rejected that thought. "And if he did he obviously didn't kill his opponent because there wasn't another body."

"What are we going to do if we find Oscar?"

"What do you mean?"

Connor kept his attention on the road as he spoke. "I mean how do you handle jailing a shifter. Won't he kill all the guards?"

"Connor, you don't arrest rogue shifters. You put them down like rabid dogs. You find Oscar, you kill him." Tiber didn't want the sheriff to think there might be a chance to save the murderous shifter. "We can't put him into rehab or a nice medical facility to get help. He's already killed several of our men. He needs to be destroyed."

Connor turned down the road leading to the vet's clinic. "I know he's dangerous, just I feel as if I'm violating the law I swore to uphold. How can I hold someone responsible for their crimes while I commit murder?"

"Connor, pack law and the rest of the world don't operate from the same rulebook. In fact, made wolves are more likely to go feral and have to be killed. You and your partner were the exceptions. Made wolves are tricky. Growing up I saw a lot of people try to bring non-wolves into our pack and change them. Only a third of the people make it safely."

"What happened to the rest of them?" Connor asked.

Tiber could tell by the sheriff's sudden stillness that he'd been unaware of his luck. He would've assumed Donny would've told Proctor who in turn would've told his old partner, but upon reflection, Tiber realized the two men didn't spend a lot of time talking.

There wasn't any way to sugar coat the issue. "They either die during transition or turn insane and have to be hunted down and shot."

"I had no idea. I thought Proctor and I were the usual." Connor's hands shook as he turned into the parking lot. "I had thought about talking to you about changing Josh, too, but not now. Not if Josh could be killed."

"A person has to be strong enough to accept their inner animal. Unfortunately there's no way to tell that until you try and convert them. I've seen strong willed people turn mad and people I would've considered weaker thrive. It all depends on what they're truly like inside."

That was the trick with shifting. If a person could accept their inner self—the good, the bad and the turning furry under a full moon—they could become one with the pack. Too many people instead couldn't handle the stress of changing into another entity. Either physically or emotionally, they either turned insane and ended their own life, or were inept and lost it doing something stupid like taking on a larger wolf. Pack life wasn't always a friendly and supportive environment like in Tiber's pack.

The sickly ripe smell of blood pouring across the dewy morning grass had greeted him more than once in his younger days, especially after the Alpha had been drinking. Tiber shook off his childhood nightmares. They'd escaped that situation as soon as the Alpha had turned his homophobic eyes toward Donny. Tiber had refused to let his cousin become another victim.

"I guess I'm lucky then." Connor's voice broke into Tiber's thoughts, pulling him out of his horrific memories.

"I guess you are." Tiber had made his own luck in life. He'd fought claw and fang to get his pack established and to keep others from wandering in and thinking they could take over. Pack members respected him, but many considered him a cold bastard. He'd take cold and forbidding to dead and bleeding any day. Donny kept the pack together. The Omega was their heart. Tiber kept everyone alive.

For the next few minutes the only sound in the cab was the crunch of small rocks beneath the truck's tires and the soft whimpers of the wolf in the back.

Connor cleared his throat. "I can't thank you enough for changing me, and Proctor. I know you might not have wanted two extra wolves in your pack, but we appreciate not being left to die."

Tiber sighed. "I didn't mean to make you feel unwelcome. I'm happy to invite both you and your friend into my pack. We're trying to add to our numbers anyway. In order to survive a pack has to grow large enough to protect the weaker members. Right now we need more strong members to enlarge the pack and keep our few children safe. Often the first thing an Alpha does when taking over is kill all the kids in order to replace them with their own."

"How does that work?" Connor asked.

"How does what work?"

"Building a pack. I mean you said a new Alpha replaced the kids with his own, but since you're gay it's not like you're going to suddenly get a mate or two and push out tons of kids."

"Right now we're spreading the word to other wolf packs that we're an all-accepting pack. A lot of Alphas are older and aren't as welcoming of same sex pairings. My birth pack certainly wasn't." Tiber didn't understand growing up why some members were banished. Not until he grew to adulthood did he learn of his Alpha's homophobia. Stilson didn't dare attack Tiber, but he'd beat up Donny a number of times before Tiber grabbed his cousin and got the hell out of town. Memories drifted like a toxic cloud through his head. He only shook it off when Connor spoke again.

"Is that why you left your old pack and came to start your own?"

Tiber let out a long breath, pushing away the bad thoughts. He'd become an expert at putting things behind him. "Yes. Donny's father tried to kill him when he found out Donny was gay. He wasn't too fond of him before that. Donny didn't grow big enough or strong enough to satisfy his father and, when he began showing signs of being an Omega, his father finally snapped. I had to get Donny out of there to save his life."

"You did the right thing. Donny is a great guy and Proctor adores him."

"Yeah." Tiber swallowed the lump in his throat. He tried not to let the bitterness grow in his chest because eventually it would eat him up alive. Still the question haunted him. Why couldn't he find a mate?

"Do you think more people will come join us?"

Tiber nodded. "Eventually. I need to get rid of Oscar before I encourage more pack mates. I can't risk families moving here, not when I can't insure their safety."

"We'll get him." Connor's confidence soothed some of Tiber's anxiety. It helped to have strong Betas on his side.

"Don't underestimate him. He won't fight fair." The newly appointed sheriff still thought like a human. Eventually he'd learn that wolves settled things by fang and claw, not generally with bullets. Although in Oscar's case Tiber would be willing to make an exception.

Tiber's phone rang. He pulled it out of his pocket and smiled when he read the display. He pressed the connect button. "Hey, Donny, back in town?"

The Omega had gone to help his mate move his stuff to Black Creek. Without their Omega the pack had lost some of its warmth. It would be good to have Donny back among the pack.

"Yep, we're back at home. For a bachelor, Proctor has a lot of crap."

Tiber heard Proctor mutter something in the background.

Donny cleared his throat. "I mean my beloved brought all his many precious belongings with him and we're trying to find a place for it all."

Tiber grinned. He'd missed Donny and his quirky sense of humor.

"We're heading over to Josh's, we found an injured red wolf shifter in the woods and we're having him checked out."

"Be careful. He could be a trap." Donny's tone lost all its good cheer when he warned Tiber.

"I will." Tiber had to admit the thought hadn't occurred to him. The black wolf shifter did have a psychopath's cunning and would be more than willing to sacrifice someone to help carry out his master plan, whatever that may be. However, glancing over his shoulder at the injured animal in the back, Tiber couldn't muster up any suspicion. The red wolf called to him at a deeper level than just from one shifter to another. Tiber would reserve judgment until he met the shifter in his male form.

After a few more warnings and pointed jokes at Proctor's expense. Tiber disconnected and slid his phone back into his shirt pocket.

"Donny's back?" Connor asked.

"Yep. You'll have your deputy back to work any day now."

"Good. With Oscar on the loose we need as many men on the ground as possible." Connor scowled. "We have to catch that bastard soon. It's only been luck that Josh hasn't been bitten yet."

Tiber frowned as he thought that over. "That is strange. He certainly had the chance a few times."

"Well from what you told me we need to make sure he doesn't get it again."

"It might not be a bad thing to hire more deputies. The pack can afford to finance them. We've done well with our investments."

"That's a good idea." Connor frowned. "I'd be more comfortable if they could be shifters. At least then they'd know what they were getting into. I'd hate to bring in some unsuspecting humans like me and Proctor were."

"Agreed. I'll put out feelers and try to find people to apply. I'll leave the final decision to you, but I'll make sure they'd be good members of the pack." Tiber knew a few law enforcement people from his previous pack who might be ready for a change. He had to be careful. He didn't want to alert his old Alpha to their location. He wasn't hiding, not exactly, but dealing with the bastard wasn't high on his list. Deal with one psycho at a time was his new motto.

Connor pulled up in front of the vet clinic. Josh, his mate, rushed out of the building and had the back cab open before Tiber could warn him. A loud, vicious snarl had the vet stepping back.

"How did you get him in the truck without losing an arm?" Josh asked

"He likes Tiber," Connor said.

"I'll bring him." Tiber climbed out of the truck and reached for the wolf. The snarling, growling beast turned to a whimpering pup when he spotted Tiber.

"Gotta love the Alpha power," Connor said.

Tiber didn't bother to correct him. He wasn't using his Alpha abilities. He simply knew the shifter wouldn't hurt him."

"Come on, boy, let's get you inside. Josh is going to check you over and fix your wound." If the vet sewed up the gash, the shifter could change into his human form without worrying about causing further damage. Without stitching the injury, converting to a bipedal shape could rip the wound wide open.

The wolf licked Tiber's cheek when he lifted him up.

"I might need you to stay close while I work on him," Josh said. "If he'll stay still enough for you, I can shoot him with the needle for anesthesia."

Tiber nodded. His hands shook a bit when he followed Josh into the building. He nodded to the receptionist as he passed.

"Don't worry, boy," he murmured to the wolf. What they would do with the shifter after that still remained to be seen.

Chapter Two

Keir sniffed at the beautiful man beside him.
Alpha.

The power pouring off the Alpha slid through Keir. He whimpered. Wiggling, he tried to get closer. He needed to touch. He needed Tiber's fingers on him.

"Shh, Josh won't hurt you," Tiber's soothing voice rolled across his fur. He itched to roll over and expose his belly, but his side hurt. He snorted his frustration.

The Alpha stroked Keir's head. It would be all right now that he'd been found. Once he recovered, he'd beg his case to stay. He had to. He belonged to Tiber.

Fighting the black wolf had injured him, but he'd held his own. The other wolf wouldn't be able to walk well. Keir had crushed his back leg with a snap of his teeth. Keir knew he'd lost a lot of blood and the weakness pulled at him to take a nap. Closing his eyes, he scooted closer to Tiber. He breathed in deeply, inhaling the calming scent of the Alpha.

"That's it. Calm. I've got you."

"Hold him. I'm going to give him a shot." The vet's voice broke into Keir's focus on the Alpha. He snarled at the interloper.

"Hey, easy. Josh is here to help. He's going to sew you up."

Keir growled lightly to show his displeasure.

"Easy, Tiber, don't get too close. He could bite you," the foolish vet said.

"He's not going to bite me, are you?"

The Alpha's sexy confidence made Keir wish he were in his human form.

A sharp pinch distracted him. The vet's shot. Warmth flowed through his body. He whimpered at the weird sensation. Closing his eyes, he let the vet work while he nuzzled the Alpha's hand. It was the only bit he could reach.

"He sure likes you," Josh said.

Tiber scratched Keir behind the ears. He closed his eyes in bliss.

"I wonder why he came here." Tiber's deep voice rumbled through Keir's drugged mind.

Keir hated not being able to speak. His canine form couldn't form words and he didn't have a connection with Tiber. Some Alphas could communicate telepathically, but only to their mates.

Alphas generally had two to three mates to increase the pack through their bloodline. Tiber wouldn't have that. Keir wouldn't allow it. He would be this Alpha's only even if he had to scare off all other contenders. He was one of the biggest wolves around; he knew could take any challengers.

With that happy thought spinning around in his mind, he let the scent of the Alpha and the drugs take him away.

It took two days before Keir's body healed enough for him to shift. Tiber had visited several times while Keir recovered. Each time he'd treasured the contact. He couldn't wait to shift and introduce himself in his human form. He hadn't been this excited since Christmas as a young pup.

Josh examined Keir's stitches carefully. "Okay, I'm going to take these out, then you can shift when you're ready."

A bit of tugging later Josh announced him healed. "All ready to shift?"

He set his head on his paws and waited.

"Oh I see how it is. You want Tiber to be here, don't you? I can't say I blame you, he is a handsome man."

Keir growled.

"Oh don't be like that. I have my own mate."

The door to the exam room opened. "Is he ready?"

Oh, the voice. Sexy. Rough. Delicious.

"He's healed enough. I think he was waiting for you," the vet tattled.

"Hmm. Is that right?"

Keir examined the Alpha's expression as he leaned down to examine him. Tiber had kind eyes. Keir had expected him to be cold and partly evil—his Alpha certainly had been. Tiber might have a tough exterior, but he had a soft heart. No man who saved an unknown injured wolf could be that bad.

"Well, if Josh says you're ready how about becoming human? I'd love to see what you look like in your other form."

Unable to resist Tiber's entreaty, Keir transformed.

His howl changed to a yelp when the newly healed wound pulled at his skin.

"Hey, you all right?" Tiber stroked Keir's shoulders with his large hands, warming his chilled flesh and taking away the sting with his touch.

"Oh yeah." If Tiber would continue to touch him he'd be even better. His cock rose in response to the scent and touch of the Alpha.

"I'll go find him some clothes," Josh said. The vet rushed out of there like his ass was on fire.

Tiber laughed. "Josh is mated to a newly turned shifter. He's still not completely comfortable with our nudity."

Keir resisted the urge to tell the Alpha he could join him if he wanted. Tiber stepped close enough for Keir to press his nose against the Alpha's neck. He clenched his hands to hold back the urge. He had to take it slowly. Although he didn't smell other wolf scents muddying up the Alpha it didn't mean Tiber didn't have someone who claimed is heart.

"Humans are funny that way," Keir said noncommittally. His erection already indicated his interest in the Alpha, words were unnecessary.

"I'm Tiber, Alpha of the Black Creek pack. What are you doing in my territory?"

Tiber didn't use an aggressive tone, but Keir's back still snapped straight and he tried to look worthy of the gorgeous man before him.

He tilted his head to one side, baring his neck to the Alpha and secretly hoping Tiber would take the opportunity to mark him. Sure it was a long shot, but Keir wasn't going to be picky.

"My name is Keir. I was heading to see you when I was attacked by a black wolf."

"That was probably Oscar. It's a miracle you weren't killed." Tiber ran a soothing hand along Keir's bare shoulder. "Why did you want to see me?"

"I heard your pack was friendly to gays. My old Alpha had a different opinion."

If Keir hadn't been watching he would've missed the quick flicker of Tiber's eyes as his gaze moved up and down Keir's body. "Your information is correct. We welcome all kinds. What happened in the forest?"

"Like I said, I ran into a big black wolf. He attacked me. He didn't give me any warning or shift and talk to me. One minute I was running through the woods, hunting a rabbit, the next I was being mauled."

"Did you hurt him?"

Keir nodded, happy to prove his worth. "I crushed his back leg. I don't know that I caused any more damage than that."

"Good work. Oscar's a rogue who's been killing members of my pack. He's insane and determined to kill us all. He seems to hate all of our kind. The person who changed him hadn't been aware of his psychotic tendencies before he converted him."

The idea of someone hunting the Alpha churned Keir's stomach. He couldn't let anything happen to this beautiful man—his man.

"I'll protect you," Keir promised. No one would harm the Alpha on Keir's watch.

Tiber raised an eyebrow at him. "I haven't accepted you into the pack yet."

"But you will." Keir had no doubt. Rejection wasn't an option. If Tiber turned him down, he'd stick around until the Alpha changed his mind.

"Will I?" Luckily Tiber appeared more amused than upset. His old Alpha would've backhanded Keir into the next day.

"Yes."

"Why?"

"Because I belong to you."

There, he'd said it. Maybe too early, from the dumbfounded expression on Tiber's face, but it needed to be said.

Tiber opened his mouth, then closed it again without speaking.

"Here you are." Josh breezed into the room, carrying some clothing. "I think you're about the same size as Connor, maybe a little bigger, but these clothes should work until we can get you something else."

"Thanks." Keir accepted the sweats and t-shirt. He hopped off the surgical table where Josh had been examining him. He purposely let his body brush against Tiber. The quick suck in of breath made him smile. Yes! Soon he'd have the handsome Alpha for his own.

Josh cleared his throat. "I'm going to go check on some sick animals. I think Tiber can handle things in here."

Keir didn't look away from Tiber's intense gaze.

The Alpha's lush mouth tilted up on one side. "Do you think I can handle things in here, Keir?"

"Oh, I think you can handle anything you want, Tiber." He couldn't help flirting a little. "Is there a significant other I need to worry about?"

"Not at this time."

"Good." He'd hate to have to kill off the competition. Red wolves didn't allow others to claim their mates. Keir had no doubt Tiber belonged to him, but he might need to give Tiber a little while to get used to the idea.

"Would you like to come back to the compound and talk to the rest of the pack? See if you'll fit in?"

"Yes. I'd like that." He resisted the urge to rub his naked body all over Tiber. When the Alpha stepped back, a sigh poured out of Keir, a mixture of disappointment and relief.

"What do you do for a living?" Tiber asked from the crushingly proper distance of across the room.

Keir pulled the sweats on. He'd prefer if Tiber got naked also, but he didn't see that happening right away. Tiber didn't appear the type to take advantage of a newly healed wolf. Too bad.

"I used to work at a tattoo shop. I did tats on all the pack members until they learned I was gay."

Sympathy filled Tiber's eyes. "Bastards. How did you get them to stay? I know some of my wolves have tried to get tattoos, but the ink fades after a few shifts."

"I've got a supplier who mixes a special ink. If you add a little silver powder in the ink it stays. It burns when you first apply it, but after a day or two the hurt fades and you're left with a kick ass tattoo. See?"

Keir turned so Tiber could see the wolf on his back.

"That's me!" Tiber exclaimed.

"Is it? I had a dream three months ago and I drew this out and had a fellow artist I trust mark me."

Tiber ran his fingers across Keir's back, tracing the tattoo and doing nothing to encourage Keir's cock to deflate.

"It's an exact image of me and a stream that is one of my favorites to run by. It has some great fishing in the summer."

"I love to fish. Maybe you can take me some time."

Tiber breathed against Keir's neck. "I'd like that."

For the first time they were both human and standing together. Keir probably had three inches and twenty pounds of muscle on the Alpha, but he'd be more than happy to give in to Tiber's power. This close, the Alpha's energy tingled along his spine.

"Do you have any tattoo shops in town?"

"No. If you want to set one up I'm sure you'd get plenty of clientele. There are a few empty storefronts in pack owned buildings, so there is plenty of space if you decide to stay."

"Thanks." Keir had practiced long and hard under the tutelage of some amazing artists to reach his level of skill. When the pack started to turn on him, he'd lost his job and his love of tattooing.

Tiber turned Keir around to face him. "I hope you decide you want to stay."

Sexual energy crackled between them even stronger than Tiber's Alpha magic. Keir wet his lips. Snatching up the top, he slid it over his body before he gave into temptation to strip the Alpha down and ride him like a desperate cowboy.

"I'm strong. I can help protect you. I'll be a good Beta."

He needed Tiber to know he wouldn't be a drain on pack resources or his mate.

Tiber stroked Keir's head, not unlike he had when Keir was in wolf form. "Anyone who can get away from Oscar with only a scratch is tough enough to be part of any pack. Let's take you back home with me. I'll give you a room to stay in while you get on your feet."

"In your house?" Keir didn't care what else happened, but had to stay near Tiber.

Tiber searched his expression for a long moment. "Yes, I have a spare room."

Keir grinned. It wasn't Tiber's bed, but it was a good start. It shouldn't be too much effort to graduate from single room to king bed. "Thanks, I appreciate the offer."

He hoped he appeared suitably appreciative instead of desperately horny.

"Come on." Tiber held out his hand. Keir accepted it eagerly, pleased when the Alpha continued to hold it as he walked him out of the vet's office.

He figured Tiber forgot he was holding his hand as he led him out to a truck. The Alpha opened the door for him. It took all Keir's resolve to release Tiber's fingers. He clenched his teeth as he slipped their hands apart, immediately aching from the lack of contact. Was this how it would be from now on? Bereft without his mate?

"Hey, it'll be all right. I promise." Tiber's reassuring smile didn't do what he probably thought it would.

Keir barely resisted the urge to beg the Alpha to fuck him against the truck. In his thirty years of life he'd never craved anyone like he did Tiber.

His mate!

A thrill tingled through him. He'd never dared hope that his plan to leave his pack and go to a new one would result in him finding his mate.

Tiber climbed into the driver's side, then started up the truck.

Keir couldn't keep his eyes off him. "What do you know about red wolves?"

He didn't know if Tiber was aware of the huge shifter differences between the two species. Although Keir was only half red wolf and grew up in a gray wolf pack, he still clung to his mother's beliefs. Red wolves believed their mates were chosen by a higher power and they would know them upon first sight.

Although Keir had never truly believed the fairy tale his mother wove during his childhood of his parents' instant love, meeting Tiber had changed all that. He held his breath when Tiber didn't answer right away.

"Well, I know generally red wolves are smaller than gray wolves. They live in Florida and western areas, have a dominant pair and are very territorial."

"All that is true, but do you know anything about red wolf shifters?"

"Not really. I mean I haven't met any personally, until now." Tiber kept his eyes on the road, but Keir knew he had all his attention.

"There aren't a lot of us around anymore. I'm not surprised you haven't met any. I'm only half red wolf on my mother's side. My father was a gray wolf. When they first met, my mother knew he was the one. Red wolves know. The shifters do, anyway. We see our mate and immediately bond." Keir smiled as he watched the scenery pass. Giddiness bubbled through him like foaming champagne, tingly and bright.

Tiber cleared his throat. "Are you telling me this because you've met your mate?"

Keir nodded. "Yes."

Tiber spun the truck around the corner in a tight turn.

Keir clutched the panic bar.

"I have to warn you that Josh and Conner are already mated."

"That's good for them since neither of them are the one." Keir moistened his lips with his tongue. "You're my mate."

Tiber swerved to the side of the road, pulling the truck to a halt. "What are you talking about?"

"You are my mate. Or I'm your mate. However you want to look at it." Keir played with the folds of his borrowed sweats, unable to meet Tiber's eyes. Shifters who weren't red wolves didn't understand the compulsion, the truth of the mate bond. "I don't know how to convince you, but it's true."

"Look at me, Keir."

The Alpha's order poured over him, compelling him to obey. Keir shivered beneath the power of Tiber's voice. His old Alpha's energy had burned like a hot knife, glowing at its highest tempering. Tiber's Alpha magic seeped into his body, warming his muscles, and sliding across his skin like a full body hug.

Gasping, he met his Alpha's eyes.

"We don't have to make any major decisions right now. Why don't we wait and see how things work between us? I'm not committed to anyone. You aren't committed to anyone. We have time."

Keir's inner wolf growled at the Alpha's presumption that he had a choice. "Sure, Alpha. There's no hurry."

Lie.

He could barely force the words through his lips. The syllables and vowels tasted like ash on his tongue. Although he'd give the appearance of cooperation, he'd be damned if he let anyone get a chance at his man.

Tiber held his gaze for a long time before a slow smile of pure joy crossed his lips and a low, chuckle warmed his ears. "I see you're going to be persistent."

"I might only be half red wolf, but I have all the tendencies. You should do a bit of research, Alpha, because if you ever let me go I won't survive. I can't be a catch and release. It's all or nothing."

Tiber lost his smile. His eyes narrowed as he examined Keir from head to toe. "I'm not playing with you, Keir, but we just met."

"We might have just met to you, but for me our souls were fated to join as soon as we were born. It's taken me thirty years to find you and I have no intention of losing you now."

A faint heart never won a kick ass Alpha and Keir wouldn't give up his man without giving it every possible effort. On the plus side, the hardest part was over. Tiber knew of his interest and he hadn't gone screaming off into the forest—yet.

Tiber sighed. "I can see you're going to be a handful."

"As long as you're the one handling me, it will be just fine."

Laughter filled the cab as Tiber put the truck back into drive. "At least life won't be boring."

Chapter Three

Tiber sighed when the main pack house came into view. He never tired of coming home, even if sometimes he longed for someone to be waiting for him. Now with Keir beside him, he had someone. Tiber shook his head. One hour of talking to a man didn't make a mate even if Keir was ready to disagree with that thought. If Keir had his way, they would be happily mated and ready for their life together. Keir was right, Tiber did need to do some research on red wolves.

Tiber knew he should take any relationship with the Beta slowly; he just found it difficult to think when Keir's scent filled the cab and his good cheer warmed Tiber's chest. Keir intoxicated him. Even with the faint trace of stitches marring his torso, Keir hadn't lost his good humor or the heated fire burning in his eyes each time his gaze met Tiber's. A look the Beta didn't turn on anyone else. Tiber had been watching.

Tiber turned off the engine. "We're here. This is the main pack house. I've got a spare room and we can pick up extra clothes to get you settled. Did you bring anything with you?"

"No. I escaped from my pack. Grabbing anything to take with me would've made them suspicious."

"Okay." Tiber bit back the protective growl simmering in his chest. His inner wolf prodded him to hunt down Keir's old pack and make his Alpha pay. Luckily his human half was in charge and had a calmer temperament.

He purposely didn't let his gaze linger across the tight fit of the t-shirt stretching across Keir's chest or check the fit of the sweats to see if a ride in the truck filled with their mingled scents had made Keir as hard it did Tiber. Yes, better to not check, because if he knew Keir's excitement matched his own they'd be making out like schoolboys in front of the pack house.

"Are we going in?" Keir's deep voice strummed through Tiber, sliding up his spine and forcing a shiver across Tiber's skin.

"I bet I could come from your voice alone."

Crap, had he said that out loud?

Keir's chuckle implied he had.

"Oh, babe, I'll take that bet. Another time, though. I'd rather make you come by sucking you off, and preferably in a nice soft bed."

Tiber made a decidedly non-Alpha whimper. He cleared his throat before reaching for the truck handle.

"Hey."

Tiber froze. Keir's hand lay across his arm to halt his actions. Tiber was unwilling to move and dislodge Keir's touch even if Oscar himself had slammed against the door.

"What?" Tiber's voice came out more a whisper than the strong question he'd hoped it would be.

"Just so you know, I'm yours whenever you want. We're wolves, we don't need the song and dance like humans. But you're the Alpha . . ." Keir let his words trail off.

Tiber's resolve snapped like a dry twig in the woods and almost as loudly. Reaching across the cab, he grabbed Keir's shirt and yanked the Beta across the bench seat.

"That's right. I am the Alpha." Tiber slammed his lips against Keir's, an aggressive claiming. Keir froze for a moment before melting beneath Tiber's mouth. Tiber lightened his kiss, still taking control, but not so dominating. The best matings were always a case of give and take. Tiber might be the Alpha, but he wasn't an asshole. He'd teach Keir later how they would be equal partners in any relationship they might choose.

Keir's low growl of desire almost pushed Tiber's needy body over the edge. Panting, he broke free. "Bed. My room. Now."

"Yes, my mate."

Tiber's cock jerked at the word. Damn, he liked how Keir said mate as if it were all his hopes and dreams wrapped in four simple letters and tattooed across Tiber's heart.

Tiber slid out of the cab. He heard Keir's passenger door slam shut soon after. Anxiety thrummed through him, but he refused to show it. Being an Alpha had guaranteed Tiber rarely showed any signs of nervousness. He couldn't lead others if they knew how shit scared he was most of the time. He'd learned in childhood to hide his fears well enough to keep his scent from giving it away. He wouldn't stop now just because a gorgeous wolf had claimed him for his own.

His cousin Donny stepped out of the cabin. "Oh good, you're back."

Donny's eyes widened when he caught sight of Keir.

"This is Keir, he's joining the pack."

Keir approached, but instead of going up to Donny, he wrapped an arm around Tiber, a silent marking of his territory.

Donny's wide smile let Tiber know he'd be hearing about that little action soon. For the first time, his cousin showed a bit of discretion. "I'm Donny, Tiber's cousin. You must be the injured wolf Tiber has mentioned."

"Yes. Nice to meet you."

As soon as Donny mentioned he was Tiber's cousin, Keir had relaxed against him.

"I told you no one here had any claims on me."

"You might not acknowledge them. That doesn't mean someone isn't scoping you out."

"He has a good point," Donny said, fanning the flames of Keir's jealousy. "I've seen Aslan checking out your ass a time or two."

Keir's low growl raised the hair on the back of Tiber's neck.

"Easy, boy. Looking isn't claiming."

Keir placed a conciliatory kiss on Tiber's shoulder.

Donny fidgeted from foot to foot as he talked, never able to stay in one spot for long, especially when excited. "We have company."

"Who?" Tiber growled. He didn't want company, he wanted Keir. He needed to drag the sexy redhead to his bedroom and fuck him through the floor. If he had to stay and be polite to someone, he wouldn't be held accountable for his rudeness.

"There are two women who I think are a couple and a pair of twin girls, about age five, I think. We haven't had much time to talk before you got here. I was about to call you and warn you when you pulled up."

"What do they want?"

"Sanctuary."

Tiber laughed. "Don't we all."

He didn't know how he could offer sanctuary to women and children when he couldn't even keep his own pack alive.

Walking past his cousin, he marched into the house, letting his Alpha power slide through the air ahead of him to herald his arrival. If he planned to lead these people, they needed to feel his ability. Keir groaned behind him, but Tiber didn't look back.

He paused in the doorway to take in the scene. The two women stood shoulder to shoulder protectively. Peeking around their legs was a pair of identical twin girls with dark pigtails and large blue eyes.

"I'm Tiberius, Alpha of the Black Creek pack. How can I help you?"

One of the women stepped forward after slowly releasing her hold on the other woman. Her blonde hair flowed down to the middle of her back, her face had more of a fox cast than a wolf's, and she smelled of summer flowers. If Tiber had been inclined to like females he would've chosen a women like this one to be his mate.

"I'm Carrie and this is my mate, Dina, and our girls, Melinda and Maddie. We're very pleased to meet you, Alpha."

"I'm pleased to meet you, too, Carrie."

She reached out her hand to shake while tilting her head in submission. Tiber accepted her hand, then slid his fingers across her bared neck in acceptance of her acknowledging his power.

Biting her lip, she stared at him with nervous blue eyes that matched the twins' before continuing. "We ask for sanctuary against the people in our pack who seek to take our girls away. In return we offer ourselves as mate brides."

That was when all hell broke loose. Keir, who'd been silent during the entire exchange, let out a full wolf growl. "He is mine!"

Tiber turned to find Keir in partial shift, ready to take out Carrie's throat.

"Shift back now!" Tiber's will crackled the air with electricity. He pressed his Alpha power against Keir's body.

The Beta wolf whimpered and shifted back to full human.

"She can't have you," the Beta insisted stubbornly. He kept his hateful gaze on Carrie as if ready to rip out her throat at any moment.

"Why don't you all have something to eat? I need to have a chat with Keir."

"I'm sorry." The larger man appeared to deflate a little. Desperation flickered in his eyes as he pled with Tiber. "Please. You can't take them as mates, please, Tiber."

Frustration deepened Tiber's voice into a lower growl than usual. "Come with me."

He refused to have this conversation in front of the others. Tiber grabbed Keir's shirt collar and dragged him up the stairs behind him. They had to settle this before Tiber had to discipline Keir in front of the pack for disobedience, a punishment he'd never exercised and didn't plan to start doing now.

Keir loped quickly after Tiber, never allowing tension to pull on the shirt between them.

Tiber reached his bedroom and slammed the door open. Dragging Keir across the threshold, he swung the door shut behind him, then shoved Keir against the wooden surface.

"You're mine, Tiber. Please," Keir begged again.

The desperation and fear on the Beta's face tore at Tiber's heart. Keir needed him more than anyone Tiber had ever met before. His desperation pulsed at Tiber like a living heartbeat.

Tiber opened his mouth only to have Keir slide his fingers into Tiber's hair. Before he could object, Keir kissed him.

Oh.

Normally he took the initiative in any lovemaking, but as soon as Keir's mouth touched his, his inner wolf became placid, more than willing to accept Keir's gentle mauling.

Tiber moaned against Keir's lips. It took him several kisses before he got the willpower to pull away. They had a few things to settle before they went all the way.

"Are you an Alpha?" Tiber didn't know how to handle the situation. He couldn't have another Alpha in his pack. No pack could handle two leaders—the battle for control would tear them apart.

Keir shook his head

"I could be, but I'm not. I don't have the drive to be an Alpha, even if I do have the power. I'm more than happy to hand all control over to you if that is what you need to accept me." Keir raked Tiber with a hot gaze, taking in every inch of his body.

The words barely left Keir's mouth before he pounced on Tiber. He had the agility of a cat more than a canine. Tiber opened his mouth to object, to say he would be in charge of their lovemaking, but... damn, Keir tasted good. He'd be an idiot to give this up.

Tiber slid his tongue along Keir's, then with a flex of muscle, flipped them. Keir's back slammed against the door. Tiber rubbed up against the redhead, unable to resist wallowing in his scent. He'd never needed anyone so desperately. Biting, licking, growling, Tiber consumed Keir with a single-minded intensity. His wolf paced restlessly beneath the surface, snarling its need and clawing at Tiber as if trying to get out.

Gasping, Tiber pulled back from Keir. "What the hell was that?"

"The bond."

Keir's ragged breathing boosted Tiber's confidence. The larger man's swollen lips and dark eyes filled with want and need distracted Tiber from his thoughts. What had he been about to say?

Tiber cleared his throat and shook his head. Maybe his thought process would improve with more distance. He took a step back. Twin growls from Keir and Tiber's inner wolf echoed in his head.

"Okay, this is officially strange."

Keir stepped forward. "There is nothing strange about being mates."

"But we don't—I don't."

"You don't what?" Keir cupped Tiber's face between his big hands, cradling him as if he were something precious.

"We don't do that. Gray wolves don't form a mate bond. I mean, we obviously have relationships, but it isn't some mystical connection."

Keir kissed Tiber on each cheek, then on the nose. "I appreciate you have different beliefs, but that doesn't change the facts. We are mates. You belong to me."

Tiber ran a hand through his hair. "Most Alphas have multiple mates." He'd never planned to, but he couldn't resist poking at the shifter before him.

His back hit the door when Keir lifted him with one hand and slammed him against the wood surface. "You only get one mate now. I'll be your only. No one else. Please, Tiber."

"Think one mate can keep me satisfied?" Tiber didn't know why he continued to taunt Keir, but his inner wolf pushed back, eager to discover what would set the red wolf off.

"Oh, I'm sure of it."

Keir cupped Tiber's butt and lifted him up. Tiber wrapped his legs around Keir's waist to secure his position. Hard muscles flexed beneath his thighs and he ground his ass against Keir's erection.

"Hmm, you might be right." Tiber had never itched to submit to anyone in his life. He suspected he'd change his mind for Keir.

A feral gleam lit up Keir's eyes. "I know I'm right. You belong to me."

They could argue later. Right now the press of Keir's body, firm, and willing, made it difficult to speak. Words couldn't be formed with such scattered thoughts. Tiber had no interest in arguing when they could be fucking.

"I want to fuck you." Tiber growled out the sentence, eager to move their private party along.

No reason to beat around the bushes. He wanted Keir to know how things were going to be. If Keir thought he could come in and claim Tiber as if he were a weaker wolf, Tiber had a responsibility to set him straight. In the end, he might take Keir as his mate, but he wouldn't take him as his Alpha.

Keir set Tiber on his feet. Stripping off his shirt, he exposed a thickly muscled chest. The wound had transformed from a wide gash to a fine line, barely noticeable. If he didn't know what he was looking for, Tiber would've overlooked the mark. Tiber wanted to hunt Oscar down and rip out his heart for harming Keir. A low rumbling rolled out of him.

Keir grinned. "You're feeling it, too, aren't you?"

"Feeling what?"

"The bond. I know you say gray wolves don't bond the same as red wolves, but our wolves feel the connection."

Tiber's mouth went dry. "I-I don't know what I feel."

"Feel me." Keir stepped forward. He pressed his strong, naked chest against Tiber, aligning their bodies together. Keir's larger mass didn't bother Tiber—he knew which of them was in control. His Alpha wolf had no twinges of distress over mating with a bigger man.

Gripping Keir's thick hair, he kissed the shifter. The slick slide of lips revved Tiber's libido into high gear. He moaned against Keir's mouth. His grip tightened until Keir couldn't step away from him even if he tried.

He lifted his mouth just enough to snarl out, "Mine."

"Always," Keir's words whispered across his lips, a soft vow formed of breath and promises.

Tiber growled his agreement.

The rest of their clothes were flung off their bodies without notice of where they landed. Tiber didn't care—he could pick things up later. Right now he needed flesh against his—Keir's flesh.

"I've waited my entire life for you." Tiber couldn't hold back the words. He had to convey how much this moment meant to him. He might not understand this instant bond between them like Keir did, but he knew all about want and need and the passion between two men.

Keir's kiss, an interesting mix of aggression and submission, tripped all of Tiber's seductive switches. Pheromones perfumed the air between them like an invisible fog of lust.

Keir dropped to his knees. Before Tiber could say a word, Keir lapped at Tiber's erection, collecting the drops of precum oozing from the tip. Tiber's head slammed against the door as he tried to stay upright.

"You are really good at that."

He didn't want to think about where Keir might have received his experience. The red wolf belonged to him now. Sliding his fingers into Keir's hair, he held him in place while he fed him his cock. Keir opened wide, allowing Tiber to use him as he wished.

"Baby, that's so good." Tiber praised Keir with words and touch, making sure the Beta understood how much he appreciated Keir's efforts.

Keir sucked harder, pushing Tiber over the edge. He spilled into Keir's mouth, pleased when the Beta lapped up every drop.

The Alpha's Only

Once Keir finished cleaning him up, Tiber grabbed the Beta by his hair and dragged him to his feet.

"You are awfully good at that." His inner wolf growled a bit over Keir's expertise, but it wasn't as if Tiber was coming into the relationship a virgin.

"Hmm, I'm glad you approve."

Tiber was about to tell him how very much he approved when someone banged on his bedroom door.

"Tiber!" Donny's panicked voice snapped Tiber out of his relaxed pleasure.

"Fuck! Leave us alone!" Keir shouted. He wrapped Tiber in a possessive grip as if worried Tiber would run off and leave him.

Donny didn't go away. "There's an emergency, Oscar attacked Beau!"

"Crap! I'll be right there."

Tiber quickly dressed, surprised when he noticed Keir pulling on his clothes.

"What are you doing?"

Keir didn't back down. "I'm not letting you confront that psycho alone."

Tiber didn't bother to argue. Keir struck him as the type where he had to pick his fights.

"Fine. You can come with."

Tiber's inner wolf growled over the idea of Keir being hurt again. Keir might think he was coming to protect Tiber, but the Alpha wolf lurking inside vowed to protect its mate.

Chapter Four

Keir grinned when Tiber agreed to let him come along. The others watched him with cautious looks, but he didn't care. He got what he wanted—the chance to protect his Alpha and guard his back. Licking his lips, he savored Tiber's flavor still coating his mouth, a welcome reminder of their time together.

Sitting in the back of the extended cab with another Beta named Aslan, Keir listened as Connor and Tiber conversed about possible reasons behind Oscar's attack. He was distracted when Aslan hissed a question at him.

"You think he'll be yours?" Aslan's narrowed gaze indicated his displeasure at Keir's presumption.

"I know he's mine." Keir's wolf sat up to growl, ready to rip out the contender's throat. It would be so easy to attack in the back where Aslan wouldn't be prepared to shift and save himself from Keir's assault. He easily had thirty plus pounds of muscle on the Beta. It would be super easy to snap the fucker's neck. Only Tiber's possible disappointment stilled his hand.

"Don't bait Keir, Aslan," Tiber warned from the front seat.

"I'm just getting to know him," Aslan replied, a sly smile curving his lips.

"You're going to get to know me from the other side of that window if you don't stop it," Keir promised with an evil smile of his own. He let his wolf peek out at Aslan, trickling a bit of power across the Beta beside him. He might not go

Alpha on Tiber, but he had no compunction on twisting Aslan into little wolfy knots.

Aslan swallowed audibly. "Got it."

Connor slowed down the vehicle as they reached the wooded area just outside town.

"Did they say how much damage had been done?" Tiber asked Connor.

"No. They took Beau to the hospital. I was told he's out of critical condition. They have a shifter doctor who just came on staff and I was able to give him the heads up about Beau coming in. I want to see if we can hunt down Oscar before he injures an innocent camper."

Keir remembered Donny's disappointment in not getting to go on their outing. The Omega had only given in when the twin girls rushed over to him with adoring eyes and asked for him to tell them a story. Apparently the Omega had sucker written on his forehead when it came to children. Keir smiled at the memory.

"What was Beau doing out here by himself anyway?" Tiber asked. "I told everyone to be careful when they went out."

Keir knew from his tone that Beau better bounce back quick because Tiber was going to kick Beau's ass for disobeying a direct order.

"He said he had to get away." Connor didn't make excuses for the Beta, he merely stated the facts. Keir's opinion of the sheriff rose.

Aslan paled. "That was my fault. We had an argument. I think he went for a run to get away from me and clear his head."

No wonder the guy was trying to pick a fight with Keir—he needed a distraction from his guilt.

"It's not your fault, Aslan. Beau needs to learn to control his temper. We've warned everyone about going into the woods alone. You can't be held responsible if he doesn't listen," Tiber said.

Aslan visibly relaxed from the Alpha's words. Keir thought it was nice of Tiber to take the guilt off Aslan's shoulders. From the limited bit he'd seen, Tiber made an excellent Alpha, nothing like the assholes Keir had dealt with in the past.

Connor parked the truck and jumped out of the cab. Keir rushed to open Tiber's door, needing to stay close to the sexy Alpha. What if Oscar had returned? He couldn't chance his Alpha being attacked.

"I don't need a bodyguard," Tiber said, his tone amused.

Keir made a scoffing noise. "Don't be ridiculous. All Alphas need bodyguards, it's the new craze. This week it's bodyguards, next week it's ascots, try to keep up."

Tiber laughed, as Keir had intended. He scanned the woods, but didn't see anything out of the norm. He took a deep breath, but again nothing new. "Was Beau attacked here?"

Connor answered. "No, further in. About a five minute walk from here."

"Okay, I'm going to change to my wolf. The rest of you stay human unless needed. Connor, keep your gun ready," Tiber ordered.

Keir watched Connor bite his lip. The sheriff was obviously struggling not to talk back to the Alpha. Keir thought it spoke volumes that the sheriff even tried. Connor had his own bossy tendencies and it probably rubbed him the wrong way to take orders from anyone.

When Tiber stripped off his shirt, Connor looked away, but Aslan's stare zeroed in on the Alpha's every move.

A snarl rolled up Keir's throat.

"Hey, you can't blame a guy for looking," Aslan said, a sheepish grin crossing his face.

"No, but I can maim a guy for looking."

Aslan rolled his eyes, but obediently kept his gaze off Tiber. "Have sex with a guy once and you think he belongs to you."

An unpleasant thought crossed Keir's mind. "You never had sex with him, did you?"

"No. I was kind of hoping we would hook up, but he didn't show interest and then you arrived."

"Yes. I did." Keir grinned. His world spun happily on its axis now that he'd cleared up that particular bit of his lover's past.

"Are we done chatting, girls?" Connor asked. "Can we now continue our hunt for a killer?"

"Yes, sir." Keir glanced guiltily around. Tiber had told him to keep his eyes open and minutes after the order he'd already forgotten. He made a horrible Alpha mate. Keir dipped his head down and focused on the ground, hoping to find some tracks or something to redeem himself.

Instead, an enormous wolf with dark fur trotted into his vision.

"Hey, Tiber, aren't you a handsome wolf."

Tiber scooted out of reach when Keir reached out to pet him.

"Alphas don't allow for scratches behind the ear," Aslan said.

"Hmm. I guess I'll save that for his human form," Keir mused.

Tiber barked. With a disdainful flick of his tail, he raced into the woods, leaving the others behind.

"Damn it, Tiber," Keir muttered under his breath. The Alpha was going to rush into trouble without Keir to protect his back. Ignoring the other two men, Keir ran after Tiber. No one was going to harm the Alpha on his watch.

Keir chased Tiber into a clearing. The Alpha wolf circled around, barking furiously. Blood coated one rock and drizzled along the dirt. A man stood over the blood marks. Keir immediately blocked the stranger's path to Tiber.

"Hey, Proctor, did you learn anything new?" Connor asked the dark-haired man standing in the clearing. The man wore a deputy uniform and had a gun on his utility belt that didn't look strictly regulation.

"No. Beau was mauled right here, but there isn't any sign of Oscar."

Keir spotted a series of paw prints in the soft earth, but they were piled on top of each other until he couldn't see which way the victor headed out of the clearing. Walking into the middle of the fight scene, Keir inhaled deeply. Tiber barked and raced off in the direction Keir had scented. It smelled like the wolf Keir had battled before.

"Oh no you don't." Keir ran after the Alpha. He heard Aslan's footsteps behind him, but he didn't bother to wait for him. Aslan would follow or not, Keir's job was to keep Tiber safe. It might be a self-imposed job, but it was one he'd do or die trying.

Tiber came to a halt at the edge of a river. Oscar had efficiently erased his scent in the water. Low growling filled the air.

"Easy, Tiber. We lost him this time. Let's go check on your Beta."

Tiber flashed a fang, but Keir knew it wasn't due to him. Frustration poured off the Alpha in waves. Tiber's emotions swept through Keir as if he was experiencing them himself.

"Come on, love. Time to go."

Keir turned back only to be slammed to the ground. A tongue lapped his ear before the heavy weight jumped off him.

"You think you're a funny wolf, don't you?"

Tiber barked.

Keir shook his head and followed the Alpha back to the clearing. Oscar was probably long gone. The wolf was smart and deadly, He wouldn't be foolish enough to attack five shifters—he'd wait until they were separated and cull them one by one. Another reason they needed to stick together.

When Keir entered the site of the attack, Tiber had already shifted back and was pulling on his clothes. Keir swallowed his instinctive protest. Covering the Alpha's body should be a crime in any state.

"I can go back with Proctor if you want to take the truck," Connor offered to Tiber. "There's not much point in collecting evidence, since we know who attacked him."

Tiber nodded. "You two want to go to the hospital with me?"

"Yes." Keir would go wherever Tiber was headed. He certainly didn't want to return to the pack house without him.

"Yeah, I want to see how he's doing."

For all that he teased Keir about Tiber, Keir sensed Aslan was concerned about the other Beta.

"Okay. Let's go stop for lunch, then we'll head to the hospital. Beau should be on the mend by the time we get there. Maybe we'll be able to take him home." Tiber led the way to the truck.

Keir climbed in the passenger seat beside Tiber before Aslan got the opportunity. He wouldn't give up his spot by his Alpha's side for anyone.

Tiber smiled, but didn't comment on Keir's action. On the way to town, they discussed the best place for Keir's tattoo shop.

"I have to get a license first. Mine expired."

"No problem. We can get you one while we're searching for the best location."

"You tattoo?" Aslan asked.

"Yeah. I have one on my back, remind me to show you sometime." The best advertisement for a tattoo artist was the ones he designed himself.

"It looks just like me. I thought it was my wolf when I first saw it."

"It is you. I saw it in a dream and had to design it. If it's your wolf when you shift, then it is just one more sign that I belong to you."

Tiber raised an eyebrow at him. "I guess that means I have to keep you."

"I guess it does."

"Eventually you can put one of you in your wolf form on my back."

Keir grinned. Tattooing his own mate was a dream he didn't dare to hope for. "I'd love to do your tattoo."

Aslan's gagging sounds in the back seat had Keir reaching back to swat at him.

"I can't help it if you two are choking me with all that sugar," Aslan argued.

"You can if I slice your throat." Keir refused to allow anyone to ruin the moment for him. Tiber was almost ready to agree to be his. If Aslan did anything to change Tiber's mind, Keir would rip out the Beta's throat, pack mate or not.

"Shh." Tiber patted Keir on the leg.

"What?"

"You were growling," Tiber said.

"Oh." He hadn't realized he'd been making that noise. Frustration did that to him. Well, frustration and the urge to kick someone's ass.

Tiber pulled in front of a diner, sparing Keir the embarrassment of prolonging that conversation. Keir hopped out of the cab and quickly walked around to open Tiber's door.

"I'm not your girlfriend," Tiber snapped.

"No, you're more precious to me than that." Keir kept close to Tiber's side, scanning the area as they walked. He wouldn't put it past Oscar to ambush them. They were down to three shifters, and a psycho with a rifle could take them out if he had his heart set on it. On full alert, Keir allowed Tiber to put a hand on his back and guide him to the restaurant entrance.

The diner had all the charm of a fifties dive, but none of the grime. Whoever decorated the place had channeled their inner Elvis. Old records decorated the walls, a shiny jukebox glowed in one corner and the booths were covered in brightly colored red vinyl.

"They have the best burgers here," Tiber said enthusiastically.

The smell of cooking meat perfumed the air like the finest fragrance. "Damn, those do smell good."

Tiber stepped aside and allowed Keir to slide into the booth before him. Aslan sat on the opposite side. "I see how this is going to be," he said.

"What?" Tiber asked as he settled beside Keir, their thighs touching.

"Me on one side. Lovebirds on the other."

Tiber snorted. "I wouldn't call us lovebirds."

I wonder if he can hear my heart breaking?

Keir bit his lip to hold back his needy words.

"Hey." Tiber cupped Keir's cheek, forcing him to face him. "I didn't mean it like that. We're mates, right?"

Keir nodded.

"Then ignore Aslan. He's just jealous we found each other."

The breath whooshed out of Keir's lungs. "Okay. I don't want to sound like a needy bitch, but you haven't exactly been enthusiastic about the whole mating thing."

Tiber kissed Keir's nose. "I'm still getting used to the idea. Don't take my silence as a show of not caring. I'm very interested in being your mate. If you say we're fated to be together, who am I to argue?"

Relief whipped through him and Keir's head spun. "Oh good. I didn't want to have to turn stalkerish."

Tiber's laughter brightened the room with his joy.

A waitress approached and from her scent, Keir could tell she was a shifter.

"Afternoon, gentlemen." She subtly tilted her head at Tiber.

"Afternoon, Nancy," Tiber greeted her. "This is Keir. He's recently joined us."

"Nice to meet you," Nancy said. She had the waitress cheeriness down pat, but Keir could feel her gaze focused on him as she handed out the menus and took their drink orders. "The special is chili with beef or prime rib."

"Thanks." Tiber dismissed her with a nod of his head.

Tiber took Keir's menu and set it on the edge of the table. "Trust me when I say a burger is the way to go."

"Okay." Keir didn't care what he ate as long as he ate it beside his Alpha.

"I agree." Aslan set his menu down also. "Their other stuff is good, but the burgers are excellent. The chef gets local grass-fed beef."

"There's an empty storefront across the street." Tiber pointed to a small shopping center that consisted of a Laundromat, a shoe repair place and a leasing sign in the window between them.

Keir fiddled with the spoon before confessing. "I need to get a job so I can earn enough to open a store. I pretty much left my last pack with the fur on my back."

He'd been lucky to leave with even that. They'd wanted to whip him for his perverted ways. Only Keir's massive size prevented the Alpha from trying to take him on. Still, if Tiber had forced the issue, he probably could've gotten enough pack members to beat Keir up.

"You don't need to earn money to open a store. Pack rules states each new pack member will receive assistance in starting a new business. Now, if the business does well or not depends on you, but we give everyone a helping hand. Donny and I know what it's like to start out with nothing. I make sure everyone in my pack gets a head start to help them to success."

"Really? It's not just because you're my mate?"

"No, man, he really means it. Beau and I are going to open a garage as soon as this stuff with Oscar is over. We've got the space ready and everything. We just don't want to leave the pack house without enough guards," Aslan said. "We still need to protect the pups."

"Maybe with Keir's help we can spread the duties around a little more," Tiber suggested.

Keir nodded. He'd be happy to help protect the pack. He'd mostly watch over Tiber, but that could spread to others if needed

"Ready to order?" Their perky waitress returned with their drinks and had her pencil primed over her pad of paper as if they were about to divulge where someone had hidden their stash of diamonds.

"Three burgers with everything," Tiber said.

"Fries or chips," Nancy asked.

Tiber and Aslan ordered fries, Keir ordered chips.

When Nancy walked back to put in their order, Keir settled down in his seat and examined the space across the street. Mentally he designed the sign that would hang over the store. "Is there a limit on the amount I'm allowed to borrow?"

Tiber squeezed Keir's arm companionably. "I'll negotiate a pack rate for the space if you like it, I know the building owner. There are a couple other places if this one isn't quite the one for you."

"Tiber got us a great deal on our garage space," Aslan said.

Keir's awe at being matched with an Alpha only increased when he discovered what kind of person Tiber was inside. Tiber cared about the success of his pack as individuals, as well as a group.

"I think you're a good Alpha, Tiber," Keir blurted out.

Instead of laughing, Tiber examined Keir with a serious expression in his beautiful eyes as if weighing his words. "Thank you," he said at last.

"Aww." Aslan made kissy noises at them. "Ow, you kicked me."

Tiber grinned. "You were asking for it. I should've done worse for mocking your Alpha."

"Ah, no. I didn't mean that!" Aslan's panicked tone made Keir smile. Served him right.

"Relax, Aslan, I took no offense," Tiber calmed the panicked shifter.

"Whew." Aslan smiled. "Good. It will take me a little time to get used to seeing you with a mate."

"Me, too," Tiber agreed. Since he squeezed Keir's leg when he said it, Keir didn't take offense. Tiber did need an adjustment period—too bad Keir couldn't give him one. If a psychotic wolf were trying to kill off Tiber, he'd need Keir as close as possible. Until they managed to kill Oscar, Keir was going to stick closer to Tiber than gum on his shoe.

They chatted about the state of the pack and Tiber's goal of increasing their numbers. When the burgers arrived, Keir all but inhaled the first bite. He hummed happily around each mouthful, interspersing it with moans and licks of his fingers.

"If you keep that up, *I'm* going to pounce," Aslan announced.

Keir smiled when Tiber growled.

"I'd suggest you rethink that idea," Tiber said.

Aslan immediately tilted his head to one side. "Sorry, Alpha."

Tiber nodded his acceptance of Aslan's apology. "Think of Keir as an extension of me."

"Yes, Alpha."

They finished their food with peace restored among them.

The hospital smelled like most places of healing, a mixture of staleness and cleaning fluid. When they entered Beau's room, Keir didn't like the wide grin the Beta gave to Tiber.

Damn, does everyone want my man?

Aslan growled a bit himself, making Keir wonder if there was something going on between the Betas.

Keir wrapped a possessive hand around Tiber's arm and met Beau's gaze.

"This is Keir, my mate," Tiber introduced him.

Pride had Keir puffing out his chest at the introduction.

"Nice to meet you," Beau replied.

Keir could smell the lie in the air. Aslan might have been kidding about his interest in the Alpha, but Beau obviously wanted him."

Aslan kept sliding glances over to Beau as if waiting for acknowledgement.

Tiber moved away from Keir to approach the Beta. "How badly are you injured?"

Beau shrugged his injuries away. "A few deep scratches and a bite on my right leg. Frankly, I think he slashed my legs so I couldn't chase him. He was looking a bit rough, like someone had mauled him earlier. I think the only reason Oscar attacked was because I surprised him."

"Where did you surprise him at?" Tiber asked.

"East of the river, about ten miles from the pack lands."

Tiber crossed his arms over his chest. "And you traveled all that way alone after I told everyone to stick together? There are reasons I give orders, Beau. If you don't find me an Alpha worthy enough to follow, then you can find a new pack to join."

"No!" Beau and Aslan said simultaneously.

Tiber raised an eyebrow at Aslan.

"Please, Tiber, he was mad at me."

"That doesn't mean he should've ignored a direct order from his Alpha." Tiber's tone didn't allow for any forgiveness.

"You are right, Tiber. I'll gladly accept any punishment you wish to give me." Tears tracked down Beau's face. Aslan rushed to stand next to him. Whatever reason Beau had for being mad at Aslan apparently vanished before the disapproval of his Alpha. He quickly accepted the hand Aslan offered. Taking a deep breath, Beau got to his feet, his fingers still entangled with Aslan's. He kept his head bowed and tilted to one side to bare his throat.

"You have daytime guard duty for the next three months. I will also delay your garage opening until I feel you are responsible enough."

"But that would punish Aslan, too!" Beau turned his tear-stricken face up at Tiber.

"Yes, Aslan didn't inform me you'd run off. There are penalties for keeping things from your Alpha."

"Yes, sir," Aslan and Beau said.

Tiber nodded, and Keir could see for him the issue had been resolved. The Betas let out a breath of relief when Tiber changed the subject. "How are you feeling?"

"I'm definitely feeling better." Beau's relief was palpable.

No shifters enjoyed staying at a hospital. He didn't know how the shifter doctor handled it every day. The smells alone could hamper a shifter's recovery.

"Then let's go."

"Do I need to wait for my doctor to check me out?"

Tiber shook head. "No, he'll understand."

They grabbed his bloodstained clothes and got the hell out of there.

Chapter Five

Tiber ran through the forest, the sounds of the pack running beside him raising his spirits. They were becoming larger, stronger and he hoped better able to protect themselves from all outside dangers.

The four new pack members were settling in well. Both women were strong Betas and had easily slipped into guard duty rotation, while their daughters mixed quickly with the other kids.

It had been three weeks since anyone had last spotted Oscar. The lack of sighting the black wolf had Tiber uneasy. No way would Oscar simply give up, not after all the killing he'd done over the years.

A happy yip turned his attention toward his running companion. Keir kept up with him in big, easy lopes, his wolf expression one of utter joy. Luckily with most of the people in town being shifters, they didn't have to hide who they were.

Other members of the pack howled and panted behind them. They were in the lead, as was traditional with the Alpha pair.

In the weeks since Keir had joined them, they had grown closer. Tiber now believed Keir's assertion they were mates. They'd begun to speak telepathically as only an Alpha could do with his bonded one.

A disgusting stench pulled Tiber away from his inward contemplation of his relationship. Keir growled low and feral, beside him.

They came to a stop at the sight of a buck torn apart and left by a tree. Its guts were splayed across the forest floor, a tempting invitation for wolves hungry from a run.

Tiber sniffed around the carcass. Oscar's scent soaked the body along with the sweet smell of poison mixed with blood. Although Tiber's Alpha senses were able to pick out the danger, not all of his pack had as refined an ability to smell as he did.

Damn Oscar.

Before he could bark out a warning, the pack stepped closer, some of the younger wolves sniffing at the meat.

Tiber lunged at the closest pup, growling and snarling at the little ones to keep them away from the carcass. When a few of the bolder pups leaned forward, Tiber lashed out, snapping his teeth and barking to keep the others away from the deer.

A few of the older adults figured out the problem and helped Tiber rustle the children back to their homes. Once he was certain they'd all been guided away, he changed back to his human form.

"He's trying to kill you all," Keir said, his face pale in the moonlight.

Tiber nodded. "He's trying to demoralize us first. He knows if I can't protect the kids, I'll prove to be a poor Alpha and he'll destroy the pack from within. He didn't get to kill Donny, our Omega, so now he's trying a different path. I doubt this will be the last time he tries to end us. This is just his latest attempt." Tiber ran his fingers through his hair as he paced. "This could've ended really badly. We've got to hunt him down."

Keir grabbed Tiber's arm, stopping his manic motion. "We are, mate. We've been looking. He's just really good at hiding."

Tiber nodded. "For a man who has a decided stench, you'd think he'd be easier to find."

"He's clever." Keir wrapped his arms around Tiber and pulled him close in a tight hold.

Tiber sighed and allowed the comfort. Even an Alpha needed a cuddle once in a while. The fact they were both naked didn't rouse his passion. Terror over possibly losing his pack to poison had killed any erection he might have had.

A scream ripped through the forest. Birds took flight from the sound, adding drama to an already worrisome moment.

"Maddie!" Carrie's anguished cry cut Tiber to the quick.

"No," he whispered, "not the little ones."

Pulling free of his mate, Tiber shifted to his wolf form. Heedless of his own safety, Tiber ran toward the loud sobs echoing through the woods. He'd dreaded this moment. Oscar had gone the final step. He'd grabbed one of the pups.

Tiber came to a sliding stop when he reached the pack. The remaining twin sobbed in her mother's arms. Short, anguished cries, tore out of her small body as if without her other half she would fly apart from the sheer sorrow of it all.

He didn't remember the change, but suddenly Tiber had hands to clench and words to speak. "What happened?"

Carrie spoke first, her eyes puffy from tears. "A big black wolf came out of nowhere. He grabbed Maddie by the back of her neck and dragged her off. We couldn't stop him."

Tiber cursed, filling the air with his fury. The carcass had only been a diversion. Tiber had no doubt that Oscar had planned to grab one of the kids the entire time.

Keir wrapped a warm hand around the back of Tiber's neck, letting Tiber know his mate was there for him. "We'll get her back, Tiber."

Tiber bit back his instinctive snarl. He had to keep an optimistic face for the grieving mothers. "Since he grabbed her, he probably wants to keep her for bait. He won't hurt her. It's me he wants."

As he said the words, the truth of them filled his mouth with a bitter taste. Oscar's goal all along was to wipe out the Black Creek pack. What easier way than to tear out its heart? Nothing stabbed a wolf faster than the loss of their young.

"He'll want to barter," Keir warned. "Trade your life for the girl's."

Keir's resolve to not let that happen beat at Tiber's mind. Tiber hated to disappoint his lover, but this time he couldn't be talked out of his path. He wouldn't give up Maddie's life to a psychotic wolf.

Relax, mate. Tiber sent the message over their shared link. Keir's fury and nervous energy jittered Tiber's nerves.

He can't have you! Anger and fear traced Keir's words with thick brushstrokes of hate.

We need to find his hideout. Tiber didn't have to tell Keir that they couldn't sit around and wait for Oscar's plan to come to fruition. Whatever the black wolf planned couldn't be good for the rest of them. As far as Tiber could tell, Oscar didn't have any redeeming qualities.

"Get all the children home," Tiber ordered. "It's time we did some hunting of our own."

There were murmurs of agreement and muffled sobs, but the pack began to move until only Tiber, Keir, Connor, Proctor, Beau, and Aslan stood in the clearing. The others had gone to guard the pack in case Oscar tried again. Tiber waited until he could no longer hear the other wolves moving in the underbrush.

"What's the plan, Alpha?" Connor asked.

Grief settled his face in lines not there when they had first began their run. Of all the Betas, Connor played with the children the most, leading Tiber to wonder if Connor had any plans to adopt a child with his mate Josh. Shaking his head, Tiber turned his attention back to the matter at hand.

"We've been on the defensive since Oscar returned to our territory. It's time to do some hunting of our own. We need to be smart and figure out where he would hide out. These woods go on for miles, but Oscar will have dug himself a den. He's been sleeping somewhere all this time. We just need to discover where."

"Let's spread out and see if we can track him first."

Soft footsteps heralded the arrival of another wolf. Tiber turned without surprise to find Dina marching toward them. "I want in on the hunt. It's my daughter he has."

Tiber nodded. "Your help is welcome."

The fight went out of the female wolf and she turned a puzzled face toward Tiber. "You're not going to argue with me on this?"

"Why? If it were my daughter, I wouldn't trust anyone else to bring her back. It would be foolish of me to deny you the chance to hunt. You'd just do it on your own anyway."

Dina cleared her throat a few times before she spoke. "I appreciate that, Alpha. You're a good leader. We've been lucky to have you, despite the feral wolf in your territory."

Tiber clenched his jaw to hold back the howl of frustration aching to get out. If he'd hunted Oscar down before instead of worrying about the size of his pack, maybe a little girl wouldn't be in that psychopath's clutches.

Keir's grip on Tiber's arm pulled him out of his cloud of self-pity and regret.

We'll get through this.
Yes, we will.

Tiber quickly assigned directions and groups. "Everyone rendezvous here in an hour. Keir, you're with me."

"Of course."

Tiber knew if he hadn't assigned his mate to his side, Keir would've come anyway. He'd learned over their short time together that his mate had selective hearing and was completely deaf when it came to being ordered to do anything that might leave Tiber vulnerable. It was like having a twenty-four hour bodyguard. Tiber wondered how Keir would pull that off once he opened his tattoo shop.

They ran together, searching for some hint of Oscar passing. Every once in a while they would pick up a faint trail only to discover it was old or ended at the river. Tiber had no doubt Oscar was using the water to hide his scent, an old shifter trick that proved once again to Tiber that Oscar might be a psychopath, but he knew what he was doing.

After the designated hour, they returned to meet the others.

"No luck?" Tiber asked.

"He lost us by the river," Connor said. The others all shook their heads.

"Yeah, us, too," Keir said.

"I've got a map back at headquarters. Maybe if we chart out where all of Oscar's attacks have taken place we can narrow down our search," Proctor suggested.

"Good idea," Tiber praised the deputy. "Everyone meet back at the sheriff's office. We've got hunting to do. Dina, you can catch a ride with the sheriff and answer any questions he might have for you."

"Yes, Alpha." Dina rushed to follow Proctor and Connor back to their vehicle. Everyone else had transportation.

Tiber headed back to his car. Keir walked beside him, their shoulders brushing companionably as they moved. Without his mate's support, Tiber knew he'd be in much worse condition. Keir's unwavering belief in Tiber's ability to save the little girl did wonders for Tiber's confidence.

"I'll always have your back," Keir said. The words, spoken out loud, had the weight of a solemn vow.

"Thanks, mate." Sometimes there weren't enough vowels and consonants in the world to convey the depth of his love. In such a short time, he'd become completely enamored of his mate. He didn't know if they were preordained to meet like Keir believed, but he did know his life would be much lonelier without the redheaded wolf at his side.

Tiber gripped Keir's shoulder before opening the driver's side and retrieving his clothes.

Keir laughed. "I love you, too, mate."

Tiber turned back to face his mate. "Didn't I say that?"

Keir's wide smile had Tiber blushing. "Shit I didn't, did I?"

"I know you're not a man who says the words. That doesn't mean I don't feel them through our connection."

Tiber grabbed Keir around the waist and held him tightly against his body. He kissed Keir, hoping to put all his love and devotion into that one embrace. When he finally lifted his mouth, Keir's swollen lips and lust-filled eyes made him smile.

"Never doubt the love I have for my mate," Tiber growled. "I'll not let anyone question the rightness of our bond, even you."

Keir melted against Tiber's body. Keeping his head down, he played with the small hairs on Tiber's chest. "Understood."

"Good." He pressed a kiss on Keir's scalp. "Get dressed. We need to meet everyone at the sheriff station."

When they arrived, everyone was already there. They gave Tiber and Keir a curious glance, but no one said anything.

"Let's see your map," Tiber said to Proctor.

They moved to a big table so the deputy could lay out the large aerial survey of the Black Creek area. Proctor grabbed a black marker and circled where there had been sightings of Oscar.

"And there," Connor pointed to where Oscar had kidnapped the girl.

"It looks like he's been traveling," Tiber said. "Going from one site to the next, probably to stay under our radar."

"He can't be that hard to find," Keir objected. "He pumps out hate like it's Pez."

"There are some old caves here." Beau pointed out a section by the river. "I discovered them a few years ago while I was fishing. They aren't very big, but Oscar might be able to wiggle in there in wolf form."

"That could be why we can't scent him," Tiber agreed. "If he's hiding that close to the water, it probably washes away his trail."

There were a series of agreements and they began to strategize their approach.

"Where's Dina?" Tiber looked up and noticed the absence of Maddie's mother.

"She was just here," Proctor said.

"Damn, I bet she headed out there alone." Why did he say she could come along? He should've kept a better eye on the grieving woman. "Let's go. There's no time to lose. Dina might get herself killed before we get there."

"I'd keep a watch on her," Connor warned. "It might just be a mother grieving, but she's acting a bit off."

"What do you mean?"

"I can't pinpoint it, but I've got a bad feeling about that woman."

"I'd go with Connor's feelings," Proctor joined in. "They've saved my ass more than once."

"I'll keep it in mind." How a hinky feeling about a grieving woman would help, Tiber didn't know, but he wouldn't dismiss anyone's instincts, no matter how bizarre. "Let's go."

They all piled into two of the sheriff's oversized trucks. They didn't want to waste time for everyone to get there separately.

"It's not your fault," Keir said. Sitting in the back with Tiber, his mate gripped Tiber's hand. "We all thought she'd have the sense to wait for us."

Remembering the grief on Dina's face, Tiber scowled. What kind of leader didn't know his people well enough to know when they were about to snap? "I should've guessed Dina would head out on her own."

"How? You aren't psychic. Let it go, Tiber. Dina is responsible for herself."

"I don't want to have to tell Carrie that I lost her daughter and her mate." Tiber tried hard to be a proper Alpha. Sometimes the position sucked.

It took them half an hour to get as close as possible to where the map indicated caves might be.

Connor grabbed a rifle out of the locker in the back of his truck and handed another one to Proctor. "We're going in as human. The rest of you . . ."

"We're going in as pack," Tiber confirmed. "Maybe we can flush him out."

Tiber's sense of justice battled against the need to rip out Oscar's throat. He pinned Connor with a stare. "If he kills me, gun him down."

"Understood, Alpha."

Connor's wolf instincts were coming along quite nicely.

Keir grabbed Tiber's hand and kissed the palm. "Let's go get our psychopath."

Tiber smiled at his mate. It took several minutes for everyone to shift. Inhaling deeply, Tiber still didn't smell anything. Orientating himself, he glanced around until he located the path he wanted. He barked to alert the others. A trample of paws against the earth followed him. Tiber's delight in a run was tempered by his matching anger at Maddie's abduction.

He heard the river long before he saw the rushing water. The recent rain made the current faster and higher than usual. Tiber hoped the caves hadn't flooded.

It took several minutes before they found the position they'd spotted on the map. Pinpoint holes in the small hill turned into larger gaping openings the closer they ran. A whiff of Oscar's scent turned Tiber's attention to the farthest one.

Careful. Tiber sent the thought to Keir. The others were naturally cautious. His impetuous mate was more likely to blithely run in.

Slowing down, Tiber carefully picked his way through the loose rocks. Oscar's scent strengthened as he approached the farthest cave. As he reached the cave opening, disappointment slid through him. He could tell Oscar wasn't there any longer. The smell had faded enough for Tiber to tell Oscar hadn't been there in a day or two. There were no scents of Maddie. Oscar hadn't brought her here.

Maybe he'd left some clues.

Stay back here. I'm going to check things out, Tiber telegraphed to his mate. *Watch out for signs of Oscar returning.*

Giving Keir the task of watching Tiber's back would soothe his mate's need to protect Tiber and keep him out of the way while Tiber investigated.

Tiber entered the cave. It took a couple of minutes for his eyes to adjust. Luckily his shifter genes gave him night vision stronger than a regular wolf's. Pitch black soon turned to semi-dark and bright enough for him to make out objects in the dim light.

A rumpled blanket lay tangled against one wall along with wrappers from various pre-packaged foods. No furniture filled the space. Either Oscar didn't need much, or he had another place to stay elsewhere.

Tiber shifted to his human shape in order to examine the small cave more thoroughly. He learned nothing more than Oscar's unnatural affection for energy bars and distaste of bathing, despite the fresh water only steps from his cave. The strong scent of Dina hung in the air, so he knew the female Beta had checked out the cave.

Disheartened, Tiber turned to go. Writing across the entrance of the cave caught his attention.

Goodbye.

In big red letters, the words mocked Tiber. Damn Oscar. He must have known he'd given his location away. Tiber snarled his frustration. He took another step and a bit of the floor gave way.

What was that?

Tiber lifted his foot to see a small trigger.

Oh crap!

An explosion rocked the cave.

Tiber stumbled back from the blast, disoriented and half-deaf from the bomb, Tiber's feet tangled with the blanket. He shouted as he tumbled to the ground. An ominous snapping noise following by breath-stealing pain in his wrist made Tiber suspect he'd broken it.

Grabbing his arm, Tiber lay on the ground in complete and utter darkness. A black so deep even his extra sight couldn't save him.

"Tiber!" Keir's panicked shout was barely audible through the wall of stones.

I'm fine. Tiber projected back to his mate. For how long he didn't know. If the pack could clear away the entrance he'd survive, but from the little bit he could make out, the wall looked sealed tight, and oxygen could become an issue.

"Don't worry, we'll get you out!" Keir said.

Tiber hoped they could get to him in time.

Chapter Six

Keir's hands shook as he reached for the first stone. He couldn't lose Tiber, not now. He'd just found his mate.

"Keir!"

He didn't bother to acknowledge the person talking. He didn't care what they had to say. He only had one goal. Free Tiber. Everyone else could go fuck themselves.

"Keir, we have to think this through."

Connor's voice penetrated Keir's fog of despair. "I *am* thinking. If we don't get to Tiber soon he could run out of air. I can't believe I let him go in there alone."

Guilt chomped him in its razor sharp teeth, then spit him back out. He'd been so careful to watch for Oscar he hadn't thought of other dangers. Who knew Oscar had the presence of mind to set a trap?

"You let him go in there because he's the Alpha and he told you to wait. We'll get him out of there. Don't worry."

"What do you mean, don't worry!" Keir knew his voice had topped over the edge of hysteria, but he couldn't help it. "My mate is in there and he could be dying!"

"Did he say he was dying?" Connor asked.

Damn the man for trying to insert logic into Keir's meltdown. "No, but do you think he'd admit it? He'd hold back because he didn't want me to worry. I can tell he's in pain."

Tiber might not tell him in words, but Tiber's physical discomfort had slithered across their link.

Connor tried again to be the voice of reason. "We have to be careful. We don't know how far the cave-in went. If you pull the wrong stone you could send it crashing down on him."

"No!" Keir wailed. His worst nightmare was coming true—to find his mate only to lose him.

"Snap out of it!" Beau demanded. "You're an Alpha's mate. Act like it."

Beau's words doused Keir like cold water, pulling him out of his panic attack. "Right. You're right. I need to think logically. How do we get him out of there without collapsing the entire thing?"

"You keep your connection with Tiber active. I'll climb on top of the hill and see if I can pry the top rock off and start them tumbling toward you. You step to the side and let me know if Tiber says anything about rocks falling at him."

"Okay." He could do that. Tiber's emotions poured across their connection, calm and collected. If his Alpha had any worries, he was keeping them to himself. Typical.

You okay, love? He sent to Tiber.

Yes. Are you digging me out?

Connor is trying to figure out how to get the rocks away without tumbling them into you.

No point in lying. Tiber would know if he tried to hide the truth.

"Stand clear!" Connor shouted.

They all stepped backward. Beau and Aslan stood on either side. Proctor had climbed on top to assist Connor.

"Keep an eye out for any other bombs," Keir shouted.

"Thanks, I hadn't thought of that."

Connor's sarcastic tone had Keir blushing. Of course a cop would think of another explosive device.

"Sorry!" he yelled back.

A low growl filled his head. Tiber didn't like anyone embarrassing Keir. Connor would be paying for that comment once Tiber was free.

Connor pried off the top stones, rolling them out of the cave. Keir rushed to help the others loosen more, dragging them off. To Keir's horrified gaze, the rocks began to tumble apart, half of them moving inside the cave.

"Tiber!" Too panicked to communicate telepathically, Keir screamed until Tiber shouted back.

"I'm fine." Tiber's voice took the hard edges off his terror but it didn't completely go away.

Calm, mate. I need you to not panic. Tiber's words filled Keir's head, sweeping away his terror and replacing it with confidence they'd get his mate out of there alive.

I don't want you hurt.

No response.

Keir bit his lip. He needed to be strong. He was an Alpha's mate. Sucking in a long breath, he dug in to help the others. He'd get his mate out of there or die trying.

After an hour they'd dug enough of a hole to see to the other side. Keir scrambled up the hill of rocks to peer through the opening. Tiber lay there, holding his arm. "You're injured," Keir accused. He knew his mate had been hiding something from him.

"Just my wrist."

"Hold on we'll get you out of there in a bit."

It could've been so much worse. The team continued to work away at the rocks until Tiber could climb through. When Tiber made it out entirely, Keir flung himself into his mate's arms and sobbed out his joy. Fuck it, the others could get over themselves. He had to feel Tiber in his arms and hear the thud of his mate's heart beneath his ear.

"You're safe." He knew he said the words over and over, but he couldn't seem to stop himself.

"I am, but we still haven't found Maddie."

The sorrow in Tiber's words reminded him why they were there in the first place.

"Crap." In his concern for his mate, he'd all but forgotten they were still missing a little girl and her mother. "Where do you think Dina went?"

Tiber snapped upright. "That's a good question. I smelled her inside. If she was there first, how did she not trigger the bomb?"

"How did it go off?" Connor asked.

"I stepped on a trip plate buried under some wrappers."

"Maybe she missed it," Keir said.

"Maybe."

"Do you think she found Oscar?" Beau asked.

"I hope not," Tiber said. "She's not strong enough to take him."

Tiber's phone rang. He let out a sigh of relief as he looked at the readout.

"That's her right now." Tiber pushed the speaker button on his phone. "Hey, Dina, where are you?"

"She's here with me."

Keir didn't recognize the man's voice, but Tiber's next words confirmed his suspicions.

"Let them go, Oscar!" Tiber demanded.

Oscar's mocking laughter sent chills up Keir's spine. "Why would I do that, when I can use them against you?"

"Do you feel tough picking on innocent women and children?" Tiber taunted.

"Innocent? The kid bit me and the woman tried to rip off my balls. They're a danger to society. I would be doing you a favor by killing them."

"What do you want?"

Tiber's shoulders slumped and he leaned against the closest tree to stay upright. Keir stepped forward and wrapped an arm around Tiber for support.

"What do I want? I want to go back to being human. However, I'll settle for making you dogs suffer for turning me into one of you."

Keir stared at the phone, almost surprised to not see it dripping with venom.

"I didn't change you. That was before my time. Let the females go."

"Why would I do that? To prove what a good guy I am? I'm not a good guy, and the sooner you realize that the better. I'd rather cut them up and leave you a trail of body parts, since you are so good at following my lead. Instead I'll make you a deal. You come and turn yourself in to me, and I'll let both of the females go. Why would I need them if I have the pack Alpha?"

No!

Keir screamed in his head. He knew before he spoke what answer Tiber would give.

"When and where?"

Keir swallowed back the bile trying to rise in his throat. He was seconds from tossing his cookies all over the sapling beside him. How could Tiber value his own life so little when he consisted of Keir's entire world?

"I'll meet you in the field north of your cabins where I left your deer present. Two o'clock. Don't be late. I'm sure I don't need to tell you to come alone. If I smell anyone else I'll kill them both."

Oscar disconnected.

"You can't go, Tiber," Keir protested. "Your wrist is damaged and you won't be able to fight if Oscar attacks you."

A wry smile twisted Tiber's lips. "I'm not sure I could take him even if I wasn't injured."

"All the more reason to not go to this meeting. It's a trap." Even as he said the words, he knew it wasn't going to make any difference. No way would his mate leave a woman and her child to fend for themselves.

Tiber cupped Keir's face. He stroked Keir's cheeks with his thumbs in a gesture so tender it made Keir's chest ache. "Baby, I don't want to leave you, but I wouldn't be a good leader if I let my people die because I was too much of a coward to face him."

"You're not a coward," Keir refuted loyally. "You're injured."

"I have to see if I can save them."

"You aren't going alone." Keir wouldn't lose his mate. He wouldn't.

Tiber's gaze, a mixture of understanding and resolve, punched Keir in the gut. "You heard him, Keir. If he smells anyone else, he'll kill them."

"And if you go alone he'll kill you." Keir gripped Tiber's arms, careful of his injured wrist. "I like Maddie and Dina, but I love you. I would sacrifice the world to keep you safe."

Tiber smiled, but through their bond, a deep sadness swept through Keir.

"I'm so glad I found you, Keir." Tiber's hard kiss did little to reassure Keir, especially when he pulled away.

Keir clutched Tiber's shirt. "Don't do this to us."

The Alpha slid his hands across Keir's head. "I don't wish to leave you, I want you to know that."

The sound of a throat clearing pulled Keir's attention away from Tiber's dark gaze.

"I hate to ruin your great romantic moment, but I might have a solution to your problem," Connor said.

"Really?" Tiber examined the sheriff as if waiting for the punch line.

"I did some research and last week I purchased a new spray developed for law enforcement. It disguises our scent so if we're hunting shifters, they can't smell us."

Keir's mouth dropped open. "That's perfect."

"I haven't tested it yet." Connor raised his hands in supplication. "I just got it in, but if it works we can at least surround Oscar in order to get the hostages. However, I don't know that we'll be able to get close enough to save Tiber if Oscar attacks. It blinds out scent, but it doesn't make us invisible."

"Let's test it out first," Tiber said. "Then we can make a decision."

Keir kissed Tiber. "First we'll get you checked out, then we'll test the spray."

The thought of losing Tiber was inconceivable. Whether the spray worked or not, he would follow. If Tiber died, Keir had nothing left to live for.

A solemn group left the forest and headed back to the hospital to have Tiber wrist checked out.

Chapter Seven

Tiber could tell by the hard line of Keir's jaw that his mate wasn't going to be reasonable about the exchange.

"It will be fine," Tiber began.

"Don't. Don't lie to me, Tiber. I can't handle it. I know you are going to throw yourself away for two people you barely know. I don't need for you to try and make me feel better."

"They are part of my pack and one of them is a little girl."

Keir deflated. The expression of defeat on his face tore at Tiber. "I know. I do. I understand why you feel like you need to take their place, but I just got you. I can't lose you now."

"You aren't going to lose me." Tiber might go to hell for the lies he was spreading around, but he'd go to it knowing he tried to put his mate at ease. Secretly he suspected he wouldn't be coming back from this adventure. He didn't dare underestimate his opponent. Oscar had proven his intelligence by the trap he'd set in his cave. The black wolf knew how packs thought and had no problem killing the others to get his way.

"If I die, promise me you'll band with the others to kill Oscar."

Keir bit his lip and Tiber tried to ignore the sheen of tears in his mate's eyes. "I swear it. If he kills you, I will make it my job to destroy him."

The kiss they shared, hard and passionate, burned through Tiber like a winter's fire.

"I love you."

There, he'd said it. No reason to hold back when he didn't plan to be alive tomorrow. He couldn't let Keir know how hard it was to let him go and meet his fate."

Tiber's hand ached and the cast itched his skin. He'd break it off in another hour. For now he had to tolerate the annoying weight and clumsy maneuvering.

"How does it feel?" Keir traced his fingers across the bumpy texture of the cast.

"Bulky."

"You can't take it off before three. The doctor meant it when he said you'll heal better if your arm is temporarily restricted."

"I know." Tiber cringed at the hard edge in his voice. Keir didn't deserve his anger or his guilt in leaving his mate behind. "Sorry."

Keir pressed a kiss to Tiber's cheek. "I know. Come on, let's get this over with."

Since they had limited amount of spray, it had been agreed that Proctor and Connor would use the chemical and all the others besides Tiber would stay at the base camp. Tiber could tell Keir hated the arrangement even as he agreed it was the best choice, but Tiber would rather fully trained cops confront the psychopath than unprepared pack members like Keir. Tiber wished they knew more about Oscar than that he'd been bitten by the crazy bug, but they had to work with what they knew.

"Are you ready?" Tiber asked Proctor and Connor.

They both nodded.

"Then let's go." Tiber kissed Keir goodbye. "Take care, mate. I'll see you in a bit."

Tiber couldn't tell if Keir believed him or not. He sent reassurance down their private connection, but he knew it wouldn't be enough. Keir wouldn't understand his choices unless he came back alive.

Connor and Proctor sprayed themselves down and scurried off through the deep underbrush. Tiber promptly lost track of them. Good. If he couldn't see them or smell them, things might actually work out. For the first time a smidgen of hope wormed its way into his chest. He could do this. He could be the leader he'd always dreamed of being.

Come back to me alive. Keir's voice inside his head hardened his resolve. He now had someone to return to. He had to be as safe as possible.

The woods crowded around him. As much as he usually enjoyed a good forest run, dread squatted at the pit of his stomach like an ugly toad squirming and hopping until he barely held strong against the urge to hurl his dinner. He probably shouldn't have eaten something before he came, but if Oscar got hold of him, he doubted the black wolf would bother to feed him. He'd be surprised if Oscar didn't slit his throat as soon as he had Tiber under his control.

"I know you're out there!" Oscar shouted.

For a second Tiber froze, unable to take another step closer. A fine tremble shook his frame. Damn, how had Oscar scented the others? Had they been clumsy and shown themselves too soon?

"I know you're out there, Tiber. Get your ass over here. You're not as sneaky as you think you are!"

Relief warmed Tiber quicker than a blowtorch. If Oscar considered walking down the path in the middle of the forest to be sneaky, he didn't have to worry too much about his Betas being spotted.

Tiber held his hands up in a sign of surrender as he entered the clearing in front of the cabin.

Oscar stood on the front step, a shotgun in his hand. Tiber's odds of escaping unharmed just sank to arctic lows. He should've figured a man who'd set a bomb to trap him in a cave wouldn't draw the line at shooting him from a distance.

"I'm here. Where are they?" Tiber didn't want to give Oscar time to think things over. If the man became suspicious, he might just shoot Tiber right there.

Oscar pushed a hank of dirty dark hair off his forehead. A sneer curled his lip as he examined Tiber with narrowed eyes. "If it isn't the high and mighty Alpha. Did you come to beg for the life of your pack? I've been culling them out for you. The ones who aren't worthy. The weak. The stupid. I thought about killing all of your dogs, but I've decided instead to try and pick out the ones worthy of being part of my pack. Too bad you can't stay. You're too strong to challenge, but luckily you're not too bright."

"Where are Dina and Maddie?" He couldn't let himself be distracted. He had to get the pair out of there before all hell broke loose.

Oscar popped the shotgun against one shoulder and scratched his chin. "Well, I suppose I should keep my word. I mean, I can always kill you afterwards, I made no promise to keep you alive."

Tiber swallowed the lump in his throat. He tightened his psychic connection with Keir until he could barely feel the link between them. Keir didn't need to go through this with him. Despite his determination that Tiber was his one and, only, surely the beautiful man could find another to warm his bed and cherish his kindness.

With a heart as big as the sun, Keir would make any wolf an amazing mate.

Tiber took another step forward. "The females."

"Come out!" Oscar ordered in a hard tone. The front door swung open and Dina and Maddie shuffled out the front door.

Dina stopped on the top step, a strange smile curving her lips.

Oscar grabbed Dina when she walked up next to him. He slid his fingers into her hair and tilted her head back. Surprisingly, Tiber didn't scent any fear. A bad premonition joined the toad at the bottom of his stomach.

"You know how you have the big old Beta for your mate? Well, a few years ago I decided I wanted to procreate and I got myself a nice pair of bitches to breed. If I'm gonna be a dog, I might as well start a kennel of my own. I was just cleaning out the area of the riffraff to make room for my family." A cruel smile crossed Oscar's face as he tightened his grip on Dina. The scent of lust swamped Tiber. Dina had half-closed her eyes as Oscar manhandled her. She apparently got off on his abuse.

"Why are you here, Oscar? Why do you keep coming back to Black Creek?" If he was going to die, he should at least get his questions answered.

"Because this is where I was reborn. I might never have wanted to be a shifter, but this is where it all happened. This is where I belong and, once I take over your pack, this is where I will rule as king of my own domain." Oscar oozed smug satisfaction.

Tiber gritted his teeth. He'd been played for a fool by a pair of women and some cute kids. Keir! His mate had arrived at the same time as the others. Was he part of the plot, too?

"What about Keir?" He hated himself for doubting the Beta as soon as the words passed his lips.

Oscar grinned, exposing teeth too sharp for a human. Maybe he'd lost some of his humanity with all his kills. When a man gave himself over so much to his inner beast, it wasn't inconceivable that it began to take over him in all forms.

"Now that could've been a coincidence or maybe I set you up with your little boyfriend. I guess that's something you'll never know."

Oscar pointed his gun at Tiber. "Now would be the time for you pray to whatever puppy god you hold dear."

"No!" Maddie jumped up and pushed the rifle up just as Oscar fired.

Tiber, who'd already began to move in anticipation of Oscar shooting, walked straight into the bullet.

He'd heard pain described as searing before, but this was more of the hot-poker-in-an-open-wound type of agony. His breath rushed out of him as he slammed into the earth. Gasping, he tried to blink the tears out of his eyes to keep Oscar in his sight.

Oscar roared with rage. He backhanded Maddie and sent the little girl flying off the steps.

Tiber had to get up. He had to save the little girl. Her mother just stood there, unconcerned at the tiny pile Maddie's body created on the ground.

A loud snarl startled him as a red blur surged out of the forest and slammed into Oscar. The shotgun tumbled down the steps, but luckily didn't go off.

Keir!

Shocked, Tiber watched his beautiful, gentle mate tear apart Oscar like he was destuffing a teddy bear. Blood, guts and screams filled the air. Dina leapt off the porch to save Oscar, but was intercepted by Connor and Proctor who arrived in time to stop her attack. A loud crack and her sudden stillness indicated to Tiber that one of them had snapped her neck.

He had to get up. He had to help Keir.

The second of doubt he'd had over his mate's timely appearance in his life vanished. He'd been a fool to have ever doubted his love.

Groaning, Tiber rolled over, but his attempts to get his knees under him failed as he slipped on the blood on the grass beneath him. Damn, it was red. Pools of slick liquid coated the bright green grass. As he struggled, spots formed in the air before his eyes.

Pretty.

"Oh god, oh god. Tiber." Keir's panicked tone pulled Tiber from his contemplation of what color red his blood truly fell under.

"I think it's garnet."

"What?" Keir rolled Tiber onto his back.

Tiber held up his hand to show the smeared blood. "I think it's a garnet color or maybe cranberry."

"Hang in there, love, I think you're going into shock. I'm going to carry you."

"You're always trying to carry me around." Tiber didn't know if he objected to Keir's habit of hauling him in his arms. It was kind of nice once in a while to give up control and let someone else be in charge for a while. Not that he had a submissive bone in his body, but sometimes he just got tired.

Very tired.

Tiber's eyelids began to shut on their own. The effort to keep them open was too much work.

"Easy, love, go ahead and rest. You'll need to shore up all your energy because once you feel better I'm going to fuck you until this entire miserable memory has been washed away."

Tiber liked the sound of that. The soothing rhythm of Keir's voice rounded the rough edges off his pain. He breathed in slowly, letting the darkness claim him, knowing he was safe with his mate watching over him.

Chapter Eight

Keir brushed his teeth... again. He'd never get the foul flavor of Oscar's dirty flesh off his tongue. Killing Oscar had been easy. Once his wolf watched Tiber fall, the only thing in his mind was destroying the bastard who dared to harm his beloved.

Now, Tiber lay in the bed, a bullet hole in one arm and a newly healed broken wrist on the other. If this was what it meant to be Alpha, Tiber needed to retire—yesterday.

While he watched over Tiber, Keir paced, cried and kept a close eye on his mate's every breath, sometimes all at the same time.

"You need to get some rest," Beau said.

The Beta had come to relieve Keir from his vigil, but he refused to go. They'd moved Tiber back to his own bed from the hospital because once they patched him up it was better not to have Tiber where the human doctors might see his unnatural healing speed. As it was, the only shifter doctor had to keep misdirecting the blood samples. They couldn't have shifter blood going to a regular lab. Sometimes it sucked to have a secret. It made simple things much more complicated.

"I can't leave him. What if he wakes up and I'm gone?"

"Then he'll send you one of those psychic communications you two do so well and he'll tell you he woke up." Beau scowled at Keir as if annoyed he had to point out the obvious.

Keir bit his lip. "Okay. Maybe just for a little bit." Keir kicked off his shoes and curled up beside Tiber on his uninjured side.

Beau sighed. "I thought you were going to leave. The whole point of taking a break was to go get some fresh air."

"If you think I'm leaving him before he wakes up, you're an idiot." Keir stroked Tiber's chest, reassured at the strong heartbeat pumping beneath his fingertips.

Beau growled and stomped out of the room.

"It's okay, mate. I'm here and I won't let poor, stupid Beau talk me into leaving." Keir rested his head against Tiber's uninjured side and closed his eyes. In no time, sleep claimed him.

Fingers trailing through his hair pulled Keir from his slumber. Blinking, he tried to focus on the face so close to his own.

"Tiber," Keir whispered.

Tiber's dark eyes were filled with so much love Keir's heart ached to see it.

"Hey, gorgeous."

"Hey, back. How are you feeling?" He kept his voice low in case Tiber's head hurt. Sometimes human medications had horrible side effects in wolves.

Tiber's slow, relieved smile warmed Keir to his toes. "Actually pretty good. What happened?"

"I don't know how much you remember, but I killed Oscar and, Connor and Proctor killed Dina. We came back here to confront Carrie, but when we told her Dina was dead, she was so happy she cried for an hour. Apparently they were using the twins as a way of controlling Carrie. She was a victim in all this."

"Are you sure?"

"Yeah, I let Connor interrogate her. He said she was telling the truth. It's up to you if you want to toss her out, though. She did let Dina bring her here with the knowledge they were going to infiltrate on Oscar's behalf."

"No. It sounds like she has had enough of a rough time, and the twins deserve a home. We'll let her stay, but keep a watch on her. Apparently she has horrible taste in mates. What about Maddie?"

"She was shaken up, but she's running around with her sister now. I think she'll be just fine."

"Good. I like those little girls."

"Yeah, me, too." Keir stroked Tiber's cheek. "You scared the crap out of me. I almost lost you twice. This mating with the Alpha thing is a lot more work than I thought it would be."

Tiber wrapped a hand round Keir's fingers. "But you saved me both times. For an Alpha, I appear to need a white knight to rescue me on a fairly regular basis."

The vulnerability in Tiber's eyes, as if he worried he might be too much trouble, cut at Keir's heart. "It is my privilege to rescue you."

Keir meant every word. The flash of surprise, then acceptance in Tiber's expression warmed his heart.

"Thank you."

Keir pressed a soft kiss on Tiber's lips. "You never have to thank me for doing what I was born to do."

"Am I allowed to shift?"

Tiber's unexpected question threw Keir off. "Yeah, the doctor said when you woke up you could change."

"Good. I'm going to wolf out and when I shift back I'm going to reclaim my mate."

Keir shivered from the growl in Tiber's voice. "I can't wait. Let me take the bandage off."

Tiber slipped from the bed. Keir admired the tight muscles displayed by his mate. He quickly removed the large bandage covering the bullet wound. Damn, even with the red scars Tiber had a fine body.

"If I slip on your drool you'll have to nurse me back to health again."

Keir met Tiber's amused expression with a cheeky grin of his own. "I'd be happy to volunteer for sponge bathing duty.

Tiber laughed.

The laugh changed to a growl with the snapping and crackling of bones reshaping. Soon there was a dark wolf panting on the floor. Its sad eyes stared at Keir in reproof.

"What? I'm not the one who tried to hurt you. Now change back."

Tiber lay on the floor for a moment. Keir could see the wolf trying to recapture its strength.

"What is he doing out of bed?" Donny asked. He stomped up to the Alpha. "You are supposed to be resting."

Keir marched over and put himself between the man and wolf. "Don't yell at him. He wanted to heal faster. The doctor told me his injuries are healed enough to shift when he woke up. I would never allow him to change if I thought he'd be further injured."

Donny deflated beneath Keir's ire. "Sorry. I know. I'm just worried. I've never seen him so damaged before."

"He's not damaged." Keir stroked the wolf head rubbing against his thigh.

Donny watched Tiber rub against Keir for a long moment. "I guess I never thought I'd see Tiber love someone more than he loves me."

"You weren't . . ." Keir couldn't get himself to finish that sentence.

Donny laughed. "No. We might be distant cousins, but I've always thought of Tiber as more of a big brother. I just never thought about how our relationship would change once he found someone for himself. He really loves you."

Tiber walked over to Donny. He went onto his back paws, planting his front paws on Donny's shoulders. He licked a long line up Donny's cheek.

"Eww, wolf germs. I love you, too, big guy." Donny pushed Tiber away. "I'll leave you two alone. Let me know if you need anything."

Keir nodded. "Will do." He wouldn't need anything. Everything he could ever want was sitting in this room. As soon as Donny left, Keir closed, then locked the door. He didn't want anyone to interrupt.

The wolf sat in the middle of the floor. It tilted its head in a gesture of curiosity, as if the animal couldn't figure out what Keir was up to. "I believe you promised to fuck me."

In a surprisingly short time Tiber changed.

Keir gasped when Tiber grabbed him with his newly formed hands and yanked him close.

"I always keep my word."

Keir melted against his mate as Tiber took his mouth in a hard, punishing kiss. His lip split beneath the force of Tiber's passion.

"Easy, love, I'm not going anywhere." The desperation in Tiber's moves cut at Keir's heart.

"I thought you were lost to me forever. I almost died." Tiber's expression begged Keir to understand how much he needed his mate.

"I know, love. But I'm here and I'm not going to let you get away from me now."

Tiber sighed. "Strip and get up on the bed. I need to claim you."

Keir was all about re-establishing the bond. He tried to undress, but his fingers became awkward in his excitement. A pair of strong hands reached around him and tore open his jeans.

"Thanks," Keir whispered.

Soon he stood naked and fidgety in front of his mate. Although physically he knew he was bigger than Tiber, Alpha's presence filled the room. He couldn't take a breath without inhaling the scent of his mate—but then, why would he want to?

Tiber stepped closer until his back brushed against the Alpha's warm front. "You can climb up on the bed or I can fuck you against the wall. Your choice."

Keir swallowed, trying to get moisture into his suddenly dry throat. "Keep that up and I'll come before you even get inside me."

It took a great deal of will power, but with slow careful motions, he stepped away from Tiber and climbed up on the bed. Not daring to look back at his mate, he scooted to the top of the mattress. When he was at a good distance to allow his mate to join him, Keir spread his legs wide and lowered his chest to the mattress. He left his ass in the air. Glancing over his shoulder, he fluttered his eyelashes at Tiber. "I'm ready when you are."

Between one blink and the next, Tiber moved from across the room to join him on the bed.

Keir moaned at the first brush of Tiber's erection sliding between his ass cheeks. "Oh."

Heat poured off Tiber and the warm rod of his cock pressed against Keir spiked his desire. An ache to be taken hardened his body until he knew if Tiber didn't speed things along, he'd spill onto the bed below without a single touch.

"Please." He barely recognized the desperate, pleading voice as his own.

"Don't worry, love, I'll give you what you need." Tiber grabbed the bottle of lube from the side table by his bed.

It took little time for Keir to be prepped. He shoved back against Tiber's fingers until the Alpha slapped him on the ass. "Patience. I won't hurt you."

"Fuck me. I need you," Keir begged. He wasn't too proud to beg. As much as Tiber needed to reassure himself he was still alive, Keir craved his touch. Only the reality of Tiber pounding into him would convince him his mate was alive. He desperately needed Tiber to pound into him.

"Relax."

Keir took a deep breath. "Okay, okay."

Be easy, my mate. Tiber's voice seeped into him, a calming presence to his stressed soul.

"I thought I'd lost you."

"But you found me again."

After prepping Keir carefully, Tiber pushed inside. Keir gasped at the sensation of Tiber breaching him. The Alpha paused once he had fully seated, giving Keir a moment to adjust.

"Now, move," Keir ordered.

Tiber took Keir at his word. After a few cautious motions, testing Keir's readiness, Tiber sped up his strokes.

"Yes. Yes. Harder."

Tiber wrapped his fingers around Keir's as he set a hard rhythm pegging Keir's prostate with each stroke. Over and over he brought Keir to the brink only to slow down enough to drive him insane.

Keir whimpered. "Please, Tiber."

Tiber released Keir's right hand long enough to wrap around Keir's erection. "Come."

Unable and unwilling to resist the command of his mate, Keir spilled his seed across the sheet below. A long groan of release poured out of him along with his cum.

"I thought I'd lost this forever," Tiber growled.

"Mark me." Keir tilted his head to one side, baring his neck in submission.

Tiber froze, his cock still hard inside Keir. Without warning, he plunged his fangs into Keir.

"Yes," Keir moaned.

Tiber splashed inside him, groaning against Keir's neck. After a long moment, Tiber lifted his mouth and licked at the mark he left behind.

Keir gasped when Tiber pulled away, then slid out of him. Empty. He was so empty.

"Hey." Tiber rolled Keir over and held him close. "I'm right here."

To Keir's horror, tears began to slide down his cheeks. "I-I thought I'd lost you."

"Never. You will never lose me."

The soft vow settled Keir's anxiety. His heart felt peaceful. "I love you," he whispered as if confessing a secret.

"I know, mate, I love you, too."

Closing his eyes, he began to fade to sleep.

"Scoot over."

Keir frowned. "Why?"

"Because I'm in the wet spot."

Laughing, Keir moved over. "We can't have that."

"No we can't indeed." Tiber kissed Keir on the forehead.

Keir fell asleep, content that everything he needed was wrapped around him.

About the Author

AMBER KELL lives in Seattle, WA with her husband, two sons, three cats and one extremely stupid dog. She loves to hear from her fans at amberkellwrites@gmail.com

*Look for other books by RJ Scott at
www.extasybooks.com*

Supernatural Bounty Hunter Series:
*The Vampire Contract
The Guilty Werewolf
The Warlock's Secret
The Demon's Blood*

*Look for other books by Stephani Hecht at
www.extasybooks.com and www.devinedestinies.com*

Archangel Series
Blue Line Hockey Series
Drone Vampire Series
EMS Heat Series
Friends to Lovers Series
Haven Coffee House Boys
Lost Shifter Series
Night Wardens Series
Wayne County Wolves Series
*Atlantis Lost
Have a Harpy Holiday
Hey, There's Fur in my Wedding Cake
Mystical Passions
Salting Zombies
Sins of an Angel
The Reluctant Incubus
The Third Floor*

Look for other books by Amber Kell at
www.extasybooks.com

Banded Brothers Series:
To Have a Human
To Catch a Croc
To Enchant an Eagle
To Bite a Bear
To Kiss a Killer

CPSIA information can be obtained at www.ICGtesting.com
Printed in the USA
LVOW12s1725221013

358078LV00001B/59/P